I0535677

JOINT EFFORT IN DEATH

Published by Airplane Books

Copyright 2015 Don Yarber
All rights reserved

ISBN: 978-0-9850695-4-4

Joint Effort in Death

Don Yarber and Allen Clarke

This book is dedicated to the memory of Junior Chandler, a good friend and a good golfer.

The character, Noble Savage, in this book is the creation of Allen Clarke, who wrote the character's chapters up to page 212. Don Yarber assumed the responsibility of finishing the novel, and with permission from Allen Clarke, wrote the remaining parts involving Noble Savage, the character created by Clarke.

Yarber created the character, Burl Britton, in the novel, and wrote all chapters featuring Burl Britton.

Joint Effort in Death

CHAPTER ONE

Burl Britton was feeling his age.

He was touched by the case he had just accepted, and deep inside he felt a little selfish for taking it. Missing teens are a dime a dozen, they are seldom found if they do not want to be found, and he knew it. The couple that had just left the office of Burl Britton, Private Detective, were in their late thirties, young, vibrant, alive. Burl was nearing 60 and feeling it every day. Yet he had accepted the retainer, a thousand dollars, and signed the contract.

He would be paid a hundred a day plus expenses. If he didn't find the teen aged girl in 30 days, his contract would terminate and he would turn over any documentation to the parents.

He really disliked missing persons cases unless he felt that the case just involved a dead beat skipping out on child support or mounds of credit card debt. Those cases he liked. They paid good, and usually weren't all that difficult to solve.

Missing teens were hard to find. He knew that of all the teens reported missing in the United States each year, only about ten percent were found alive. The other ninety percent remained missing or returned on their own. Some of them were likely dead, some huddled together in abandoned houses, subway tunnels and makeshift camps in the woods somewhere, most living on prostitution, theft and minor hold ups or burglary.

There was something different about the case brought to him by Mr. and Mrs. Arthur Banquell. Their daughter, Lisa, was sixteen. She told her mother, Dora, that she was going to spend the night with a girlfriend, Mona, in the Augusta suburb of Whispering Meadows. She said that she would be home in time for supper the next day, Saturday. There was no mention of a party, no boys involved, and Dora had no reason to doubt Lisa. They had a good relationship, loved each other a great deal, and both of them loved Art Banquell with all their beings.

Art was the perfect Dad. He was an accountant, upper middle class, church going, active in the community, devoted to wife and daughter, didn't drink and didn't smoke, and did something most fathers never do. He spent a lot of time with Lisa. He was involved in her life. He helped her study, he gave her attention, he listened to her daily. He knew who she went out with, insisted that her dates pick her up at their home, and checked the background of each boy with the careful magnifying glass of someone who really cared.

That is what Britton was told. That, too, might prove to be a different case.

But Lisa did not come home Saturday. She didn't call to explain why she wouldn't be home. Dora called Mona's home and was shocked to find that Lisa had not been there. That was the thing that nearly broke Art and

Dora's hearts. Lisa had lied to them. Or did she?

Burl Britton sighed. His practice had gradually declined over the past two years or so, from peaks of near a hundred grand per year, he was now averaging only forty five. His car was three years old, a Honda Civic Hybrid that he purchased for the good mileage, not the comfort.

Lisa Banquell's case wasn't one that he wanted, but he couldn't afford to turn it down.

He locked his office and shuffled slowly out to the old Honda parked at the curb, glanced back as if he remembered something that he didn't do, and then shrugged his shoulders and got in the car.

It was after six and he hadn't eaten since breakfast. He was hungry, tired, and disappointed that the only case he had picked up on this quiet Monday was a missing teen case. Oh well, he thought, I'll start on it tomorrow.

He put his old Samsonite briefcase on the seat beside him, opened it and took out the picture of Lisa Banquell. She was posed with her short cheer leader skirt, legs spread wide apart, arms extended fully to each side, hands holding pompoms. Her long, dark hair hung over each shoulder and down over her chest. She smiled at Burl Britton from the photograph, a full smile, revealing beautiful white perfectly aligned teeth.

Burl thought about his own daughters, now grown, married and with children of their own.

He sighed again, dropped the photograph back in his briefcase, snapped the lid shut and fastened his seat belt. He glanced at himself in the mirror. His hair had turned almost completely white. His blue eyes didn't see as well as they once did. His cheeks were a healthy color, tanned by summer sun and his passion for tennis.

He needed to go play a few sets, shower, get something to eat and go home. Home to the empty house, the blathering television with nothing fit to watch, the emptiness.

CHAPTER 2

My name is Savage. Noble T. Savage, if you can believe it. And, if you haven't guessed by now, yeah, I'm a red man. The T stands for doubting Thomas. And, I suppose that I've had a whole bunch to disbelieve lately. Yeah, I know I shouldn't be crying in my soup and crackers. Even though, the truth is, my cupboards have been a little skimpy these days.

I'm what one might call a private dick. Some might just call me a dick. That's a matter of personal opinion. The truth is, if you can get past my callous heart and thick skin, you just might find a genuine human being in there somewhere.

The nature of my business is tough. By the way, that could also be my middle name, as well as `trouble`. I'm trouble to whoever wants it that way. On the other hand, I can be a real pussy cat. At odd times you might see me crack a smile but the punch line has to be of an exceptional nature.

My phone's been silent. That's not a good sign. I don't much like it when things get too quiet. I got to get out of this stinkin` hole of a reserve. I'm tired of watchin` the grass grow. Life on the rez can get to a guy after awhile. You might wonder how I got to be a private dick. Well, I couldn't afford education through conventional means, so I tried correspondence. Two weeks later, they sent me a certificate which hangs proudly on my office wall.

Once in awhile I'll get into my 56` Pontiac and rumble into town. My office is a crawlspace which I rent for fifty bucks a month. My shingle's been up for a couple of months now, but still no takers. Maybe nobody believes in the shadow man anymore. I'm on the net. You'd think my inbox would be glutted with urgent messages by now. I guess you might say I'm still waiting for That Great White Buffalo to make my day. Talk to you later. I've got some grease bread to fry!

CHAPTER 3

Tuesday morning Burl Britton went through the rituals of showering, shaving, and getting dressed for work. After a bowl of oatmeal he felt better and when he picked up his briefcase and headed for the old Honda in the driveway, he even allowed himself the luxury of a positive thought. He thought he would find a lead to Lisa Banquell today.

At his small office, Britton reviewed all he had on the case, checked his message machine and then called the Banquell residence and asked if he could see Lisa's room. He knew what he would find there might be something that the Banquell's had overlooked. They had not gone to the police yet, and he had asked them to postpone filing an official missing persons report until he had a chance to do some preliminary investigating. There were two reasons for that. First reason was that Police work invariably clouded up the issue. Police tasks are regimented, follow certain inbred patterns, and seldom turned in directions that aren't part of that procedure. He had learned years ago to follow his instinct instead of procedures.

When he was a rookie cop he already had the instincts of a seasoned private detective, but then that isn't what the Augusta police force expected of a rookie cop so they frowned on any individual thinking. A phrase heard on television a lot nowadays is "think out of the box". That's what Britton did. He couldn't help it. It was a part of his nature to think of things that others might never think of, to follow leads that might not appear to be a lead. That is one reason he was a lousy cop and a great private detective.

The Banquell's lived in an exclusive part of Whispering Meadows. You might call it an estate instead of a home. The house sat a third of the way back on the five acre lot, a long, shiny brick driveway rolled through brick entryways that had four rail white vinyl fence extending from them, across the front and down each side of the driveway. It reminded Britton of a horse ranch, but the Banquell's owned no horses.

He parked the car near a four car garage, but out of the way of the doors so that anyone wanting to leave could do so. He walked the short distance to a side entrance of the large brick two story home and rang the doorbell.

"Good morning Mrs. Banquell," he said as Dora Banquell answered the door.

"Mr. Britton," she said. Her voice was hollow and weak. He knew that she hadn't slept much. Her eyes had little dark circles under them.

"Come in," she said, holding the door in her right hand and motioning with her left hand. Britton went in and was immediately impressed with the interior of the Banquell home. Upper middle class residence, impressive furniture, exquisitely decorated.

"Ill show you to Lisa's bedroom," Dora Banquell said.

"Thank you, Mrs. Banquell," Britton said, politely, "I hope that I am not disturbing you, I won't be long."

He followed her through the rambling home, up a flight of stairs that curved left from bottom to top and emerged on a hallway that ran athwart of the living room area below. The second door on their right was open and Dora motioned towards it.

"I haven't done anything in here," she said. "It's just as it was the morning she left."

"Thank you," he said. "I won't be long."

He went in and the room was almost exactly as he had thought it would be, decorated nicely in school colors of Whispering Meadows High School. Maroon and gold. The bed was made, next to it was a small computer desk, a screen saver program scrolling across the screen read "English Lit test Friday". He glanced over his shoulder and saw that Dora had left him alone in the room.

One of the first things that he looked for was e-mail. There were several, none of which held a clue as to where the beautiful young lady had gone.

He opened a Facebook page and looked at Lisa's messages. One caught his attention. It was from a boy named Larry who wanted Lisa to go to the prom with him. Britton took a notebook from his pocket and copied the email message verbatim. He closed Facebook and went back to the email program.

Lisa used Outlook Express as her email server and Britton clicked on the "View" at the top of the toolbar. A drop down menu appeared and the first entry was "Current View". He clicked on that. The first three lines of that menu were "Show all messages" "Hide read messages" and "Hide read or ignored messages".

The hair on Burl Britton's arms rose slightly and he felt the familiar tingle that he experienced every time he knew that he was about to uncover something of importance in a case. His eyes followed the cursor as he swept it to "Show all messages" and clicked. The little black dot next to "Hide read or ignored messages" disappeared and appeared, as if by magic, on the line he chose.

A new page of email messages appeared.

The first one he read held the clue he knew he was going to find.

"Lisa darling, I will pick you up at the designated spot on Saturday. Don't worry about clothes, we can hit a Wal-Mart store and get whatever you need, toothbrush, whatever. Please don't worry, this is going to work. We'll be together forever and that is what counts."

The email was from someone named James Enderly.

Britton put the cursor on James Enderly and did a right mouse click and clicked on "properties". A box opened on the screen with two tabs, "General" and "Details". He clicked on details and the page opened with all of James Enderly's email properties on it. Britton laboriously copied every word on to the page in his notebook. It would have been easier to print the page, Lisa Banquell's printer was on a shelf below the monitor. Britton preferred to write it down. He had always had the ability to remember most of what he wrote. If he was going to take a test in school and there was something that he knew would be on the test, he would copy it verbatim onto a piece of notebook paper and when time came for the test he would remember most of it.

"Snap out of it, Burl," he said to himself, "You're a long ways from school."

Feeling confident that he had what he had came to find in Lisa's room, Burl Britton rose from the chair and glanced around. He riffled through books, opened clothes drawers and peeked in. He felt weird looking at Lisa Banquell's underwear, and quickly closed that drawer.

He dropped to hands and knees, stretched his body prone on the lush carpet and peered under the bed. There was a pencil and paperback book under the bed. He retrieved both. A standard #2 pencil. The book was a paperback copy of "Birth of a Nation" by D. W. Griffith." and when Burl Britton riffled it with his thumb a note fell out.

"Lisa, this is the book I was telling you about." It was signed "Michelle" in the block style handwriting that is prevalent. Parker penmanship is no longer taught in school, Britton reflected. Shame, too.

Britton carried the book with him when he left Lisa's room and went down the curved stairway. Mrs. Banquell was in the living room, staring at the dark screen of a 52 inch television set. A cup of coffee sat on a table to her right.

"I found this book under Lisa's bed," Britton said, and watched as Dora's head turned slowly.

"Is that important?" She wanted to know.

"Do you know who 'Michelle' might be? There's a note in it from 'Michelle'."

"More than likely that is Michelle Montague," Dora said. "She is Lisa's friend from school. Her best friend."

Britton opened his notebook and made a note.

He didn't mention the small plastic envelope he had found in the book with a white powder substance in it. He would find out what the substance was before he told her about it. No need opening a can of worms for nothing.

"Did Lisa ever mention a boy named James Enderly?"

"No, I've never heard that name before," Dora said. "Who is he?"

"I don't know yet," Britton said. He wasn't ready to give her any hope at this point. Too many times he had given parents a name and they had started their own investigation. By the time he tried to follow, the trail was muddied. He didn't tell her any details, just that it was someone Lisa knew, as evident by an email he had found on her computer. He didn't tell her what the email said, he had some checking to do first. Curiously she didn't ask about the details of the email.

He asked Dora about the boy who wanted to take Lisa to the prom. She knew the boy and gave him a rundown on the boy's family, a general idea of where he lived and that he was a running back on the football team and considered very intelligent.

Dutifully Britton jotted that information into his spiral notebook.

By the time he said his goodbyes to Dora Banquell, Britton's spirits had lifted considerably. He had some clues. He had some leads. He had some work to do to keep his mind occupied and off of his own loss.

CHAPTER 4

Canwood, Saskatchewan is a one-horse town. Doesn't that little tidbit of local geography excite you? Nah, I didn't think so. I blush a deep shade of red when I think of its implications. There's nothing here but miles and miles of farmland. Canwood pub is the central hub of activity. I roll into town at about 3:oo p.m. Screeching to a stop in front of the post office, my 56`Pontiac farts to a halt in a cloud of blue smoke. Quite unceremoniously, I drag my lazy carcass from off of the red, velour seats and onto the sidewalk. The postmaster, J.P. Grimley, almost kills me dead with his usual "evil eye." I always suspected he didn't like the colour of my skin. I kinda think he was secretly jealous of my perfect tan.

"Well, good morning`, girly-girl!" I say to the postmistress. She had the look of a youngish Marilyn Monroe.

"Morning, sir." she breathed.

"Say, howz about a date?" I whispered slyly.

"Sure, Mr. Savage, how about the twelfth of never." She giggled girlishly.

"Aww ..now you done hurt my widdle feelings." I said, trying my best Tweety Bird impersonation.

"Actually, Mr. Savage, my doctor told me to cut back on...ahem, red meat"

"Now, now, now, girly-girl, the parson wouldn't be too impressed to hear you talking that way to a distinguished gentleman. Would he now?"

J.P. Grimley came out of his little perch, with his face exasperated and beet-red.

"Now, Noble, you scat! Pick up your mail and get outta town!"

"You'd best be minding your p`s and q`s, J. P.!" I barked.

At that precise moment, he made the stupid mistake of trying to manhandle me out of the Post Office. He tried his level best to hug me not so tenderly and I danced out of his grip. In a split second, I planted my size 14`s where the sun don't shine. I left him rolling in the dust screaming in a falsetto vein.

Scooping up my mail, I paused at the doorway long enough to bid Marilyn adieu.

"Now, remember, girly-girl, if you ever get tired of life in the fast lane. Look me up. I'm in the yellow pages."

On the way out of town, I cracked open my mail. There was a letter all the way from the Windy City. Chicago, the moider capital of the Noo-nited States of `Merca! A picture fell out just as I went to open it. It was of a young man, a teenager. Either that or he was the next Dick Clark. A wholesome looking kid, I surmised. `Precious` was written on the back. I took out the letter and read the barely legible handwriting. Again, I surmised that this was the infamous scrawl of a very well paid physician. Actually, I didn't think anybody wrote letters anymore. The letter was not crisply presented. It had the look of something which had been wrinkled over. It read;

Chicago, Illinois

July 4, 2012

Dear Det. Savage.

    We are in a desperate situation. Our son has gone missing for the past week. We are in no position to offer you a substantial fee for his safe return. We are by no means wealthy by today's standards, but we will pay you for your travel and accommodations. As for your regular fees, we can only promise you that we are doing everything in our power to acquire sufficient funds to meet your needs. As a gesture of good faith, please find remitted in U.S. Funds via traveler's checks the amount of $500.00. Please, Mr. Savage, we have exhausted all other means to secure services such as you are able to provide. We have approached so many other agencies and we have come up empty. You are our last resort. My wife is an emotional wreck. And, I feel, at this writing that I am not too far behind her.

                        Desperate , yet Hopeful

John and Marilyn Enderly

    Well, call me an all-day sucker. I guess I've just been hired. On a separate sheet of paper, I found all the particulars of the case. It took me less than a day to take off my shingle and put out a "Gone Fishing" sign. I guess my usual pork and bean Friday night supper would have to wait for awhile. I had to wonder though if my old Pontiac would make it there and back.

I guess I was about to find out. I didn't pack heat. If need be, my fists would have to do the talking.

CHAPTER FIVE

Burl Britton had a friend who ran a computer repair shop in Augusta. He headed the Honda towards the parkway out of Whispering Meadows and pointed it up the onramp towards Augusta.

Thirty minutes later he opened the door to the shop.

"Burl, my favorite Private Eye," Roger Stone said.

"Hi, Roger."

"Has your laptop gone haywire again?"

"No, it's doing fine," Britton said as he ambled towards the counter in the back of the shop.

"OK, just a friendly visit this time? You want some coffee?"

"OK thanks, Roger. What I really came for is some help. Can you take a look at something and tell me what you make of it?"

"Sure, let's see it."

Burl opened his spiral notebook and showed Roger the page with the information he had laboriously copied, the email properties for James Enderly.

"What do you want to know?"

"Can you determine from that where it came from?"

Roger glanced down the page. His practiced eye found the line that read "received from WesTelproxyserver.com" and he sat at his computer and typed a few words.

The result of his Google search for WesTel.Com showed a small communications company with a network of users in the Chicago area.

"It came from Chicago, an internet service provider named WesTel. This was handled by a proxy server in Augusta but it originated in Chicago."

"Chicago, huh?"

"Yep. Does that help?"

Britton accepted the coffee that Roger poured for him, took a sip and grinned. "It may help a lot. Do me a favor and see if you've got a white pages listing for surname Enderly in the Chicago area."

The keys on Roger's computer clicked and clacked, hesitated, clicked a few more times and clacked several times.

"There are several listings," Roger said, "One, two, three...." he went down the list, counting out loud.

"Any James?"

"One."

"What's the number?"

Roger rattled off the Chicago area code, and a seven digit number. Burl wrote it down in his notebook.

"Thanks, Roger."

"You're welcome. What kind of case are you tackling now?"

"Kid missing over in Whispering Meadows. Girl, 16. I think she ran away with James Enderly. I found an email in her computer from him. That's where I got that stuff." He motioned towards the page with the "properties" of James Enderly's email.

"You going to Chicago?"

"Not if I can help it," he said. "I'll try making some phone calls first, see if I can find out anything. If not, I'll get in touch with an investigator I know in Chicago, see if he will help."

"Well, good luck with it," Roger said. "I've got a bunch of work to do, Burl. Good to see you again. Come back when you don't have so long to stay."

Burl drank the last of his coffee, sat the cup down and grinned at Roger. "Up yours too!"

He sat in his Honda thinking that he would wait until he got back to his office to call Chicago. His cell phone was low on minutes and he had a plan on his office phone that let him call long distance at a rate so low it wouldn't bankrupt him. A penny saved is a penny earned, he thought.

It was nearly noon when he got back to his office and dialed the Chicago number.

"Hello."

"Is this the Enderly residence?"

"Yes, who's calling?" A female voice.

"Is there a James Enderly living at your residence?"

"Yes, that is my husband. Who wants to know?"

"Mrs. Enderly, my name is Burl Britton. I'm a private investigator from Georgia, and I'm working a missing persons case. The young lady who is missing received an email from a James Enderly in the Chicago area. I'm trying to get a lead on that person."

"Well it isn't MY James!"

"Mrs. Enderly, I'm sure that it isn't your husband. Is there a young James Enderly? A son perhaps?"

"My husband has a nephew named James. We haven't seen him in a few years. We don't associate with my husband's brother very much. They've not spoken in five years."

"Can you tell me anything about your husband's nephew? How old would he be? Where he goes to school, is he out of school, where he works?"

"I can only tell you that he's about eighteen." She said.

"You don't know if he's still in school?"

"No. I told you, we haven't heard from that family in at least five years."

"What is your husband's brother's name?"

"John."

"Well, thank you, Mrs. Enderly. I appreciate your time."

The line went dead.

Apparently Mrs. Enderly wasn't anxious to help if it meant dealing with the family of her husband's brother.

CHAPTER 6

I hit the eastbound blacktop at around 8:45, the morning after I received my retainer. In a sick sort of way, I felt like I was going to miss the flatlands. What the heck for, I don't know. I guess some things in life can't be easily accounted for. If the boy was from the wrong side of the tracks, I could easily relate. No one knows deep poverty quite like us redskins. If it wasn't for bologna and macaroni, the Cree Nation, would likely be extinct. Listen to me, I'm not even in Chicago yet, and I'm already singin` the blues! Wait`ll they get a load of me!

I read somewhere (probably in Reader's Digest) that the town of Chicago can be quite deadly. That's quite alright with me. I'm in my element, when things get vicious. That's just my game. I've got warrior blood coursing through my veins. My heart is a beating chunk of ice, cause once I get you down you're not coming back up the same way you went down. Somebody comes at me with a weapon, they better be able to make the first shot count, cause they will spend the rest of their natural life in a wheelchair.

The miles keep whipping past me as I roar down the wide open plains. At dusk, I pull off the road at a truck stop close to the Manitoba border. I fill up my guzzler, and go into the confectionary to buy a ring of garlic and a loaf of day-old rye. People think I'm cheap, but, I prefer the word frugal. Staring off into the distance, I see a blue moon riding on the clear night sky. It's beautiful out here on the prairie. It's so unconfined. It makes a man want to reach out and touch the stars. Back home, most folks will be curling up in their warm blankets. I sigh deeply, and I think of home, luxuriating in a few moments of peace. I see a young couple on the other side of the highway trying to flag down a ride before darkness falls. I snap to it, as I realize I'm losing precious time. At 57, I feel I can no longer dilly-dally, even at the simplest of chores. I look in the rear-view, and I barely recognize the man staring back at me under the shadow of a dark brown fedora. The light in the cab glitters off the beaded hatband and the wisps of silvery hair at the sideburns.

Pouring a hot cup of java, I see the steam curling up to merge with the smoke from my cheroot. I don't really like to smoke, but I like the way it makes me look tough. It's all part of the illusion. At least, that's what I want them to believe. I figure by the time they figure out it's no bluff, it's too late. By then, they're usually trying to process what just hit them. I'm part con, repo-man and snake charmer. In my experience, there's a lot of two-legged snakes, so you always have to be keen to their tricks. By the way, I also have this uncanny sixth sense, I kinda inherited from my granpappy. It's kinda like this small voice in my head that senses the imminence of something bad about to happen. I usually get that strange little "twinge" on the inside of me. Whenever I feel it, I know I'm about to step into some pretty deep, "ca-ca"

Wha!...hold on, here it comes! This big buck jumps out from the tall grass, and barely misses ruining the finish on Old Betsy! I careen wildly for about a hundred yards, before regaining my composure. I figure if I would have been holding my java, I might have scalded my weeney! The whip I drive is a souped-up muscle car. It's like a shiny black ghost swiftly eating up the wide open prairie. It's got a deep-throated rumble from a pair of genuine Hollywood mufflers. It's a big V-8, and it's punishing on my thinning wallet. I chose to sacrifice frugality for power. I've got my window wide open and I'm just now getting used to the smell of putrefying swamp water coming up from the ditch. Needless to say, the raunchy odor keeps my beautiful brown eyes wide open.

I got the speedometer at a steady 120 clicks. I'm the bloody Red Baron, and I'm coming after you, babies! Towards early morning, I run out of prairie and I'm deep into the woodland. I'm praying that the moose are still sleeping. The lush green of pine blurs on either side of my journey, mile after lonely mile. I turn on the ancient radio and it crackles and sputs to life.

"This is C.G.B.B! The Voice of a Thousand Lakes! We got us a reequest from Margie to Donny to play, "Yer Cheatin`Heart" by old Hanky Panky Williams! You all enjoy this moldy an` oldie, but a goody! Yee`haw!!

I'm not much for "corn" but it was the only reception I was getting, so I just let it play. Finding some comfort in the sound of another human voice, I found myself singing along like poor old Kawliga. It was at that moment that I started to think about this young guy I was supposed to locate. I wondered where he was tonight. Maybe he was sleeping in some dumpster, or maybe in a culvert with the mosquitoes feasting on his hiney. Funny, how the mind can start to play with you after 8 hours behind the wheel. In the instructions, they had told me to meet them at a designated bus depot deep in the heart of Chicago. They thought that I would arrive by Greyhound. I wasn't too keen on the idea of riding in the belly of a big dog, so I decided to drive.

Before hitting Winnipeg, I exited off to a side-road, and got some beauty sleep, not that I needed it. I guess it would have been easier to fly but the miser in me won out. I knew I'd be fit to be tied after this long road trip, so I planned on taking in some of the sights after I finished my business. I barely remember going through International Falls, before heading south. Finally, I reached the city of my destination. I had quite the time peeling myself off the red velour seats as I got out of Old Betsy and walked into the Greyhound terminal. I phoned my clients and within half an hour they came to meet me at the bus depot. When I finally made their acquaintance, they looked very tired and old beyond their years. It seemed to me like they had driven all the way from Saskatchewan.

CHAPTER 7

Burl Britton hung up the phone, said something ungentlemanly about Mrs. Enderly under his breath and wondered why people, especially relatives, just can't get along. He recalled bits and pieces of the conversation. He had learned that there was a James Enderly who was the son of John Enderly living in Chicago.

All of that fit.

He checked the list of numbers that Roger had rattled off from the Chicago area white pages. He found John Enderly and dialed that number.

The phone rang and rang. No-one was answering. He let it ring several times, hoping to get an answering machine or something so that he would know it was still a good number. Just as he was about to hang up he heard a muffled sound.

"'Lo"

It sounded like a woman's voice.

"Mrs. Enderly?"

"Yes."

"Mrs. John Enderly"

"Yes, who is this?"

Burl thought to himself for a second, "who is this" always sounded to him like the person speaking didn't know who THEY were. He let it slide.

"My name is Burl Britton," he said. "I'm a private detective from the Atlanta area. I'm trying to find a young lady who has been missing since last Saturday. I found an email on her computer from a James Enderly in the Chicago area. Would you be any relation? He is about 18 years of age."

"John!" Burl heard the phone hit the table top, a wall or the floor, definitely the sound that it was dropped.

He waited.

He could hear muffled voices in the background. Then he heard footsteps thumping then a man's deep gruff voice practically yelled into the phone.

"HELLO."

"Mr. Enderly?"

"Yes. You have news about my son?"

"Is your son James Enderly, approximately 18 years of age?"

"Yes, yes. That's my son. What do you know? What can you tell us about him. Is he all right?"

"Hold on a second, Mr. Enderly," Burl said. "I'm investigating the disappearance of a girl in the Atlanta, Georgia area. I found an e-mail....."

"My son is missing too," the gruff voice interrupted.

"Your son is missing?" Burl asked.

"I just said he was," the gruff voice retorted. "I've been asking you if you know anything about his whereabouts or if he's OK."

"I don't know anything at this point," Burl said. "He may or may not have met with the girl I am seeking."

Burl told John Enderly about the email and what it said, without glancing at his notes. He knew that he had recited the message virtually verbatim.

"That's Jimmy!" John Enderly said. "I know it has to be him. But he doesn't even have a computer. How could he be sending messages if he doesn't have a computer?"

"He may have a friend who has one," Burl said. "Or he may be using one in a local library. Does your son frequently visit the library?"

"Not to my knowledge," John Enderly said. "He's not a very bright boy, dropped out of school last year because he said it was boring. I would be surprised if he knew any one who has a computer. He works at Pizza Parlor on the other side of town. Rides the El to work every day early. Comes home early in the evening and when he gets paid he usually gives me his paycheck. Except this past Saturday he didn't come home."

"I think that has to be the James Enderly who may be with the girl I'm seeking," Burl said. "Thank you for your time, Mr. Enderly. May I call again if I have any further questions?"

"Hell yes," Enderly said. "If you find anything or hear from Jimmy, please call me. I've got a private detective I'm supposed to meet tonight at the bus station. Some Injun from out in Western Canada. He's the only one who would take the case. Rest of them want too much money up front. We paid him $500 cause that's all we can afford right now, told him we'd pay his regular fee when we can."

"You've hired a private detective?" Burl Britton asked.

"Yes. Name of Savage. Noble Savage is his name. Funny name for an Injun, don't you think?"

Britton didn't answer. He hated the word Injun. His great-great grandmother was a full blooded Chickasaw on his father's side. His great- great grandfather was Cherokee on his mother's side. He didn't like the phrase "Native American" either. He preferred tribal names.

"Well, I'm sure that he's qualified," Britton said. "Thank you for your time, Mr. Enderly. If I find anything I'll let you know."

"Thank YOU!" Enderly said.

Britton hung up the phone and wrote the name "Noble Savage" in his notebook, drew a squiggly line under it and next to it wrote the word "Tribe" with a half dozen question marks after it.

He regretted telling Enderly that he would let him know if he found anything about James. Enderly wasn't paying his bills and he owed him nothing. It was just the despair in John Enderly's voice that made him want to try to help. He didn't have any idea about the abilities of Enderly's choice for an investigator, but then it wasn't any of his business so he put it out of his mind and closed his notebook, made a mental note to try to get in touch with Noble Savage at some point or another. Savage might have information that would help him solve his own case. He didn't think for a second that he might have information that would help Savage with HIS case.

CHAPTER 8

"Mr. and Mrs. Enderly, I presume?" I said , trying to sound cosmopolitan.

"That is correct, sir" gruffed Mr. Enderly, in a voice like gravel pouring into a vat of cement.

"My name is Noble Savage, pleased to make your acquaintance."

"Funny, I expected..."his voice trailed off into the Old West, as I finished his sentence for him.

"Someone a little more civilized?" I ended on a blunt question.

The woman gasped at my audacious interjection.

"Why don't we just dispense with all the formalities and cut to the chase. I just drove halfway across the backside of my country to get to you. Is that, O.K. with you, sir?"

"Certainly..I..I..didn`t mean.." Again I cut him off.

"Sir, I couldn't care less about your personal prejudices, I'm just here to carry out my part of our agreement. Is that quite alright with you, sir?" I noticed he was looking at my hat as though he was looking for..a ..feather, perhaps?

Mrs. Enderly chimed in and saved his soul.

"Mr. Savage, we are so very grateful that you could come all the way from...Skaskitchewin..oh, dear. I mean..

She turned a deep dusty rose.

"Don't bother trying to pronounce it, let's just say I'm the Indian from Canada, and be done with it!

We moved over into a booth in the bus-depot cafeteria. We ordered a big breakfast of ham and sausage and four eggs. God, I hadn't ate like that in a coon's age! I looked over and they had barely touched their plates. I surmised that their loss of appetite was part of the grieving process. When the bill came, I was ready to peel off a hundred dollar bill. Mr. Enderly quickly shushed me away from the waitress and insisted that they would pick up the tab.

"Of, course, we insist that you room with us for the duration, or at least the greater part of your time with us. We refuse to take no for an answer." It was the woman's voice of charity.

"If you insist." I said, secretly tickled that I would be put up until I finished the job.

"We insist, don't we, John? She stared at him with laser eyes.

`Thank you, ma'am." I said with a debonair tip of my fedora.

The next morning, I sat down with the Enderlys and the puzzle slowly started to take shape. Their son, James, was adopted, but they loved him as if he was their own. They had gotten him from an orphanage deep in the heart of the inner city. From a child, he seemed to be somewhat disturbed. At times he would experience uncontrollable fits of rage. They hadn't wanted to admit it but the tests came back to the affirmative, James was indeed an Auspberger case as well as bipolar. He could be quite unpredictable in his behavioral patterns. In fact, he could be quite violent, and seemingly without provocation. It appeared as though the couple lived with their son under a constant black cloud of trepidation.

I had a heart of stone, but, somehow, something touched me deep inside about this case. Was it because of my own socially disadvantaged background? I don't know. I shook off those tenderizing thoughts. I was a tough, and that's the way I wanted to go. I despised softness with a quietly steaming passion. Of course, I didn't mind it in a woman. My mother was a woman. I just figured everything has its` proper place and time.

After all, I'm still a man and I had learned about the birds and the bees a long, long time ago. I guess that's what makes a couple do some pretty schizoid things sometime. I found my way to the bathroom and tried to smile at that guy in the mirror, but, he wouldn't smile back.

"Ah, up yours, too, Tonto!" I said and I went downstairs and crawled into bed.

CHAPTER 9

Early the next morning Burl Britton woke up from a restless sleep. Something had kept him from sleeping well. He remembered waking up all through the night, a nagging feeling of impending doom lingering like bad breath.

He sat on the edge of his bed and turned the lamp on. It was 5 a.m. He was usually awake at 5 or 5:30 every day, but most days he felt better. Today he felt like leftover pizza, stale and odorous.

He dragged his 6 foot frame into the shower and after 10 minutes of soaping and rinsing and a thorough shampoo, he felt a little better on the outside but his mind was still in a blue funk on the inside. There was just something bothering him.

He fixed himself a bowl of cold cereal and carried it into his living room and sat on the edge of a chocolate brown leather divan, picked up the remote and clicked it at the small TV in the entertainment center. He had never cared much for the huge wide screen TV's and after the passing of his wife, he sold the big set and bought one that fit back in the entertainment center. He seldom watched TV at night, too occupied with sorting out the events of whatever case he might be handling. Morning news was about all he ever watched on a regular basis.

This morning's news was a shocker. His clients, Mr. and Mrs. Banquell were found dead in their home by a maid. Both had been shot. Mr. Banquell had been shot with a shotgun,

Dora had been shot several times with a small caliber handgun. Coroner's reports were due by the end of the week, but police had already ruled the deaths homicide, ruling out the possibility that one had killed the other then committed suicide. The case of the missing daughter, Lisa, according to police, may have played a part in the death of Lisa's parents.

So that is what it was that had flickered like an old silent movie through Burl Britton's mind all night long.

He knew that his case was still valid, his fees would be paid from the Banquell's estate. He also knew that the police would soon come calling for details in the missing persons case. He wasn't sure how much he could withhold. Sometimes his cases were hampered when the police were brought in.

In the thirty odd years that he had been a Private Investigator, he had never had a client murdered. It dawned on him that his fingerprints would be scattered like peanut shells at a Braves game throughout the Banquell's estate like home.

Fortunately he had the recording still on his office phone where Dora Banquell had phoned him and requested that he come to their home for the purpose of contracting to find her missing daughter.

Britton walked back into his kitchen, rinsed his cereal bowl and spoon and put them in the dishwasher. Then he realized that the dishes in the dishwasher were clean, he had started the cycle before he went to bed the previous evening, so he removed the bowl and spoon and set them in the sink.

He walked through the house to the den. Most of the furniture had been removed from the den. Britton always wondered why his wife had insisted on having a home with a den and a living room. You either lived in a living room or stayed in the den. They had always stayed in the den. After his wife passed away, Britton couldn't see any need for a living room that wasn't lived in, so he moved the furniture from the den and set up his exercise equipment there.

He had kept himself in good shape since he left the police force. His six foot frame carried a neatly packed 180 pounds of lean, muscular meat. A full length mirror on one wall reflected his form as he sat on a rowing machine and worked out for ten minutes, then a bow flex for heavier work.

Tennis kept him quick and flexible, but lately he had started to get a little paunch around his middle. Too many beers, he thought, and made a mental note to cut back on the beer. He didn't smoke and watched what he ate, but ate what he wanted. Having never been a big eater, his portions were normal and he seldom had seconds, although he nearly always had a dessert after his evening meal. Oprah said that he shouldn't eat and go to bed within two hours of each other, so he had started eating his dessert after supper, then retiring around 9 or 9:30 each night, unless working a case that required later hours.

His morning workout did not help erase the feeling of doom that had settled over him during the night. The deaths of the Banquell's just seemed like a bad omen to him. Something was amiss. He felt sure that this case was going to be one that would push him closer to retirement, and he wasn't sure that he was ready to retire just yet. He had few hobbies other than tennis and an occasional golf game, did not socialize much except for Sunday morning Church services, and an annual trip to South Texas to play golf with his brother.

"We'll see what happens," he said aloud, and left the exercise room and headed for the shower.

CHAPTER 10

I awoke to the smell of freshly brewed java and the drone of a pesky fly. Back on the rez, I was usually up at the crack of noon. The White Man's clock lied to me. It was plain to see that I was indeed on Indian Time. I got up off the floor. My subconscious must have been working overtime again. I was still wearing my black, thick- rimmed, Indian Affairs issue specs. Sometimes, I fall asleep with them on to see what I`m dreaming about. I must have been re-living one of my many illustrious street-fights once again. I shook off my semi-dream state long enough to hear the chaotic sounds of a woman highly distraught. Mrs. Enderley tried to keep her obvious alarm to a loud whisper.

When I appeared in the doorway of their living room, they suddenly muted their conversation. The cordless on the floor gave me my first hint that something had gone suddenly awry. Rule no. 1, according, to my crime correspondence textbook, read: "If things appear to be suspicious, then, they probably are. Proceed with all due caution." Somehow, I felt like a little boy who had just walked in on a very sensitive moment.

"Care to enlighten me as to what the hey is going on?

"That was...the ..p.p..p...police." she sounded like a thoroughly angst Porky Pig.

"Yes, and they want you to buy some Girl Scout brownies? C'mon, out with it!"

"It's about Jimmy!"

I faintly recall, with heavy eyelids, going through their family albums, the previous evening. The idea was that I was trying to get a deeper sense of who I was supposed to find. I went through a scattered montage of posed photos. In all of them, Jimmy rarely smiled. I just supposed his mental disposition had everything to do with the absence of human warmth in the photos. I knew all about the absence of human warmth. I would have made a great blues wailer. A picture can tell a thousand motives,` as my instructor wrote. Just then, I had an," aha!" moment.    There I went, surmising again. I must be the world's greatest surmiser! Read my thick brown lips, `Little Jimmy, wasn't happy here, or quite possibly anywhere on earth." It was difficult to imagine how every gesture might be perceived by him to be of suspicious nature.

My mind drifted back to that lil' sweetie in Canwood.   I mean, after all, I, too was a teenager, not so many moons ago.

"Detective Savage, are you still with us!" It was the lord of the manor.

"Wuh?..yeah, I was thinking about something pertinent to this case."

"What you talking about?" I was a little slow without my morning java. People on the rez called me Java Man, most likely after the prehistoric gentleman.

"I'm sorry, I'm so sorry, it's my baby! Jimmy has been arrested! They caught him in a stolen car, somewhere near Atlanta. Please, Mr. Savage, you got to help us!" This time it was Mother Hen talking.

"I don't mean to sound heartless," I lied, "but do you think I can have my morning java first?"

I hated drama queens. I hated wussy jokers, and I had a pair of them falling apart right in front of my beautiful brown eyes. I took a stiff shot of premium Columbian java, and felt a twinge of warmth in my stone-cold pumper. I shook it off as I got dressed to meet the next piece in the puzzle.

CHAPTER 11

We drove to the police station in an agonized silence. I couldn't fully ascertain if it was depression or sorrow which hung palpably, given the narrow confines . It likely was a mix of both. I didn't mist over easily. I could be a callous bastard. A man needs to be tough in this life. And, I didn't much give a damn what I had to do to overcome the obstacles that came my way. I was weaned on violence at an early age. Over the years, I learned how to take my licks. And, in due time, I became quite expert at dispensing my own inimitable brand of hand to hand mayhem!

"Keep eyes on opponent!" the sharp command jagged my spine.

"Yes, Sensei!!"I would acknowledge his superior wisdom.

"Flow like water! Not like clumsy fool!"

I became suddenly silent, not knowing what to say next.

"When enemy comes at you with knife, you become like sword! Flow forward, flow forward, overpower like tiger!!`

His words cut into me like obsidian blades. Until, I flowed like swift water! The kata I learned in the shadow of wisdom became my weapon. I was schooled thoroughly in the beautifully poetic motions of Tae Kwon Do. The old man smiled secretly as I advanced through the deadly forms known to my teacher.

"When you strike, it must be with power and swiftness as lightning! Show no mercy to those who desire to send you to shadow-world!"

"Yes, Sensei!" I accorded respect to the old man who fought as no other.

"And, above all else, listen to your inner man!"

I didn't get what he meant, until years later, when I squared off with the town bully. He was a walking, boisterous side of beef. But, I left him in the dust, weeping like a baby. In a few deft movements; as water meets with fire, I snapped both of his wrists like brittle, autumn twigs.

"Mr. Savage! You've taken the wrong turn. We passed the 12th precinct a block ago!"

Presently, my mind whipped back to 2012. I pulled the big steering wheel a half-turn and headed back to the 12th. For a crazy moment, Sweetie from Canwood whispered into my mind..."How about the 12th of never?...."
I stopped abruptly in the police chief's parking spot and we piled out of Old Betsy.

"Anybody got a nickel for the meter?" I bellowed, in a not so mellow vein.

"The meters haven't been a nickel since the 40`s, Mr. Savage." I would have blushed, but I had long ago forgotten how. And, if I could, my face would probably glow, a distinct dusty rose.

We walked into the precinct and it was almost like drifting onto a set on Barney Miller. This was the place of Al Capone, Baby-Face Nelson and John Dillinger. I had tried to dress accordingly. I had a penchant for double-breasted pin-striped suits straight from the racks of Value Village. Some say that my clothes smelled like someone crapped into the pockets. That was just the moth-balls. I guess my nose just grew accustomed to the malignant odor. But, nothing quite matches the malodorous stench of human misery. Growing up on the rez, for a hundred years, a guy just kinda gets used to it. We had our own little mafia on our home turf. They were called chief and council.

"Hey, Chief! Howz about a rain dance? Weez been kinda dry around dis neighborhood, lately." It was the desk Sergeant, typically gruff in all his urbane glory.

"Mister," I gritted, through clenched teeth," If I want crap from you, I'll scrape it off your teeth!"

He motioned toward me like he wanted to tear me apart like a cheap guitar.

"Oh, I wish you would try what you're thinking." I said with an abrasive, icy edge of cool.

"Gentlemen, please, please. we are after all, civilized!" It was the chief of police.

"Tanksh!, but I assure you, I can take care of myself." I said calmly, in the language that only real men perceive.

"What may we do for you, sir?" the chief wore a stone mask, thinly glazed over with his own personal dislikes.

"I'm Det. Noble Savage, and this couple, the Enderlys`, John and Marilyn, are my current employers. They have procured my services as P.I. Pardon, my Canadian, but, I'm on the hunt for a James Enderly. He's the Enderlys' adopted son. Would you like me to do an etch-a-sketch to flesh out the reason for our little visit?"

"I take it, you're speaking of the James Enderly who just walked out of here about an hour ago?"

"What?" It was Mother Hen again.

"How did he....?"the rooster crowed with roughed up crest.

" Yeah, miracle of miracles, he made bail! Good luck in finding him!"

"Who was he with?" I said sounding like I genuinely cared. I didn't recognize the voice of genuine concern. It was becoming obvious, I was getting a little soft. I didn't exactly cherish the feeling. In my world, you get too soft, a guy might end up visiting the little fishies on the bottom of the Hudson.

"A woman, nice looking."

"How did she make payment?" I tried to dig up some bones.

"Oh, I don't know, maybe with a truck-full of re-cyclable cans, I don't know, Mr. P.I., that's your job to find out. There , ask your buddy, Casey, the desk sarge."

Obviously, it was time to eat crow. I was secretly hoping he wouldn't ask me for a date, in return for the info.

I tried to be genteel. Yet, sometimes, I have to go a little savage.

"Listen, Sergeant, I'd like to apologize for my rude conduct as it pertains to our .....He cut me off.

"What the hell are you? No stinkin` savage is supposed to talk like that. How about a..How!..or at least an "ugg".or something like that?"

I snapped. I grabbed his crisp, blue tie. Rule number three. Be careful to respect officers of the law with which you make contact. I made contact. I'm quite certain that he was adjusting to a different point of view as I constricted the blood flow to his Neanderthal brain. He was turning purple by the time I released him from the Vulcan death grip.

"Do you have something to say to me, Sir?" I inquired, as a gentleman should.

"She...pp..pp..p..pp.pp...paid in. money order. Wells Fargo, I think." He slumped down in a heap as a new man.

Marilyn Enderly had fainted dead away, and John was trying to revive her with a cool, wet handkerchief. He was remarkably composed for someone who had just seen his world turned upside down. When she came to, I tried to reassure Marilyn that everything was going to be alright. Funny thing was, I was starting to believe it myself. But just between you and me, I never did believe in fairy tales.

"Come on guys, let's go home." I said, trying to shake the feeling that the trouble had only started to reveal its ugly little head.

CHAPTER 12

The Whispering Meadows Police Department headquarters building looked like one that you would see in Andy of Mayberry. Tall columns of concrete on either end of the building, steps all the way across the front. It looked more like a courthouse than a police department.

Britton walked to the counter and addressed the desk sergeant on duty.

"I'm Burl Britton," he said. "I figured I'd come in before you send a squad car out to pick me up."

"Oh, Mr. Britton," the sergeant said, rising. "Yes, we do have some questions we'd like to ask you. Right this way, Sir."

He led Britton down a hallway on the left, and past two doors before knocking on the glass window of the third door.

He pushed the door open and stepped inside.

"Mr. Britton is here," he said. Britton walked in. He was surprised to see that the Detective Sergeant Miller, whose name was on the door, was a woman. She stood up and extended her hand.

"Thanks for coming in, Mr. Britton," she said.

He shook her hand. She had a medium strong grip, like she really meant it, instead of offering just her fingers in a handshake like a lot of women do. She smelled good, a gentle hint of honeysuckle perfume. He guessed that she might be in her early 40's, tall, honey-blonde hair that was cut above her shoulders and nicely coifed.

"I'm Beverly Miller," she said. "I guess you know why we wanted to talk to you, and thank you for coming in on your own."

"You found my prints at the Banquell's home," He said. "I was there at their request. They hired me to find Lisa Banquell, reported missing last Saturday."

"We had no report," Sergeant Miller said.

"I'm aware of that," Britton said. "Mrs. Banquell didn't want to publicize the fact that her daughter may have ran away from home. That kind of news doesn't set well with the Sunday go to meeting crowd."

"Yes, well..."

"You want to know if I've found Lisa yet, is that it?"

"Actually, Mr. Britton, we didn't know about your involvement with the Banquell's. Your prints showed up. It didn't take long to match them with our computer base, since you are a licensed Private Detective and prior to that you were on the police force."

"Figures," Britton said.

"Our officers surmised that you were there on business."

"I bet." Britton said. "I know that bunch of yes men on your police force. They know me. They probably suspected that I was having a fling with the lovely Dora Banquell. Is that it?"

"That possibility was posed," she said, blushing. "Of course we do not jump to conclusions in this department, if I can help it. I would have surmised that your visit there was a business one.'

"It was."

"So you were hired to find the missing daughter?"

"Yep."

"They just have the one child. Lisa, age 16, high school cheerleader, well liked. No problems reported at school, we've checked all of that. What have you found?"

"I've found that Lisa may have gone to Chicago with a boy named Jimmy Enderly."

"Can you elaborate on that?"

"I found an email on her computer. She had it in a hidden file, like she didn't want anyone to see it. I had a friend trace the email properties, he said it was from a small internet service provider in Chicago. I looked up Enderly's in the white pages and started calling. I got lucky. Contacted a lady who is married to Jimmy Enderly's uncle. Eventually I got through to the right Enderly, a John Enderly. He reported his son was missing."

"Anything else you want to tell me, Mr. Britton?"

"Just curious why you aren't putting out an APB on Lisa Banquell."

"Oh yeah," she said. "Of course I meant we'll pick up the two of them for questioning."

"That means you haven't already?"

"What does that mean?" Sergeant Miller asked.

"Don't be coy with me, Sergeant," Britton said. "I know where the money is in this town. The Banquell's come from a long line of money. Arthur's father, Jobe Banquell, has got enough money to burn Texas if it is soaking wet. Are you trying to keep anything out of the local papers?"

"You are pretty astute, Mr. Britton," she said. "OK. We've already picked up the boy. Jimmy Enderly has been questioned and released to the Chicago police department where he was wanted for car theft."

"Jimmy and Lisa had an internet romance going, according Jimmy. According to Chicago police, Jimmy stole a 2008 Buick Lucerne and drove it down here to Georgia.

"So you were one step ahead of me," Britton said.

"We got lucky, too." She pushed a piece of paper across the desk to him.

He picked it up and read it.

It was a traffic violation. Jimmy was stopped by a Georgia State Trooper for speeding on the interstate between Atlanta and Whispering Meadows. When they asked for Jimmy's drivers license and registration, he couldn't provide the registration. They ran a make on the car and found that it had been stolen the previous Friday from a Pizza Parlor parking lot in Chicago.

"So I guess my case has ended," Britton said.

"Maybe not," she smiled at him. "Jobe Banquell called shortly before you came in. He has no idea where his granddaughter is. When we told him that your fingerprints had been found at the Banquell house, he requested that we call him when we picked you up for questioning. The desk sergeant called him when you came in. He's on his way here to talk to you. I'm guessing that he will want you to find Lisa."

"What if I don't want anything else to do with this case?" Britton asked.

"That's up to you, Mr. Britton," she said. "If I were you, I'd talk to Jobe Banquell. He doesn't like to be shunned."

"Let's get something straight," Britton said, standing. "I don't owe allegiance to Jobe Banquell, to the Whispering Meadows police department, or to the State of Georgia. If he wants to talk to me, he can find me."

"Thanks again for coming in," Sergeant Miller said as Britton left her office.

CHAPTER 13

We drove back to the Enderley home in the rain. For some strange reason, this old song kept playing, in my mind over and over again. "Rainy night in Georgia...rainy night in Georgia, and it feels like it's raining all over the world."

The couple in the back seat were silently weeping. Their tears mingled soulfully with the rain slashing back and forth on the windshield.

A drum beat, in the back of my mind, deeply hollow in its resonance. The sorrow chant echoed across the valley of weeping in the landscape of my jaded mind. A faded black and white photo of a little orphaned boy rose up out of my darkly shadowed past. It was me! My grandfather held my hand as we stood at my mother's graveside. From that moment on, my heart began to turn to stone, and the years went by.

I was as tough as they come, and my mission in life was to re-unite Jimmy Enderly with his family or die trying. From that critical pinpoint in my investigation, I didn't really care anymore if they gave me sweet squat for my services. Someone, out there had called my play to come deeper into this mystery. I never back down from a voice I can't attach a face to. I was piqued. I felt I owed it to myself to see this through to the end, come what may.

It seemed eons until we saw the bright lights of home. We got out of the old Pontiac feeling like zombies who had done some unforgivable wrong. It was good to get inside and to warm our hands beside the fireplace. John put on the coffee, and slowly, Java man came back to life, just as frisky as ever. I felt the life creep back into my hands, and I proceeded to make some phone calls. The Enderlys were going to have a phone bill to remember for many years to come.

The Enderly case seemed to be a simple one. Bored teenager gets the urge to merge, finds a soul-mate on the internet and he's off to the wide blue yonder. This one blazed a trail from Chicago down to the land of plantations and cotton fields. M..mm..m..mm, I could already smell the chitins and gravy and black-eyed peas. Now, according to the Whispering Meadows Police Department our Bonnie and Clyde showed up on the roster as a couple of in-love juvies. I put 2 and 2 together and I ended up with 3. Math was never my thing. But when something doesn't add up, it just doesn't make sense. Don't get me wrong, the only way I learned about l`amour was reading about it in True Confessions. The truth, is, I was too embarrassed to ask my grandfather.

Why does life always seem to be so complicated? My image of Jimmy as an innocent was slowly starting to fall apart. Mind you, the way his mind processed information would be worlds apart from a "normal" person. Besides, what the hell is considered normal these days?

"Noble, would you like another coffee?
"It was my gracious host.

I was worried somewhat, because I was getting a little attached to my employers. It wasn't like me to get to like someone who hired me. I knew this could mean complications. I knew I eventually would have to get back to the Prairies. So, once again I had to pull on my stone mask and turn to ice. I knew it was a losing battle, because the warmth of the sun was starting to shine through.

Then they told me about this Burl Britton. The only Burl I knew was the singer. Yeah, you know...`a little bit of tear let me down...spoiled my act as a clown," Oh, what was his last name again? You know. the big fella..the big guy..O.K. Crackerby! Burl Ives, yeah, yeah, that's it!

CHAPTER 14

When he has trouble thinking a case through, Burl Britton's favorite spot is the county library. He will often study the principals in the case, their heritage, their accomplishments. So it was that he found himself at the library doing a little research on Jobe Banquell.

Jobe had started a small peanut farm in the 50's and by the time he was 30 he had bought several thousand acres of land from surrounding farmers, most of whom had retired and put the land in soil banks. His peanut farms were producing the product for Jobe peanut butter factories in Georgia, a company that shipped peanut butter to every state in the Union, and some foreign countries. Now he was extremely wealthy.

Britton didn't envy wealth. He thought that every man has a chance to accomplish something in life, and each individual is faced with choices as to whether or not he wants his dreams to be reality. The first choice that has to be made is whether or not to work. He couldn't remember a day when he hadn't worked. At an early age he worked in his father's fields, the whole family did. His father sharecropped a big farm. All of Britton's siblings were put to work at about the age of 5. Either you fed chickens, slopped pigs, picked peaches, or worked inside the house, you worked.

Britton learned later that the old man believed that poison from insecticides would cause cancer. They never sprayed a drop of it on the farm.

Now he was reading about Jobe's peanut butter factory and how that old man had worked to accomplish his dreams

He was deeply engrossed in the story and didn't see two large black men walking silently towards the table where he sat. One stopped on one side of his chair, the other stood directly behind it.

"Mr. Britton, you should come with us," one said.

Britton turned and looked at the man. He was as big as a barn door, wore a fine suit, and dark glasses.

"Who are you?"

"We work for Jobe Banquell," the man said.

"Mr. Banquell wants to talk to you, Mr. Britton," the other man said.

"You tell Mr. Banquell to come to me," Britton said, and turned back to the book he was reading.

He felt something touch his back, right in the middle of his spine. It wasn't the first time someone had poked a gun in his back, and he knew it immediately.

"It is in your best interest to come with us, Mr. Britton," the first black man said quietly. "Please don't make us hurt you."

Britton pushed his chair away from the table and stood up. He knew that he was in no danger of being shot in a public library, but he also knew that these two men could put something over his face to make him sleep, or inject him with an instant knock out drug. He was smart enough to realize that it was futile to resist.

He smiled up into the face of the huge man.

"Looks like you've made your point."

They led him out of the library and to a limousine that waited at the curb. One opened the door for him and he got in next to a heavy man wearing a dark blue suit, brilliant white shirt, and a dark blue and red striped tie.

"Mr. Britton?"

"Yes, and you must be Jobe Banquell."

"Yes I am," the man said. He extended his hand and Britton shook it.

"What can I do for you, Mr. Banquell?" Britton asked. "I don't really like the way you summoned me, but discretion is the better part of valor, and rather than cause a disturbance in the public library, I've decided to talk to you."

"Yes," Banquell said, and Britton could tell that he was thinking that Britton didn't have a choice.

"You've no doubt heard of the death of my son and daughter in law?"

"Yes, I've already talked to the police about that. I'm sorry for your loss."

"You were hired to find Lisa. Do you know where she is?"

"No," Britton said. "So I guess I should finalize my statement and mail it to you?"

"That's what I want to talk to you about. I want you to find her and bring her to me."

"What if she doesn't want to come? Or what if she's dead?"

"If she's dead, bring her body. If she's alive, bring her. You're bigger than she is, do whatever it takes to get her to me."

"What's in it for me?"

"I'll pay you $25,000 if you can bring her to me alive before the police find her."

"That's a tall order, I'm one man. Police are all over the country."

"I know how Police departments work," the old man said. "They have rules and regulations, they have protocol, the have procedures. I know that you don't have to follow the same rules that they follow. That's why I'm offering a very lucrative sum. Do you understand me?"

"I understand perfectly," Britton said. Twenty five grand was a very generous offer. It might cost him a few thousand for expenses.

"Plus expenses," Banquell said, as if he was reading Britton's mind.

"Deal," Britton said. He extended his hand. Banquell shook it.

"I'll put it in writing and once you've signed the contract, I'll start looking," Britton said.

"Agreed," the old man said.

Britton told the senior Banquell about the e-mail he had discovered on Lisa's computer, and about the boy being picked up by Georgia police for driving a stolen vehicle. "The police turned the boy over to Chicago authorities. The car he was driving was stolen there. She may have went to Chicago. Did she have money?"

"She always had money," Banquell said. "Her allowance is $2000 per month. I don't know how much money she had, but she had a debit card to get more if she needed it. Money's never been an object in Lisa's life. She's been spoiled since she was born. I should have never consented to let her go to a public school. I wanted to put her in a private, all girls school. Her father, my son, convinced me that she would develop more normally in public schools. I always worried about kidnappers, Arthur felt that it would have been difficult for anyone to kidnap her since everyone knew she was my granddaughter and the consequences of hurting her would be instant and final retribution. He even said that he would personally kill anyone who harmed a hair on her head."

"You couldn't protect her from herself," Britton said.

"What does that mean?"

"When I searched her room, I found a small packet of white substance. I took it to a private company for analysis. It was cocaine."

"Cocaine?" The old man muttered, putting his head down and shaking it back and forth.

The limousine had circled the library several times, down one street, a right turn, down that street and another right, now they were slowing to a stop in the same spot where Britton had got in.

"When can I expect to see our agreement in writing?" Banquell asked.

"Today," said Britton. "I have a messenger service that will bring it to you, Please sign both copies and have one returned to my office. When I get it, I'll start a ledger with everything I know about your son, his wife, and

Lisa. You will get weekly updates until such time as I've found Lisa or you terminate me."

The old man sighed again and pressed a button on the arm of the seat where he sat.

"Stop the car, let Mr. Britton out," he said.

Britton got out of the car and walked to his own. When he got in his Honda it felt like he was sitting in a bumper car after being in the limo. Money, he thought. Can't buy happiness. Money isn't everything.

Yeah, he thought, but it's way ahead of what ever is in second place.

He drove back to his office and after drawing up his agreement with Jobe Banquell and sending it on its way by messenger service, he called Delta Airlines and made reservations for a round trip flight to Chicago. What the hay, Jobe Banquell was paying for the flight so he booked it first class. The flight was scheduled to leave at 6:15 and it was now 11 a.m. He would have plenty of time to go home and shower, change clothes and pack a few things. He didn't know how long he would be in Chicago, but made reservations at a hotel near the airport for two nights.

When the time came to be at the airport for security check in, Britton was there. He got a brush through security by showing his PI license to a NSA guard that he knew.

"Have a nice flight, Burl," the guard said.

"Thanks," Britton said and walked to the waiting area for boarding.

A half hour later he was at 10,000 feet and enjoying the luxury of first class with a Jack

Daniels and water, reading the swimsuit issue of Sports Illustrated.

Chicago was drizzling rain when the flight landed. It was dark and too late to do anything, so Britton took an airport shuttle to the hotel and checked in. He found the dining room, ordered steak and lobster, and made a mental note to charge the meal to Jobe Banquell.

In his room he put a call through to John Enderly.

"Mr. Enderly, this is Burl Britton, I talked to you a few days ago about Jimmy. Remember me?"

"Yes, Mr. Britton," Enderly said. "Have you any good news for me?"

"You mean Jimmy isn't with you?"

"No, I haven't seen him. We got word that the Chicago Police had custody of him, but before we could get to the precinct where he was held, someone bailed him out. Mr. Savage asked some questions and was told that a woman put up the money for his bail. We haven't seen him, though. I wish he would have called or something."

"A woman bailed him out?" Britton asked.

"Yes, that's what we were told. Hold on, I'll let you talk to Mr. Savage. He's handling the missing persons case for us, to find Jimmy."

The line went silent for a minute.

"Yeah?" The voice was deep and vibrant. It sounded like it was coming from a barrel-chested man who could sing bass in a barbershop quartet.

"Mr. Savage?"

"That's me, who'm I talking to?"

"This is Burl Britton," Burl said. "I'm working the other side of your case, trying to track down Lisa Banquell. Mr. Enderly just told me you found out a woman bailed out Jimmy Enderly from a Chicago precinct holding tank."

"You heard right."

"Have you any idea where the two are at this time?"

"That's a dumb question, Britton. If I knew, wouldn't I be there getting Jimmy? That's what these good folks are paying me to do."

"Sorry, I guess you're right on that," Britton said. "Anything at all that you might have regarding my case, I'd appreciate the tip. If I find anything on Jimmy, I'll be sure to let you know. We're both after the same objective."

"No, were really not," Savage said. "You're looking for Lisa. I'm looking for Jimmy. I could care less if you ever find Lisa unless she's got Jimmy with her. I'm not beholden to you or whoever hired you."

"I understand," Britton said. "I'm just offering to help. And I'd appreciate your help."

"I'm not sure I need your help, Mr. Britton," Savage said, roughly. "I work my own cases, ask my own questions, and have a way of dealing with folks who don't give me the right answers."

"OK, have it your way, Savage." Britton said. His tolerance level had nearly peaked. "I don't really need help from you, either, but since we have a common objective, to find two runaway teens, I thought we could make it a joint effort. If you don't want it that way, then good luck."

He hung up.

He sat on the edge of his bed for a minute thinking about what he had just learned. What should his next move be? It would take a month of Sundays to check all of the motels and hotels in the Windy City, looking for someone who may not even be around town. He was starting to doubt his reason for the trip.

His mind raced around, seeking help from some source. It was pretty obvious that Savage wasn't going to be much help. What Savage had said about working his own cases was still irking Britton. Tonight was the first time he had ever been turned down when he offered to help another PI on a case in return for help on his case. And since the two cases were tied together like a bow on a tennis shoe, he was irked that Savage wouldn't help him. He'd just have to find his own sources, make his own way.

While watching an old re-run on television, his mind finally made the connection he was looking for. He had a friend at the Atlanta television station WGTV, a public broadcast channel. Her name was Donna DeLong. They had gone out a couple of times and enjoyed playing tennis on Sunday afternoons. She might know someone at the news channel that could get Chicago to run a spot asking if anyone had seen Lisa Banquell or Jimmy Enderly, to call a hotline. The hotline would be his cell phone.

He called Donna, talked sweet to her for several minutes and she agreed to make some phone calls.

By eleven o'clock a Chicago news broadcast was showing pictures of Lisa and

Jimmy and asking anyone who had seen them to call the hotline, Britton's cell phone. Of course no one but him knew the call would only be answered by him. Donna had contacted Atlanta PD and got a picture of Jimmy when he was arrested for car theft. Britton had then contacted Jobe Banquell and asked that he fax a picture of Lisa to the public broadcasting station, where it was passed on to the Chicago station.

Britton watched fascinated as the news reporter rattled off the standard line: Missing teens, Jimmy Enderly and Lisa Banquell may be in the Chicago area, according to local sources. Anyone who has seen either of the teens whose pictures are being shown on your screen at this time, please contact the missing teen hotline.

Feeling completely satisfied with his ability to find a way when no way seemed possible, Britton undressed, crawled in the king-sized bed and was soon fast asleep.

CHAPTER 15

At six the next morning Burl Britton was awakened by a rapping on his hotel door. He sat upright in the bed instantly, wide awake. Who would be knocking at this hour?

The door rattled with the force of the knock.

Britton got up and pulled on his pants, yelling at the person knocking on the door.

"Yeah, just a second," he said.

He unhooked the security chain and turned the knob.

A man stood at the door. He was shorter than Britton by about four inches, but stocky, broad shoulders and narrow waste. Britton guessed that he would be about 50 years of age.

"Britton?" The man said.

"Yes."

"I'm here to offer an apology. I saw your message on local TV about the missing kids. I don't know how you managed it, but it was a damned good idea."

"You're Savage?" Britton said.

"Not in the literal sense of the word," Savage said. "But yeah, that's me, Noble Savage."

He stuck out his hand and Britton shook hands with him. His grip was like steel and Britton noted that Savage had hands that looked like those he had seen on professional boxers. Knuckles wide spaced, fingers thick and strong.

"Come in," Britton said and stepped aside.

Savage walked in, glancing left and right quickly like a man well trained to watch for things that might present a danger.

"You saw the blurb on TV?"

"Yeah," Savage said. "I was beating myself to death because my investigation was going no-where. I'm sitting in a chair at the Enderly's place, thinking that I might make a trip to Atlanta. The TV was on, although the Enderly's had retired for the night. Then, BAM! It was right there on TV, pictures of the missing kids. It didn't take me long to figure that you had something to do with it."

"How did you find that out?" Britton asked, curious.

"I called the station. They told me the news release came from Atlanta, some woman who works for a public broadcast company, name of Donna DeLong. I called a friend in Atlanta and had him look her up. She didn't want to talk to me at first, but when she found out I had talked to you, she opened up. She said it was your idea."

Britton was taken aback. He thought that Savage's ability to find out who was behind the TV blurb was pretty good detective work.

"That's good work," he said.

Savage smiled. "Not as good as yours," he said. "I apologize for being a little gruff last night. After thinking about it, I realized that you are right. We can help each other. I'm sure that you're client will pay you a lot more than mine is paying me, but then I've grown to like the Enderlys and its not so much the money with me."

"I'm willing to share whatever fee I get," Britton said. Half of something is better than half of nothing, he thought.

He was beginning to like this rough looking man. Anyone who has a heart big enough to feel compassion for a couple that spends their last hard earned savings to find a missing son was first rate in Britton's book. And, it looked like Savage could use a few dollars. He was dressed in dark slacks that were wrinkled, a black jacket and a Fedora style hat with a beaded band.

"That's big of you, Britton," Savage said. "How much is your client dishing out if you find the girl?"

"Dead or alive, he's on the hook for twenty five grand," Britton said.

Savage let out a long, protracted whistle.

"Twenty five grand?" He shook his head back and forth. "I would get half?"

"That's what I'm offering," Britton said.

Savage thought about it for a long minute.

He didn't like the idea of working a case with anyone else, but twelve and a half thousand was more money than he had made all of last year since he had hung up his shingle.

"You'll put that in writing?"

"No problem," Britton said. "It'll have to wait till I get back to Atlanta, though. I don't have any consulting agreements with me, they are in my office back in Whispering Meadows."

"A handshake will do for now," Savage said, offering his ham-sized hand again.

Britton shook it again.

Savage reached inside his jacket and pulled out a pint of something dark and unscrewed the cap.

"Here's to a joint effort," he said, taking a swig and offering the bottle to Britton.

Britton looked at it, thought "what the hell?" and took a swig. He sputtered, shook his head and coughed.

"What is that?" He asked.

"Home made," Savage said.

CHAPTER 16

I went on the hunt for Britton knowing deep down that eventually I`d need to work with him. I knew that big cities was his turf. He had inroads to places and people that I may never see. Let's face it, my credibility as a private dick was on the line. I wasn't making any headway in my lone quest for the always evasive truth. Finally, I had to concede that the city of Big Shoulders was a white man's turf. I didn't much like the idea of playing shadow man. It was a blow to my Id. I just wanted to get on with it.

Besides, I was anxious to get back to the flats. My sense of wishful thinking deceived me into believing that girly-girl would be waiting for me when I finally made it back home. It was quite possible too that my professionalism might be questioned once they got a load of the feather in my hat. As well, my financial woes, were becoming way too obvious. My piggy bank was getting a little on the lean side, so I thought I'd better try to get a hold of him. I was in the process of trying to look presentable, when I gave it up, knowing that it's..(ahem).. tough to improve on perfection. Taking my tube of Brylcream, I greased up. I slicked my hair back almost to the point of starting to resemble some kind of free-wheeling gigolo. I took one last look in the mirror and thought out loud.

"You know, Savage, you're not too shabby for a senior citizen."

The guy in the mirror was much too serious. The leather I wore still smelled like

Value Village. I tried to mask the odor of my rank poverty with a spritz of Lilac Glory, but the stench persisted. So, instead, I opted for a dark corduroy sport jacket. I didn't like the feather much. I felt it was too stereotypical. The beaded hatband was native enough. At this point, I almost dropped my piece of humble pie when I saw the newscast.

"Holy smoke signals!" I, ky-yiyed.

There on the six o'clock news were Bonnie and Clyde! Yeah, you're right! What respectable native will admit to waking up before noon? Immediately, I got down to the task of zeroing in on Britton's location. It didn't take genius to look in the phone book. However, in the city of Chicago, there's got to be half a million hotels. I started calling the obvious ones near the airport and asking for a Burl Britton. Bingo! I hit the jackpot.

Sitting across from him, I did my own personal analysis of my new found business partner. You can usually tell where a person is coming from within the first few minutes of the initial conversation. If he looks you in the eye, and doesn't appear too nervous he's probably going to be a straight shooter. Anybody that would cut me in on 50 percent of his own personal preserves couldn't possibly be a bad sort. As it is with strangers, and particularly with men, there was a slight undercurrent of tension. In the real world, deals can go horribly wrong. In this case, I didn't get a sense of any subversive scheming from this man. I figured he needed help, and there certainly isn't anything wrong with that. No man is an island, right?

We sat down around the table and hammered out the details of our business agreement. He told me what he knew of the case and I exchanged my findings with him. I could tell that this was a man that I could learn much from. The naked truth is, I didn't have very many friends, and those I did have, sooner or later were a big disappointment. From what I could gather, we were in for a few long nights of digging for solutions.

I didn't mind that part, I was a nighthawk through and through. Even as a child on the rez, my grandfather had to keep chasing me off to sleep. The night was my friend and I came alive in it. Stealth was my thing. I was on top of you long before you heard the whisper of my moccasins on the grass. My ancestral past was shrouded in the fine art of horse-stealing. Like I said before, a warrior's blood courses through like fire in my veins. I endured pain when other men would be sobbing to Mama. When it came to fighting, I fought to win and I didn't much give a damn how big they seemed. Mr. Britton had just bought himself a helluva pardner. I would be there to the conclusive end, come what may.

Britton promised to put our agreement in writing as soon as he got back to Atlanta, but for now we shook hands like gentlemen. I wondered momentarily if this would be another white man's treaty to be broken, but I had to trust him for now. Then I offered Britton a sip of Saskatchewan's finest. Taking the bottle, he downed a hearty swig as if it were finely aged Kentucky bourbon. He tilted his head back and learned the true meaning of fire-water. He winced, coughed and handed it back to me.

"What the heck was that?" He said with a sour look on his face.

"That there is my grandfather's own personal recipe for whatever ails you. Yep, it's home-made, straight from the tater!"

CHAPTER 17

I was sitting in the den, by the front picture window, deep in conversation with Marilyn and John. Then, I heard it. The couple seemed to be oblivious to the cracking sound against the glass. Immediately, I sensed, deep down, that there was going to be bad news on the doorstep at any given moment. Talk about the surreal. I felt like I was sitting dead center in some sort of bad dream. I looked over at Marilyn, and I choked down the rising lump in my throat. Right at that moment, I would have given the world to change what I felt was certain to transpire. I excused myself, and went outside to check on the noise.

And sure enough, I found a dead sparrow, laying on the grass where it had landed after hitting the window. Now, I'm not a superstitious man, by nature. But I knew something was about to happen that I couldn't control. Was it Nietzsche who said, `When you look into the abyss, then the abyss will look into you? Well, lately, I had plenty of time to do some deep soul-searching. Funny thing was, every time I`d dip deep, all I ever got was cold, hard ice.

"Noble! Go to bed right now, or else, I'm going to get my belt!" It was Gramps.

"Yes, sir, right away sir!" I yelled. He was the only one who could put the fear of God into my heart in double quick time.

"What's wrong, Mr. Savage?" It was the lady of the house. At that moment, I didn't know what to tell her. So, as always, I got away with a lie.

"Oh, it's probably nothing, it's just a bird."

"Well, come back in, you'll catch a chill." Nobody ever cared for me like she did. Again, I was a million miles away. I was suddenly five years old, and my mom had just whispered, "goodbye` into my ear.

"Mom, no...no..no..please don't leave me!" Someone had to pry me loose from her. I looked up, and it was Grandpa.

"She's gone, son. It's too late, she's gone." He wrapped me up in his strong arms, and that was the last time I ever cried. From that moment on, I swore that no one was ever going to hurt me ever again. Slowly, I started to build walls around my heart, and partitioned off the secret part that every man has, deep within his being.

"Noble, it's your turn!" This whole thing had turned into a waiting game. We waited for the phone to ring, in between games of Scrabble and Chinese checkers.

Finally, I had enough. John looked at me over his bifocals, as if he could understand what was going through my mind.

"Listen, folks, you may as well go to bed. I'm going for a drive." I had surreptitiously borrowed photos of Jimmy.

Marilyn handed me the house keys. John glanced over at their ornate Grandfather clock, and made mention of the late hour.

"Don't worry about me. Just say a prayer for Jimmy."

I drove up and down every back alley that I came across, or so it seemed. The night life, and the wildlife were out in full force. Twice, I narrowly escaped getting a brick or something or other thrown into my windshield.

"Where the heck are you, Jimmy?" I spoke into the chill of the night.

I had had the genius of making duplicate photos of Jimmy at Wal-Mart. I had gone there on the pretence of shopping for socks. I'm not at all sure that Sherlock would have done the same thing, but, I thought I'd give it a try. I passed these out on the mean streets, just to see what might turn up. Invariably, someone would ask if there was a reward. For once, I told the naked truth, in saying, 'Mebbe'.

One hooker took a look at the photo and said, "Hey, he's kinda cute. What about you, blood? Are you looking for action?"

"No, thanks, I moonlight as a priest. Ever feel like fessing up, give me a ding-a-ling, O.K., sis?" I handed her my 101st card of the evening. I may be native, but I wasn't stupid. Sex, these days, is like playing Russian Roulette with six bullets in the chamber.

The sun was hiding behind the skyscrapers when I got home the next morning. Hmm..home..sure would be nice, I thought. I walked in to the Enderley residence like a catatonic zombie. I got no sense of rhythm, but I managed to shuffle off to bed alright. I had a fitful sleep. I dreamed I was psycho-analyzing Freud. Go figure. And, then, my nocturnal ramblings turned really strange.

I saw my body floating on the ceiling of this cheap, motel room. The next thing I knew I was looking down at the body of Jimmy Enderly. He was curled up in a corner in a fetal position. I recognized him from the photos. He called out my name, which I thought was strange enough, because I had never met him before in my life. I saw two other bodies there. I couldn't tell whether they were male or female. I couldn't get a clear view of their faces. The only distinction of the two was that one them held out a blood-stained hand, and appeared to be clutching a heart with a crack in it. They spoke in a gibberish that I couldn't decipher. And, then, Freud chimed in.

"Mr. Savage, you are in violation of the Universal Law!" he said firmly resolute.

"And, just what the hell is that law?" I asked.

`You can't, and shan`t speak to the dead! Why everybody knows that!" Sigmund asserted.

`Well, excuse my Cree, but you're dead aren't you? And, I'm speaking to you, aren't I!"

"Well, that's...that`s..different!" he returned with extreme exasperation.

"How?" And then, I woke up. On the floor!

Somewhere down the valley of cob-webs, I heard the phone bleeping. I heard the shuffling of bedroom slippers, then someone picked up the receiver. Still half-asleep, I heard the voice rise and fall, as if greatly disturbed. My eye-lids were about to shut down again, and then I heard a loud thump in the living room floor. In my stupefied state, I jumped off of the floor, and ran into the living room. There, on the rust-coloured shag carpet, lay John Enderley.

Immediately I checked his pulse and he appeared to me as though he was still in the land of the living. I picked up the phone and some grunt was asking if Mr. Enderley was still there.

"Yes, and no!" was my truthful answer.

"Whadya mean, mister, are ya tryin' ta jack me around!"

"Mr. Enderley, is somewhat indisposed, at the moment."

"What d'ya mean? Is he taking a crap or something?"

"You could say that."

"Who am I talkin' ta? The butler?"

"No, my name is Detective Noble Savage. I'm a P.I. from..Sask...oh, never mind...I'm from Canada! I work for the Enderleys. Anything you have to tell them, you can tell me!"

"Well, we believe that we may have found Jimmy Enderley. There was a brief moment of silence. "I mean. his body. We regret to inform the Enderly household of his demise."

"Thank you, sir, is there anything else?"

"We need someone to come down to the 23rd precinct on Chesterton Drive to make a positive identification."

"Yes, of course, someone will be there within the hour."

I hung up the phone, feeling numb. Funny, a guy never gets used to being the deliverer of bad news. I should have known from the moment the bird hit the window.

The elders weren't talking into the smoke when they used to tell us about these things. Personally, I didn't adhere to all that hocus-pocus. Although, sometimes, I had to wonder. It seems to me, that once in a lullaby, I used to hear stories. Stories about how some of the old men used to change their form. I think they called them shape-shifters, or something of that nature. Lately, I was too consumed with solving this case that I forgot, or neglected those things that I couldn't readily explain. Then, the tough, emerged once again and , like a punk whistling in the dark, I whispered into the advancing nightfall... "Well, I guess there goes my supply of pork and beans."

Stepping out onto the front step, I tilted back my fedora, lit up a cheroot, watched the smoke curl and wisp away. Isn't that just the way life is, I thought. Like a puff of smoke. A shiver went through me, and I pulled up my collar. Suddenly, I felt a deep sense of longing to see the prairie one more time. I would wait outside, and allow the news to sink in to them, and go back in to see if I could say something that might make a difference at this time. The truth is, there aren't any words that a man can offer at such a time as this. I knew that all I could for the Enderleys was just to be there.

Whoever it was that had put away Jimmy Enderley didn't know that they had bought themselves a world of trouble. The big Indian from Saskatchewan was going to see to it, personally. My middle name meant Trouble. Big time!!

CHAPTER 18

Britton's plane did not arrive back in Atlanta on Sunday morning in time for him to attend church services in Whispering Meadows. There wasn't time for a trip home, a shower, breakfast and then being at church by 10:30. By the time he got home it was nearly 12 noon. He fixed himself a small lunch, a salami sandwich and a small bowl of cottage cheese. He drank a beer with it and sat down to watch golf on TV.

He was thinking of what he would do next when the phone rang.

"Hello."

"Britton, it's me, Savage."

"Hey," Britton said.

"That's for horses, aint it?"

"Just a southern way of saying 'howdy'" Britton said.

"I'm not in much of a mood for formalities," Savage said. "I found Jimmy Enderly. I didn't find him, really, some maid found him in a cheap motel on Chicago's south side. Dead."

"Dead?"

"That's what I said, dead. Somebody slipped him some kind of poison. Poor kid died of cardiac arrest, but poison is what caused it. I'm thinking it was the Banquell girl that did it."

"What makes you think that?"

"Before Jimmy died, he wrote a note on a pizza napkin, used a lipstick to write it. It said Moose Moseley."

"Moseley? The football player from down here?"

"That's him."

"What would Jimmy Enderly have in common with Moose Moseley, and why would he write Moseley's name on a pizza napkin?"

"I'm guessing that Moose was in Chicago with Lisa Banquell when she bailed Jimmy out of jail."

"Lisa bailed Jimmy?"

"That's what I'm thinking, but something don't fit."

"What doesn't fit?"

"The cops told me a woman in her mid 30's bailed Jimmy out."

Britton sat silent for a minute, thinking.

"Why do you think Lisa would want to kill Jimmy? By the emails that I saw, they were pretty fond of each other."

"Can't say," Savage replied. "I thought you would like to know about it, that's all. If I find that Lisa Banquell is responsible for Jimmy's death, I might do something that I would regret later, like staking her out over an anthill and pouring honey on her pubic hair."

"Hold on, Savage. That wasn't part of our arrangement. I want Lisa alive."

"You told me her Granddaddy said bring her back dead or alive."

"That was a figure of speech, Savage, and you know it."

"I don't know anything except that a young, innocent kid is dead. His parents are heartbroken. I guess I'm getting soft, but I have feelings for the parents. I don't like killers, no matter who they are. I know the system. I know that if Lisa Banquell killed Jimmy, her granddaddy will hire the best lawyers and get her off Scott free. If that happens, I'll extract my own kind of revenge on behalf of Jimmy's folks."

"You can't be serious, Savage."

"Serious as a heart attack, Britton. We agreed to work together on this, but if you don't like my ideas, I'm not beholden to you, and half of your fee for finding Lisa isn't enough to buy me off. You got that?"

"Why don't we talk about this. I'm not in for any of your vengeance tactics, regardless. I want to bring that girl back to Atlanta and turn her over to her grandfather. That's the sum total of my interest."

"I'll be in Atlanta tomorrow, Britton. I'm going to a funeral today. The funeral of a kid who got messed up with something. He didn't have any idea what a Southern rich girl and her Negro boyfriend could do. He fell for the oldest trick in the world, doing someone's dirty work for them."

"What do you mean by that?"

"Here's what I think," Savage said, sighing. "I think Lisa Banquell was tired of her parents telling her who she could and couldn't go with. I think she got on the internet and convinced this lonely boy to go to Atlanta and help her and her boyfriend get rid of her parents. That's my theory on this thing."

"You got any proof?" Britton asked.

"Proof? I don't have an ounce of evidence. All I've got is a napkin with a name on it. Moose Moseley. I found a yearbook on the internet from Whispering Meadows high school. It had a picture of Moose Moseley in his football uniform with the caption, "Most Likely To

Succeed". He was the homecoming King. Guess who the Queen was?"

"That's not hard to guess, Lisa Banquell, right?"

"Give the man one of my cheroots."

"That doesn't prove a thing."

"I told you, I aint talking about proof. I'm talking what we call spirit sense. You might say sixth sense, but my people call it spirit talk. Just a feeling. See you tomorrow, Britton."

The line went dead.

Britton sat there for a long time, thinking of the call. Weird. He didn't figure Savage for a vengeful type. It irritated him that Savage would be thinking of hurting a young girl, no matter what she did. In all of his years as a police officer, then a private detective, vengeance had never played a part in his motive for finding thieves, killers, missing kids, dead beat dads, or shop lifters. His motivation had always been money. He would contract for a case, solve it, and get whatever money he had agreed upon. Hurting teenage girls just didn't seem right to him.

But Jimmy Enderly was dead. Maybe Savage was right. Maybe Lisa Banquell had enticed Jimmy to kill her parents, then fed him some poison to shut him up. It wouldn't be the first time a woman found a Patsy to do her dirty work. Before he went off on a wild goose chase, however, he intended to find a motive for the Banquell's deaths.

He picked up the phone and called the Whispering Meadows PD. He didn't expect to find Beverly Miller in her office, but someone might know where he could get in touch with her. He was right. The desk sergeant gave him a phone number.

"Detective Miller," the honey dipped voice said.

"Mrs. Miller, its Burl Britton," he said.

"Mr. Britton. Correction, Sir. It isn't Mrs. Miller. My husband and I have been divorced for two years. He didn't like the idea of me being his boss. He started running around while I worked, I found out and divorced him."

"So its Miss Miller, then?"

"Yep. Now what can I do for you, Mr. Britton."

"It's Burl, Burl Britton. Mr. Britton was my father. He's been dead for nearly 50 years. And there is no Missus Britton."

"Ok, Burl." She said. "Now that we know that we are both single, what can I do for you?"

On impulse Britton said that he would like to talk to her about the Banquell case, but would rather talk in person. He then asked her if she would have dinner with him.

"I'd be glad to dine with you, Mr. Britton," she said. "I seldom mix business with pleasure, but I've had enough Slim-Fit frozen TV dinners to last anyone a lifetime, and I haven't lost but six pounds. At that rate, I'll have to eat another five thousand four hundred and six of them damned things to get back into a size six."

"You didn't look fat to me," Britton said, chuckling into the phone.

"You didn't look good," she said. He wondered if she meant that he hadn't looked at her good, or if she thought that he didn't look good.

"So I'll pick you up at 6? Tell me how to find you."

"Four eleven Par Four Drive, near the country club. Do you know the area?"

"I've driven past that house for ten years on my way to play golf. I'd say I know the way pretty well by now."

"It was our dream home. We traded up for it right after I made Detective. Then when we divorced, I got the house in the settlement. He got the new car. A Cadillac Escalade that was paid for. Sometimes I think he got the best deal."

"Any favorite foods or restaurants?" he asked.

"I'm partial to Italian," she said. "My maiden name is Palomira."

"That's Italian?"

"That's what Daddy used to tell me," she said. "I never had cause to doubt him."

"Six, then?"

"Sure, Burl. What kind of name is Burl? Or Britton?"

"Burl was my grandfather's middle name. Britton is English, I guess. I'm not much into genealogy."

"OK, Burl," she said. "But I've got some work to do at the office, suppose I meet you at Gioanni's at 6?"

"That's OK with me."

"See you then."

She hung up.

CHAPTER 19

I stood tall, hard and resolute at graveside. There fell on the small gathering a fine mist of cool rain, just enough to hide the tears. Mary could not hide hers. John kept whispering "My baby, my baby..he`s gone..he`s gone, if only, if only."

A quite rage started to burn deep down within me. If it was humanly possible, I could've kicked myself. I should have been there. I should have tried harder to get to Jimmy, before the wolves got to him. Then, the tough rescued me from my own personal hell. I heard that icy voice way on down in my conscience. 'It's not your fault, suck it up, just suck it up!` I moved over to the Enderly`s side and tried to console them. It was impossible. I didn't even really know the meaning of comfort. It was useless.

That part of me hadn't worked for years. My grandpa had tried to be somewhat of a surrogate mother to me. In his own gruff way, he tried to save some rag-tag bits of my humanity. But, to no avail. There had been too much trauma in my life. That was complicated by many years of sensory deprivation. My saving grace was in inflicting hurt on those who might try to hurt me.

And there was a long line-up of those most unfortunate characters, both white and brown. In a twisted kind of way, violence seemed to be the only way I felt I could connect with the human race. In most instances, those six degrees of separation usually closed in like a clap of lightning long before they had a chance to re-assess their options. More often than not, I would certainly be the last man standing. But, to be honest, and on occasion, I might slip and hit someone on the fist with my jaw.

The minister's dry monotone made me believe that he might be dead on his feet. He was quoting from a big black book, something about wandering through a shadowy valley of death. He spoke too late. I had been there and done that. While I was musing, I suddenly felt a soft shoulder lean on me. It was Marilyn.

"Oh, Noble, what am I going to do without my Jimmy. How am I going to live?" Her body was racking with deep, heartbreaking sobs. Then the ice man left. momentarily. I held her close to me, and for the first time in my life, I held a woman in an embrace totally devoid of lust. It was a strange feeling, but she wouldn't let me go. With my other hand, I pulled John to my side and then I made an oath. I said in no uncertain terms:

"I promise you, that whoever did this to Jimmy is going to pay a bitter price. I promise you, I'll track them down like dogs and stretch them out somewhere where no one will ever find them!"

"Noble. please, there's been enough sorrow. We don't want to see you behind bars!" It was like my mama talking.

"Mary, I don't plan on getting caught. You don't understand. I've been trained to kill without leaving a trace of evidence. They'll never know what hit them."

"And what about your conscience?" It was John this time.

"Don't you know by now, John? I don't have one."

"You're just as crazy as they are!" he said, choking back his passionate tears.

"Why don't you wake up and smell the stink of your judicial system, John."

"Well, maybe there's a way we can..."

"There is no way! Don't you understand that? Judges are bought off all the time!"

"Maybe not this time, Noble! Please, let's just sit down like rational human beings...."

"Rational? What the hell are you talking about? They poisoned your son like a damned rat! Is that rational, huh? huh? I'll give them rational down their throats until it comes out of their ears! Got it!"

I was beyond livid. I was shaking and cranked on high octane and I knew there was no turning back.

And then I heard the voice of reason. It asked me about my professionalism. And, then, it went further to try and skew me about honour. If you do something rash, it will come back to haunt you, came the whisper of sanity. How in the world did I end up in the middle of this situation? I got soft, that's what it was! I then started into a slimy sense of self-loathing. Look at you...big tough man. Why don't you go back to finding missing cows in Canwood? That's more your speed! You wanna know something? You can't argue with the voice of reason. So, by degrees, my heels started to cool off. I knew then, that I had to keep a cool head about me. Still, I wanted more than anything else to see justice served.

Somehow, I knew that I had to reach high enough on this house of cards. If I could then I would pull the King with the black heart down to where I could see his face. I had to go see the peanut man in Atlanta. I was sure that he would then lead me down that yellow brick road to where I could locate the human cockroach that cut out the hearts of the Enderlys. That's when I would shine. Something had been building up inside me for a long time. Atlanta was where things would come to a head. I felt it in my spirit. This drum kept beating in my head as though I was being guided by a force that I was foreign to. I wasn't into the traditional ways. Not by a long shot. I was still Indian, and a man can't deny what he is. Even though I wore the whiteman's clothes, I was still a red Indian deep inside.

I stayed up most of the night after the funeral. I stood guard over these special people who had welcomed me into their home. They didn't have to, but, they did. And for that reason, they became very near and dear to me. That was my secret, because the tough didn't allow me to let my feelings show. After a sleepless night, I prepared for my trip to Atlanta. I packed my pathetic little suitcase and threw it into the trunk of the Pontiac. The Enderlys gave me some travel money, after I assured them that I wasn't going to murder anybody. Mary packed me a nice lunch with a thermos of java. I turned the key. Old Bess fired up and I waved see ya later to John and Mary and headed for yet another strange city in my illustrious itinerary. I reached into my lunch bag and pulled out a big can of pork and beans. In her haste to pack, she must have forgot to loan me her can opener.

Passing by one small town, I saw some of the hicks out on a football field. I slowed down considerably when I saw the bevy of cheerleaders prancing around on the sidelines. Mary had made me meatloaf sandwiches which I promptly wolfed down. What was she trying to do anyway? Trying to get me to stay on in the big city? Fat chance, I thought, as the pigskin bounced off my hood.

"Hey, watch it! What the heck do you think I am?"

One of the girls ran out, smiled sweetly and retrieved the pigskin.

"Sorry, mister, say, that's a real nice tan you got there!"

"Thanks! I use Coppertone." I yelled, as I drove away in the general direction of Atlanta.

CHAPTER 20

Burl Britton felt like a teenager on his first date. He couldn't explain it to himself, but he was really looking forward to meeting with Beverly Miller, the Whispering Meadows detective, in charge of the Banquell case. That is why he was in the eating establishment a half an hour before Beverly showed up. He didn't want to be late. He had just finished drinking a glass of Oak Hills cabernet sauvignon when he saw her appear at the matre d's desk, say a few words then stride purposefully towards his table near a window in a secluded, dimly lit area.

He rose and spoke to her then pulled her chair away from the table, helped her scoot up close, and then sat back down.

"What's new in the Banquell case?" he asked.

"Nothing like getting right to the point, Britton," she said. "I was in hopes that you wanted to have dinner with me because you were interested in me more than pursuing the Banquell case."

Britton blushed. It was true, he definitely was interested in her, and he wished he could grab the words he had spoken, as if they were a balloon in a cartoon, and hide them under the table and start over.

"I'm sorry, Beverly," he said, shaking his head. "Please forgive my manners. Truthfully, I was looking forward to seeing you again, and I don't know why I blurted that out."

"Forget it, Britton," she said. "Or would you rather I call you Burl?"

"I prefer Britton," he said. "Burl always sounded like a knot on a tree to me, and I've never really liked the name."

"Or a knot on a log," she said, smiling.

"That too," he said, and smiled back.

"In answer to your question, there have been a few developments in that case."

Burl Britton's ears perked up.

"Can you share them with me?"

"Will you at least order me a glass of wine first?"

"Oh hell. I'm sorry. Of course, I'll order you whatever you want."

"What I want will have to wait," she said, smiling again and winking at him.

He felt a red blush creep up his chest and knew that his face was probably going to get red. He raised his hand and gestured to a waiter standing next to the matre d's table. When the waiter arrived, Britton told him to bring the lady a glass of wine, whatever she wanted.

She took her time perusing the wine list and finally settled on a Pinot Blanc. The waiter disappeared.

"I'll accept questions now," she said, "ask away."

"What do you have that might help me find the missing girl?"

"Can't help you with that, kind sir, but the murder investigation has taken a new light."

"OK."

"We know that Mr. Banquell was shot with a 12 gauge shotgun at close rang, while in his bed, probably from the door of the bedroom.

Mrs. Banquell, however, was shot with a 32 caliber revolver, even though the shotgun still contained two live rounds. It is hard to figure why a killer would blast away with a 12 gauge, drop the gun and pull a 32 out to kill the woman."

"Two different shooters?" Britton asked.

"That's what we think, but why?"

"You've got me there. The only thing I can figure is that when the killers walked in they had all intentions of killing the man, but not the woman. Then the woman either begged them not to shoot or started talking. Maybe they asked her about money in the house and when she said there was none, the second killer got angry and blasted her?"

"What was taken?"

"That's the strange thing. Mrs. Banquell's purse was on the floor next to her nightstand. It contained over $700 in cash. That leads us to believe that robbery was not a motive."

"How about the husband, was his wallet found?"

"No. His wallet was missing. We searched the house and didn't find a trace of it. Maybe he carried so much money that the killers were satisfied with that, and wanted to get out of the house. Strange."

"Jewelry?"

"None missing that was apparent. A jewelry box on Mrs. Banquell's dresser was full of good things. A Longines watch worth about 4 grand, several gold rings, some classy diamond earrings."

"Empty cartridges found?"

"One."

"In the shotgun?"

"Well, two then, the empty round in the shotgun and an empty 32 case on the floor, although Mrs. Banquell was shot twice."

"I thought you said she was shot with a revolver?"

"She was. We found the gun. It had four live rounds in it."

"Mrs. Banquell was shot twice, you found one empty cartridge on the floor from the revolver, and there were no empties found in the gun?"

"That's weird isn't it? You would think that we would have found the gun with four live rounds and two empties. It's almost like someone took the two empties out of the revolver, and either accidentally or purposely dropped one on the floor. What they did with the other one is a matter of conjecture at this point."

"Where did you find the gun?"

"In the stolen car that Jimmy Enderly was driving."

"Have you ran a trace on the gun's serial number?"

"Yeah. It belonged to Jimmy's father, John."

"So you're thinking that Jimmy Enderly killed Mrs. Banquell?"

"Looks that way, doesn't it?"

Britton was silent. The waiter arrived at that time and politely asked if they were ready to order.

"I'll have veal parmesan," Beverly said.

"That sounds good," Britton said. "I'll have the same."

They sipped their wine in silence for a moment.

"So naturally you got a warrant for Jimmy's arrest?"

"We started to. Then we got the news that he was found dead in a sleazy motel room in Chicago."

Britton sat silently contemplating the series of events. They chatted amicably about other things, her divorce, the unfortunate demise of his wife, their children. She even opened her purse and showed him pictures of her kids, two boys. Both were in college, one a senior and the other a freshman. She was proud of them both, but the younger one wanted to be a cop. The older one wanted to be a lawyer. She admitted to Britton that she had more trust in cops than she did lawyers.

"What's worse than a bus load of lawyers going over a cliff?" she asked.

"I don't know," he said, waiting for the punch line.

"A bus load of lawyers not going over a cliff," she said, and laughed heartily.

By the time their food arrived, Britton felt as if he could sit and talk to this lovely lady the rest of the evening. She was charming, attentive, and by her winks and touches, definitely interested in knowing him better.

When dinner was over, and they had an after dinner drink, they walked hand in hand to the parking lot.

"Where's your car?" he asked.

"Right over there," she said, pointing. "It's the red one."

He walked her to her car, she unlocked it with a remote key and he opened the door for her.

"I've had a great time, Beverly," he said. "I hope to see you again soon."

"You will if you follow me home, Burl Britton," she said.

CHAPTER 21

On my way down the yellow brick road to see Mr. Peanut Man, I had plenty of time to chaw down my pork and bean lunch. I also had a whole pile of questions to ask the man. It's funny how the filthy rich can get so screwed up. With all of their play money at their disposal, somehow, a guy might suppose that they'd be happier. Not so. Look at how fouled up old Howie Hughes was toward the end of his life. Apparently, after he amassed all his billions, Hughes," owned lives", and, yet, paradoxically, he became so afraid of life.

In due time, he lived on the top floor of one his penthouse skyscrapers. It was commonly reported, that until the day he drew his last breath, he lived in a virtual state of self-imposed isolation. He refused to cut his hair. His strange phobia of catching disease caused him to practically shun close human contact. He would not cut his nails, again, fearing a snip which might lead to infection. All his meals were prepared with the strictest of hygienic standards. Of course, he had to pay some willing soul to taste his food for him (just, in case).

The children of the super-rich didn't fare any better. In the case of Lisa Banquell, I suspect, that, right about now, she'd be mired in her own personal hell. Hers was a fairy tale gone horribly wrong. Once upon a time in the kingdom of Her Life, there lived a King and a Queen. They had a princess upon whom they lavished all that she ever desired. Until one day, she met, and was wooed by a Black Prince, who dwelt amongst the common folk. He was a peasant and she was a princess. The King and Queen would not have any of that. They forbade her to ever see him again. And, then, the snow started to fall all over their once happy Kingdom. And, Lisa became hopelessly addicted to it. The snow, I mean. Of, course, the Black Prince; saw to it that Princess had a steady supply.

Still, I felt I needed to know more about the Princess and about what made her tick. The worst case scenario would be that she might turn out to be a walking time-bomb. I guess we all know that there's some things that money can't buy. While it is true that the "long green" can rent a helluva lot, there are certain commodities in life that it can't touch. One of them being, peace of mind and, of course the mother of all necessities...sanity. I knew that Peanut Man probably loved his granddaughter, and would most likely do anything for her. If she was found guilty as sin about this case, then, I would have my hands full trying to wrestle this self-made billionaire down, before I could get to The Lovely One. If nothing else, this case was going to prove interesting to solve. I felt it in my bones.

It had been awhile since I'd been with a woman. Of late, I had been suffering the frisk. That hooker, in Chicago, almost had me convinced to get down and dirty, but I wanted to live to collect my pension. The problem was that the longer I resisted my natural urges, the edgier I got. I had a penchant for getting downright dangerous, when I got into that wandering state of mind. A cold shower might hold back my stallion.

But, for the near foreseeable future, sooner or later the impish grin, was sure to come a-calling. The hooker kept dancing in my face. She was thick with make-up. That`s the way I like `em. Her red dress clung to her like a second skin. She had a set of pearly whites that threatened to eat me alive. Her full figure went beyond an hour -glass. She was licking on a banana as I was speaking softly to her. I achieved wood in a minute. It`s true about us natives, we could be as hard as petrified wood. So, there was a certain amount of truth to their reference to us as , "wooden Indians.". Ha!! Look out, baby, here I is!!

The road to Atlanta, my friend, is a long one. Old Bess kept up. I couldn`t begrudge her for that. Her brakes had been a little spongy lately, but the old girl kept plugging away, mile after mile. The Georgian countryside is beautiful, and wouldn't be a bad place to set down some roots. That`s if skin colour wasn't such a big deal. So, this was the land of chitlings, gravy and black-eyed peas! Made me hunger just thinking about it. So, I pulled into this roadside cafe. It was a hot, kinda blistery day, and I didn't have any A.C. Besides, anyone who's in the know will tell you that Indian A.C., is driving down the road with all your windows wide open.

At this point, I was feeling a little home-sick. But, hey, don`t tell no one, O.K? It'll spoil my tough guy image. Got it? So,  here I am, deep in red-neck country and I`m craving and hoping for some real home style Southern comfort.

I could feel the sweat trickling down my back. I bought Old Bess to a sputtering halt just outside of Mama Parker's Eatery. I dusted off some of that good old Georgian dirt with my fedora. Running a greased comb through my salt and peppa, I tried to look presentable for my public. I shuffled through a pair of western style quarter doors on squeaky hinges. The overhead fans creaked, turning out a lazy spin. I moseyed over to a booth and flopped down, saying, `Hi! `to the flies, I turned my coffee cup, right side up. I noticed the place got suddenly silent. In my ignorance, I assumed, everyone, was observing a moment of silence; for a recently departed member of the community. Or was it that someone was about to die?

"When you go to the dark places, look for the light, and it will find you."

"Yes, Sensei." I answered the old man. Still, I didn't know what he meant. Until today.

It was the usual redneck joint. Instantly, I could sense the animosity. If I could spread it on a slab of bread, it would cover like thick peanut butter. I felt as though Canwood had followed me to the ends of the earth. Canwood, what a peach of a town! It was the asshole of the Parkland.

"Ya`smell somethin` kinda rotten, Cleetus?" The voice came from two booths over to my right. Except for the geographical location, this little scene was no different than a thousand times before.

"Always think two steps ahead and one step back. Your kata, your chi must flow. Do not resist the Tiger that lives in you! Let it strike! Let it strike!"

"Yes, Sensei!" This time, my response, was automatic. Even in my seated position, energy surged through my being. It seemed to be like a river of strength that was always there when I needed it. I will never understand why it never failed me. The red flags came up and I was ready.

"Yep! Smells like one of them dead reservation dogs." Cleetus chimed in. He couldn`t have had the faintest clue that he would not be driving his tractor home with two good hands on that fateful afternoon. I sat there, somehow serene as deadly thoughts started to whirl around in my mind.

"Well, Jordy, time to take out the garbage." I could hear Cleetus dragging his steel toes over to my booth.

"Hey, chiefy, yer a long ways from the rez, ain`t ya?" Jordy had snuck up on my left.

Cleetus was probably 250, yep, and, apparently, they piled it that high, at least in this state. This boy was a tough, hardened by years of farm labor. A scruffy hank of dirty-blond hair, half- covered, his pink ham of a homely face. His beady eyes of blue darted nervously about me, sizing me up. It seemed to me he was looking for a hidden whiskey flask under my sport jacket. He wore a straw hat and dirty, blue cover-alls and looked like he just walked out of a Norman Rockwell painting. He should have stayed there. My adrenaline was just now kicking in.

Anybody that knows me, or has had the unfortunate liability, to look up at me, from the dust of the earth will tell you to beware of my twitch. You see, that`s the only warning I give out.

Jordy was a slim farmhand. Probably out of Tennessee, would be my guess. But, then again, what would I know, I was just a peace-loving Canuck, just passing through and just wanting a pleasant bite to eat. His movements were more fluid than Clete's. I noticed the steel tipped cowboy boots at first glance. They were made of the finest rattler-skin this side of the Pecos. He wore black leather gloves, which I figured I might use after the dust cleared. On second thought, I figured he might be using his right hand for his own pleasure, so I decided against taking any spoils after the fact. He was just a punk. Even at that, I knew I had to be cautious.

Jordy was about 20, or so, baby-faced and pimple-scarred. He was a ginger. Red-hair under a John Deere baseball cap. I didn`t think anyone wore them anymore, but he had on a baggy scotch- plaid pair of pants, patched at the knees. I hated to teach him this lesson in respecting his seniors, but, hey..what the hey!

As he approached closer, I noticed his hawk-like features and so fittingly predatorial in the act he felt obligated to complete. Perhaps it was just that his lack of caution was a result of too many hours in the combine. I read the label on his blue chambray shirt, that took me for a loop. It was written white on red- FOREMAN- and below it, still further, was stitched: Banquell Peanut Farms. So, I surmised, that I was getting closer to my destination.

I took off my specs. Next, off came the hat. I thought of taking the tie off, but I just couldn't be bothered. I felt the wind coming in from behind like a slow winding train. The darkness had spoken, and I saw the light. It was on the floor. His shadow betrayed his intentions. I jumped and spun around catching him by the throat. Jordy squealed like a stuck pig and went down choking. He spewed out his dinner, as my tiger claw rendered Cletus to a whimpering heap. I swiftly pulled at his mule ears and his head bonged the laminated table of my booth. Another southern comforter swooped in from out of the shadows, but I deftly dispatched him with a kick to the kneecap. He screamed like a school-girl, and rolled over, playing possum. The nameless, rambunctious do-gooder would now be shopping for a pair of crutches.

I looked around at the dinner crowd and facetiously inquired, "Next?"

"Don't y all worry none bout us, mistah!"said a mousy looking man in the corner over by the entrance.

"That's right, that's right!" someone else said, somewhere over by the soda pop machine." Those bitches had èr comin' far quite a month of Sundays, Thank ye`mistah!"

"Well, that suits me to a T, thank you all!" I returned.

"Say, ye all from Canada, are ya?" said Mouse. `Say do you guys still...."

"No, sir, we do not, by any means, still live in tee-pees!"

It was good to be out on the wide open again. The people at Momma's were kind enough to send me on my way with a hearty bagged lunch, Southern Style. The fried chicken was better than the Colonel's. There was a heaping tub of mashed potatoes with home-made gravy, with chitlins, and, of course black-eyed peas. Someone else threw in for a watermelon.

I was feeling a bit gorged when, at last, I pulled up to the stately mansion of Jobe Banquell. I got on the intercom and buzzed. No answer. Nightfall was descending. I assumed that the lord of the manor was out for the evening. I wasn`t about to drive back to Chicago empty-handed, so I persisted in my quest.

I hadn't used it for awhile, but I had a little pup tent in my trunk, so I brought it out. I had quite the time setting it up, but I managed. I sort of half-remembered what survival skills I had learned in Boy Scouts. Rule no. 23, stated, "When on stake-out, be persistent. Exercise patience with all due caution." It was kinda nice out there. I had wanted to go camping for quite some time. I just didn't know I would be doing it outside of a billionaire's private property.

I heard dogs barking up by the Banquell Residence. I also had a little Coleman which I brought out to make a little pot of tea. Oh, yeah, I had never unpacked my camping gear, so it came in right handy. I curled up inside my bedroll and I drifted off. I had a dream of a girl in Canwood. She was a beautiful vision in white, just a-waiting for me at the altar. Never mind that she was 15 years my junior. That`s the beauty of imagination. A guy can get away with practically anything.

I woke up abruptly with the shining headlights of a long, sleek Mercedes shining straight into my beautiful brown eyes.

"Detective Savage, I presume?"

"You presume correctly. And you, sir, must be Jobe Banquell?"

"That I am,"

Behind him I saw a pair of flashing teeth, and heard a savage growl.

"Down, Sheba! Now! Heel!"

Immediately, the Doberman retreated, and sat on its haunches, all whiney-like.

"Clement! Get this damned schnauzer out of here! Now!... I'm so sorry, Detective, I..I.. didn't expect you to arrive so soon. You must forgive me."

"Certainly."

"Well. let's see if we can improve your accommodations, shall we?"

"Yeah, well this isn`t exactly the Dubai Hilton." I faked an attempt to be facetious.

"Yes, yes ,..quite." Jobe Banquell chuckled. "I appreciate a man with a sense of wit and humour. I haven't much had reason for mirth of late."

"I understand, sir." I said as I rolled out of my warm blankets.

"Come along, you can leave your vehicle and your gear here. I`ll have the servants come for them shortly."

Getting into the limo, I felt like Cinderfella. Inside, was a fully stocked bar. There was a high def T,V., full stereo surround sound right in front of me. My old black and white console back home looked sick compared to this set-up.

Jobe Banquell was not a particularly attractive older man. Not that I swing that way, but he had preserved well. I guess money can do that for a guy too. He was immaculately dressed.

He wore a dazzling, white dinner jacket that looked like it was hand-tailored, custom made, which I figured must have run the till to somewhere around 5 grand. Opulent wealth fit him well. Banquell had black dress slacks, again hand-stitched made out of finely spun Egyptian cotton. I could not hazard a guess as to their cost. He wore black and white brogue lambskin leather shoes, custom made with soles that floated and quite possibly never squeaked. I remember buying a pair of gray Hush Puppies in Canwood at the C and H. They looked fine and fit great. But as soon as they got wet they smelled like pig-shit! What a huge disappointment!

"Nice threads." I complimented the gentleman.

"Oh, these old rags. Nothing but hand-me-downs." he snickered. I was beginning to feel somewhat like the court jester.

In the glow of the limo's interiors, I caught the silvery glint of a Rolex, studded with diamonds. I surreptitiously gauged the timepiece at around 50 grand. My, gosh, what peanuts can buy, I secretly conjectured. Even the air smelled like money, like crisp 100 dollar bills.

"Well, here we are, Mr. Savage," he said as we pulled up onto the cobblestone driveway," Or would you prefer, Detective?"

"Well, as long as you don't call me late for dinner, either, or, will be fine."

"Oh. Pardon my ignorance, have you eaten? You must be absolutely famished, coming all the way from Saskatchewan."

`You, sir are a wonder. You are the only person in the entire United States that knows how to pronounce the name of my province!"

`Well, it`s nothing really. I go big- game hunting there every winter. I've been to fly-in-camps in Lac La Rouge numerous times. I'm a world traveler."

`That`s very interesting, sir."

"Well, next week, if things transpire to a satisfactory degree, I intend, on going to the Serengeti, to bag leopard."

"With whom?" I couldn't resist asking.

"Well, at the moment, it's a toss-up between Bill Gates or Sheik Abduh Ben Arahmin of the Royal Emirates."

"Oh. really?"I said, as I thought, of my yearly fall rabbit hunt.

"I don't much like to go with Bill. He can be quite temperamental, you know. He detests anyone who is a better marksman than he is."

As we stood at the door of the Banquell ancestral home, I felt like a beggar come to call for donations. However, in spite of his obvious personal solvency, Jobe Banquell was a down to earth gentleman. I gathered as much when he jiggled with laughter when I joked that he must have "banked well", in order to amass such opulence. He was about `6`2`, the very picture of the perfect grandfather. He had a full head of silver hair and laughing hazel eyes. He had come straight out of the Great Depression, and so he knew something of the misery of those years that stretched the patience of men`s souls. He had never forgotten what it was like to subsist on rations of boiled potatoes for weeks on end. For this reason, Jobe Banquell was a secret philanthropist. He gave exceedingly back to society to places of deep poverty. He gave hundreds of thousandths of dollars to various charities over the years. And he did so secretly. For some reason, he refused to give money to organizations that supported minority projects.

Jobe was not a handsome man, per se, at least not like yours truly. But, still in all, he was certainly not an unattractive man. I think that what made him attractive was his heart. Some thought of him as a bastard, but I suspect that perception only came by means of his shrewd business dealings. After all, business is business. He sported a pencil thin moustache reminiscent of Errol Flynn. He had the usual southern drawl, although not in a pronounced way as is commonly portrayed by Hollywood. He had laugh lines and certainly the wrinkles that come with age. At certain times, especially during the evening as he sat by the glow of the family fireplace, nursing his after dinner brandy, he often took on the aspect of one who was silently mourning for a long lost love, perhaps. But, this evening, Jobe, was in high spirits.

That evening, I was treated with such southern hospitality that I may never forget. Not forgetting that I was the tough, I was nonetheless appreciative of a soft bed and food in my belly. Before I went to bed, Jobe Banquell thanked me for taking such pains to travel all the way to Georgia. I told him plainly that I was there to help to find the truth behind all that he had heard thus far.

"We'll discuss our business further in the morning," he said, and he was all no-nonsense again.

"Goodnight" I said, but he was gone before I had a chance to say anything further.

I had spent the night on a sumptuous bed as big as Texas. No matter which way I turned, I couldn't find the edge of the bed. So, for once, I hadn't fallen off of the edge and thusly on to the floor. The butler rapped on my door respectfully.

"Sir, Mr. Banquell requests your presence at breakfast, if you please?"

"Thank you, Jeeves." I couldn't resist.

"Actually, it's Clement, sir."

"Thanks, Clem. I'll be there in a few minutes."

When I walked into the dining hall, Jobe Banquell was already digging into the French toast.

" Oh, there you are. Wonderful, sunny morning, isn't it?"

"Better than any I've seen in Canada."

"Come, sit over here by the portal window."

The view took your breath away. I looked out onto a serene lakefront property. I had figured on something a little more like a bayou.

"Is that a lake out there?"

"Yes, it was just a little something I had my grounds crew dig up for me last year. Of course, I had to dig into my piggy bank to pay out of my spare change."

"Well, isn't that something grand?"

"Yeah, Mr. Savage, I like to live big. The bigger the better I always say. And what about you, what kind of a home do you have up in Canada?"

"Oh, it's nothing more than the size of your average teepee." I offered facetiously.

He tilted his silver mane back and boomed out with a sudden burst of laughter.

`That's good, that`s good! I like that!" he said, appreciative of my home-spun humor.

"Oh, Clement, come and serve Mr. Savage. Quickly, man, he must be absolutely wasting away after his long drive."

Well, I tell you. I ate as much as in a month of Sundays. The coffee was just capital!

Too soon it was time for business. We retired to the smoking room after a breakfast that might have blown up a horse's stomach.

"I suppose that the time has come to speak of my princess." Jobe Banquell softened at her name."Lisa,.. she, was named after my mother, you know."

He became quietly introspective. A shadow crossed his face as he continued.

"I can hardly believe that she would run away from all of this." he said as he gestured to the surrounding, rich air. "Can you, Noble?"

He startled me with his use of my first name.

"How did you know my first name?"`

"Oh, I assure you, I have my ways."

"Then, why do you need me to find your granddaughter?"

"Because she'd never suspect a...."

"A savage to find her." I spoon-fed the words to this immensely wealthy man.

"Oh, my god, man! I never meant to say that!"

"So, what did you mean then?" The words hung in the air, and it was as though the easy, comfort had been sucked out of our conversation.

"I apologize for my seeming presumption, sir. And just for the record, I have sat in the company of kings and world leaders, and not once have I ever, ever apologized to any of them or their interpreters. For that reason alone, you should feel very honored."

"Well, O.K. I guess I over-reacted." The tough was back. Still, I didn't like the way things were developing, as far as my rapport with Jobe Banquell was concerned.

"By the way, here's your dossier. My friends at the Central Office had it delivered by special courier yesterday." The manila envelope had the C.I.A. official insignia on the folder.

"And, so, I must beg the obvious question as to why they can`t find your precious princess."

"Oh, those bunch of idiots! They couldn't find their demented Grandma in a small town shopping mall."

We both had a loud hacking laugh about that one.

"So, tell me, Jobe, did ..did..the cloak and dagger guys uncover any evidence about my cattle rustling up in Canwood?"

"Actually, no. Just one question though. Who is girly-girl?"

"Those sneakin`sons a ....!" I whispered.

We called Clement for more coffee and continued our parlay about Lisa.

"Tell me something, Jobe."

"What is it, Noble?"

"What's going to happen should I uncover something ugly about Lisa?"

He turned and walked over to the window overlooking Lake Lisa and was painfully silent.

"I'm sorry, Noble. I can't tell you at this point in time. Did you know that I play golf with The head judge of the Supreme Court every other Thursday?"

"I take it that you get along quite famously with the judge?"

"Oh, shit, Harry and I have known each other forever. He owes me one or two. If the truth be known, I've got him by the knockers over a few indiscretions. That's if you know what I mean." He winked slyly like a silver fox.

"Now, what about Lisa?" I said, and it somehow burst his bubble, I think.

"O.K. Noble, what do you want to know?"

"I want you to give me the straight goods, and none of this subversive crap! O.K?"

"You got it, my friend! Let's get to it"`

"I need to do a profile sketch and any recent photos would help immensely."

"Yep, can do."

"How old is she?"

"She's 16 going on 21. But she'll never get old. She'll stay a beauty forever."

"I certainly hope that you're not right on that one. What about friends?"

He pulled out a list as long as his arm. No doubt, some were true and some were false. Banquell knew that the rich always had social leeches. They hung on to them for as long as the wine flowed. There was one he thoroughly detested with a venom without antidote. He had aptly dubbed him as the Black Prince.

His name was Moose Moseley. He was the star quarterback for Pleasant Meadows High. Jobe had hoped better for Lisa's choice for her beau. In his opinion, Moose Moseley was definitely not Ivy League material. And, Banquell, was definitely not excited about the prospect of bouncing mulatto children on his slightly arthritic knees.

"Place of birth?"

"Here."

"O.K., that makes it nice and simple, doesn't it? Tell me something, Jobe. What makes you think that she'll want to stay, once I deliver her back to you?"

"Well, I'm hoping that she`s getting just a little tired of being on the run. Wouldn't you rather sleep here than out in some damned culvert?"

"Here, of course, but, hell, she's just a kid. She's probably living in her own little pretend world, as we speak."

"Well, geez, man, I don't know, Lisa is Lisa, she always did whatever she wanted to do anyway. Sad to say, I made her that way."

"Wha...wha..wha..hold on! Is this fess up time or what? Are you saying you want me to talk her into coming back once I find her? I'm not a damn social worker, She's of age. There's nothing to hold her here."

"Well, I was hoping that eventually,... love would conquer all."

"Hold on, now, Jobe. You're starting to creep me out, man! You're beginning to sound like the freakin`Wizard of Oz or something of that freakin` nature."

"I know, I know life isn't played out like that. It never does. What else am I supposed to do, huh? Cut her loose? I do have a sense of family honor, you know!"

"Please, Mr. Banquell, I'm trying my damndest to be professional about this whole thing!"

"Alright. Alright. What else do you want to know?"

"Where do you think she might head?"

"She's staying with total strangers for all I know. Geez! What a scary thought! But then, again, Lisa was always a resourceful little girl and definitely not stupid."

"O.K., now that we've established that Lisa is not stupid, I need to chart out a plan to lure her back to you."

"How do you propose to do that?"

"You've got to cut off her allowance. I can almost guarantee that she'll be phoning you once her purchases start coming back N.S.F."

"That's absolute genius, Savage! Why didn't I think of that?" He said in his eureka moment.

CHAPTER 22

Britton felt like an eighth grader with a new girl friend. He wasn't sure what his emotional involvement was yet, but he knew that his physical involvement was shifting gears. After following Beverly Miller home, he was invited in for a night cap, wound up on the couch watching an old movie and participating in some very heavy petting like two sex-starved teens at a drive in. He knew enough to know that he wanted to see Beverly again, and again.

Since the death of his wife nearly five years past, he had gone out with a few women who he had met at Church. Their attitudes were always "wait and see" when it came to sex. His attitude had always been don't buy a suit until you've tried it on. Beverly seemed to agree with that attitude. He was almost certain that his next date would result in a sleep over with the lovely lady.

For the immediate time, however, he had a case to work.

Noble Savage had called him and suggested that they meet for breakfast to go over the case and make some plans as to who was to investigate what. Britton agreed to meet Savage at a Denny's for breakfast, and was there early, sipping on a cup of coffee when he saw Savage walk through the door. Heads turned and watched the Canadian detective, he walked with the fluid movement of someone half his age and Britton recognized the way that Savage's eyes continually glanced around as the habit of a man who had spent years on the defense.

"Ah, my favorite pardner," Britton said. "Good morning. Drag up a chair and join me. I'm just having my first cup of coffee this lovely morning."

"Howdy Britton," Savage said. "Do people in this town always look at strangers like they had crawled out of the swamp?"

"Pay no attention to it, my good fellow," Britton said. "Folks around here are just curious. Anything or anyone who shows up in this town are automatically objects of speculation. These folks don't have much to do around here except speculate on what other people are doing. They will assume that you are either a cop or a consultant now that you have been seen with me."

"OK," Savage said. "What's good in here? And are you buying? I'm a little on the strapped side until we solve this case and you pay me."

"Right. I'll splurge. Have whatever you'd like. I'm going to have bacon and eggs and hash browns with sourdough toast."

"I'll have what he's having," Savage told the waitress, "and coffee, please."

"So what's the game plan, Britton?"

"Well, I understand you spent the night at the Banquell mansion. Did old man Banquell give you any ideas that you might pursue?"

"No, as a matter of fact I gave him one."

"What's that?"

"I told him to cut of Lisa's funds," Savage said. "When the well runs dry she'll come home to drink."

"Good idea," Britton said.

"Thanks."

"Where she went from here is anyone's guess, but my guess is that she'll show up back here in Whispering Meadows very soon. This is home. All of her friends are here."

"Do you think she knows about her parents funeral arrangements?" Savage asked.

"That might be a good place to start. The funeral home."

"Do you want me to handle that, or are you going to?"

"I'll do it. I know the folks there. They'll be more likely to talk to me than they would a stranger."

Britton looked up and saw Beverly Miller walking across the room towards their table. She stopped as she neared them, glanced at Savage, and smiled.

"Good morning," she said, smiling.

"Good morning to you," Britton said. "I'd like you to meet my associate from Canada, Mr. Noble Savage. We are working this case together."

"Hello," she said, extended her hand.

Noble took her hand and shook it. "Very pleased to make your acquaintance," he said.

"Mr. Savage, this is Beverly Miller. She's the detective sergeant in charge of the Banquell investigation for our local police department."

"How do you like our charming little town, Mr. Savage?"

"I spent yesterday evening at the home of Mr. Peanut," Savage said. "Those are accommodations a man could get used to very fast."

"Yes, he's the pride of this part of the country. Wealthiest man in Georgia as far as I know," Beverly said, conversationally.

Beverly had a gleam in her eye as Burl Britton asked her to join them. She had enjoyed the tryst the night before with Britton and was looking forward to seeing him again after hours.

Britton got up and pulled out a chair for her. She sat down and glanced at the menu briefly. "I've got time for a cup of coffee and a doughnut, that's all," she said.

"We've already ordered," Savage said. "Surely you can have bacon and eggs with us this morning."

"Mmmm, sounds good, but I'm a little short on time."

After several moments of banter between the three of them, their food arrived and they fell silent while eating.

"What are your plans for today, Britton?" Beverly asked.

"I'm going to find out if Lisa has contacted anyone in regards to her parents funeral," he said. "My first stop will be the funeral home. Then I'm going to talk to some of my informants and see if any of them heard anything about the Banquell shooting. Motive seems to be the big mystery right now."

"Keep in touch with me," Beverly said. "That's where we are headed too, trying to find out why someone would want to kill those fine people. Murder in this town is almost unheard of."

"Didn't you tell me that the revolver was found in the stolen car that the boy was caught in, and traced back to the Enderly man in Chicago?"

"I did," she said. "Looks like Jimmy brought his father's gun with him when he came to Whispering Meadows. That alone doesn't tell me that Jimmy killed Mrs. Banquell."

"Hold it a minute," Savage said. "Jimmy Enderly's a suspect in the Banquell shooting? The poor kid is dead. John Enderly is grief stricken over Jimmy's death."

"We don't know anything for sure," Beverly admitted. "Only that the gun was tied to the cartridge we found on the floor of the Banquell bedroom."

Britton pushed his chair away from the table and rose.

"Take good care of this lady, Savage." he said. "I'll be back in my office at three. We should meet then and compare notes."

"Sure," Savage said.

In his mind, Noble Savage was thinking that he was glad Britton was the first to leave the scene. Now he could talk, undisturbed, to the lovely lady who had just walked into his life.

Later that evening Britton was eating supper at a local Deli. He sensed someone approaching just as he took a big bite from a tuna salad sandwich. He was thinking that waitresses always seem to time it just as you've got your mouthful to say something stupid like "Is everything tasting OK tonight, Sir?".

He looked up. It wasn't a waitress. It was a cop.

"Mr. Britton?"

"Yes."

"You don't know me. My name is Joe Miller. What I'm going to say is something you may not want to hear."

"Why are you telling me, then?" Britton chewed some more then swallowed the mouthful of food a little before he wanted to, but then his mother had always taught him not to talk with a mouthful.

"I know you had dinner with my ex-wife the other night," Joe Miller said.

"And?" Britton tensed. Ex husbands sometimes have a manner that is not conducive to good public relations, particularly when it is about someone dating heir ex wives.

"Just a word of warning," Joe Miller said.

Britton tensed some more. He wasn't in any mood to fight, particularly with an armed police officer, and at the same time he did not like to be bullied or told who he could date and who he could not.

"Look, Mr. Miller," he started.

"This isn't what you think, Sir." Miller said, hastily. "I'm no threat to you. I couldn't care less who Beverly sees, our relationship ended a long time ago."

"Then what is this about, Joe?" Britton asked, relieved.

"I don't know you, but some of the guys on the force have told me you served some time as a police officer. That makes me respect you. What I have to say is that you should not get too serious about a woman who plays men like they are her personal slaves."

"Joe, I think you are out of bounds," Britton said. "First, I had dinner with Beverly as a means of finding out what the police knew about a case I'm working. I happen to think that she's an attractive, intelligent woman. What holds for us in the future is my business."

"That's true," Joe said. "And I don't give a big rats ass about your future with Beverly, but I think you need to know that she will bleed you for all she can get, just like she did me, and when she's done with you, she'll dump you on the shit pile along with all of the rest of her suckers. Beverly wants one thing out of life, Mr. Britton. Money."

"Being a police officer is hardly the place to accumulate money, Joe."

"That's just a game she enjoys playing. She likes to be the boss. She relishes being able to pull peoples strings. It is just a step for her to bigger and better things. She wants control on the police department so she can manipulate the people that she thinks can further her career."

"You sound like a jealous man, even though you say you are not, Joe."

"Maybe. I had hopes of becoming Chief of Police someday," Joe said. "I wanted the job that Beverly got. I didn't want it bad enough to sleep with the right people, though. I've always had my eye on politics here in Augusta. My grandfather was a City Councilman, and I have my personal ideas about how to serve in politics. Beverly just wants the political life to rake in the money. It took me a while to realize that."

"Look, Joe, I really don't think we should be having this conversation. If I did, I'd invite you to sit down and I'd buy you a sandwich. Beverly may have an entirely different slant on things. Maybe she just got tired of you."

"She'll give you a different viewpoint, I'm sure," Joe cut in. "What she tells you is only what she wants you to hear. I'm just advising you to watch your step."

With that, Joe Miller turned on the heels of his highly polished black policeman's shoes and walked away.

CHAPTER 23

I waited until I knew Britton had left the premises. I was hot for the kill, but I didn't want her to know it until she gave in. This one wasn't going to be easy. She seemed too prim and proper. But, I knew that most women have a dark side and I knew all the right moves to open her up like a fresh can of pork and beans. I had an excellent batting average when it came to l'amore. I had recently purchased a Virgin Mobile cellular, but I was, by no means, a virgin.

"More coffee?" said the busty waitress with laughing eyes. I nodded to the affirmative.

"Let's do it." I whispered, as she poured my hot java.

I surreptitiously watched her walk away with a piece of my heart. The rest of it, was throbbing for this fine lady, sitting across from me.

"Mr. Savage, if I may have your attention for a few moments." she sounded like the wife I never had.

"You already have that, and then some." I thought I saw a trace of a smile at the corner of her luscious ruby reds. She couldn't help it, but she blushed. I knew then that I had jumped through the first hoop.

She cleared her lovely throat. Easy now, old boy. You don't want to lose her. Britton was going to mass murder me for what I had in mind.

"So, what's your part in all of this? What is it that compels a man to drive to the ends of the earth to find a kid who is already cold in the ground?"

"That's a question that I've been asking myself for the past little while"`

"Well?"

I knew the voice of one caught in the spider's web of intrigue. Though, she would never admit it.

"Let's just call it a sense of honour. And, besides, I happen to love the Enderleys to pieces. Is that what you wanted to hear.?"

"Maybe, maybe not. Actually, I just wanted to hear the good old-fashioned truth."

If she wanted to hear the truth of what I was thinking about her at that moment, she would probably have me arrested and put away for her own personal interrogation. Mysteriously, my specs were starting to fog up.

"Well, aren't these eggs nicely prepared," She was trying to change the subject, but it was too late. The chase was on.

"Yep, I've always been fond of fried eggs myself. Usually, twin fried eggs. And the sausage is to die for."

"Please, Mr....."She seemed to squirm in her seat, struggling to keep from losing her professional demeanor.

"Noble, please, I insist." I pressed hard into the inflection of what I had to say.

"Burl should be back soon." She said, looking around for him.

"Well, I did say that I would look after you. Anyway I can. Ma`am."

"Might I remind you, sir, that I am an officer of the law!" She said, fanning herself with the menu, like some kind of Southern Belle.

Her last authoritative remark seemed like a sharp smack to the face. I snapped back to reality. Or should I say, I geared down my advances, to a silently humming lower gear.

`Oh, yes, where were we? I believe we were discussing the latest developments of the Enderly case."

"I have it on record that you are in the employ of John and Marilyn Enderly."

"Actually, our agreement was that they were going to pay me according to their budget restraints. I'm working for less than peanuts. In other words, I'm working gratis.

"Well, I am impressed." I felt her heart soften. I smiled like the wolf, deep down inside. At this point, it wasn't only my heart, that was throbbing.

"Excellent! Shall we proceed further?"

"Let's shall."

"Alright, we know that Jimmy Enderley was the prime suspect. But what would have been his motive?

"You can start with this." I said and slid a recent picture of Lisa Banquell across the table.

She gasped at the beauty of the girl.

"She looks just like..."

"A young Liz Taylor" I finished her thoughts for her.

"No wonder he was so enthralled about her. She is a raving beauty."

She had no idea that she was more beautiful. Even tough guys can gush, you know. She was not quite out of my woods yet. I would have to be especially marvelous in my comeback. And, no less spectacular with my coup'd'gras.

"O.K. what about the possibility of matricide..slash..patricide?"

"Savage, are you mad! Are you suggesting that.....?"

"Someone so beautiful could be so ugly on the inside...? Yes, that's exactly it."

"Well, I suppose stranger things have happened." She came upside to the real world according to Noble T. Savage.

"Except for one fine distinction, murder just doesn't happen. People make it happen."

"Yes, quite right. And this, would have to be the handiwork, of one sick son of a......!"she trailed off to the land of daily, gratuitous violence.

"Gun?" I offered.

"Speaking of which, it's quite possible that Jimmy Enderley had never fired off even a pop-gun in his entire life!"

"Yeah, just look at that face." I suggested as I slid a fresh-faced photo of Jimmy across to her.

"Yeah, but, how do you explain his fingerprints all over the shotgun at the crime scene?"

"Well, suppose you fell asleep somewhere. However, let's not get into that, just yet. Wouldn't it be simple enough for someone to slip the murder weapon into your hands? Think about it."

"Savage, you're starting to think like a....."

"A white man,?" I finished her sentence.

She seemed to be somewhat disturbed by my brusque comments. She mumbled something about this being the 2000`s, and that things had changed vastly since the days of lynching blacks as a casual sporting venture.

"Well, you must realize, officer, that I am somewhat integrated, and I`d have to say more so, than most natives."

"What do you mean by that?" She asked with her pouting lips, begging to be kissed.

"Well, let's just say I'm a dark cup of java, and no matter how much whitener you pour into me, I'm still going to stay brown."

"You're such a bull-shitter!" She laughed.

"Sooo,..the lady does have a smile, then? And, I see someone's been spreading some vicious truths about me."

Again, she started jiggling with girlish gaiety. I think she was somewhat shocked at the sound of her own laughter. I knew, then; that I had broken through to the inner sanctum.

"Really, Detective, I'm not supposed to be enjoying any of this! This is a very serious murder case."

"Stick to the facts, ma`am, just the facts." I sounded like a half- passable Dragnet character.

"Oh, now, I'm starting to be convinced that you are an incorrigible nut!"

"No, seriously, though, getting back to the issue of Jimmy Enderly`s supposed part in these obviously grisly murders." I was mildly surprised by my sudden elapse of subtle raunch. Ms. Miller was doing things to me that kept interfering with my professionalism.

"Yes, yes, of course." She smiled with a pleasure; subtly peculiar to the female of the species.

"I submit, respectfully, that Lisa Banquell, and her well-trained monkey, went to her parent's home, unannounced." I led into my well thought out suppositions.

"An argument ensued, which led to some vicious innuendo, on both sides." It was now the soft, yet deadly earnest voice of Bev Miller.

"Arthur Banquell tried to phone the authorities to have Lisa and her boyfriend removed," I asserted.

"And the couple in love reacted in a very uncivilized manner; and, promptly shot the Banquells at point blank range and in cold blood! But not before Moosey went over to the stereo and turned it up full blast, so the gunshots wouldn't be heard." She said.

" Arthur Banquell made the fatal error of announcing to his unlovely daughter that she was dangerously close to being disowned." I must admit I sounded like Perry Mason. She read my mind(scary thought) and followed suit.

"And, that, she was about to be removed from the will as lone beneficiary. Arthur thought Lisa would snap out of her fantasies when she heard his final disclosure." she surmised. Her quick mind, clicked swiftly, with the gears of reasonable conjecture.

"Unfortunately, Arthur Banquell went to his grave believing that he had gotten through to his beloved Princess. But her love of snow, and her lust for the Black Prince won her over in the end." I said, with more, than a tinge of sadness.

After having shot the Banquells, Moose Moseley, drove them to the Empty Arms motel, a seedy out of the way place on the South side of Chicago.

"Jimmy Enderly walked to the door of the cheap hotel room, knocked, and Lisa met him and led him inside. And with her feminine wiles, convinced him to have a drink, from a glass of vodka; mixed with a lethal dose of arsenic." Her voice trailed off with the horror of such despicable treachery.

"Jimmy Banquell fell asleep in the arms of a woman he thought had come to cherish him. Within moments, his heart stopped beating." What was this? Tough guys don't mist! I felt a slight lump in my throat.

"Oh, just one final detail." she contributed.

"Ah, yes, the crowning piece of evidence!" I acknowledged.

"The ring! Lisa dropped her class ring on the carpet floor of the hotel room. What an incredibly stupid thing to overlook!" she exasperated.

With a sweeping gesture of sheer unprofessionalism, I leaned over and gave her an unceremonious smack on her cheek.

"Your absolutely bee-you-tiful!" I gave her my best rebel yell!

Just then, Burl walked in.

CHAPTER 24

Burl Britton did not like funeral homes. As a matter of fact, he hated them. He thought that they were the epitome of a rip off. The high cost of dying. Coffins that cost $200 to build selling for $2000. Concrete vaults that are nothing but concrete, selling for $1500 to $2000. Services, including organ player, chair setup, limousine, motorcycle escort, flags, bullshit, all at a grand total of $20 G to $30 G.

But he had gone to high school with the owner of the funeral home, a sleazy character named Potts. That was a good name for a funeral home owner, Potts and plants, Britton was thinking. Pott them and plant them. From what he knew about J.R. Potts from high school, he wouldn't doubt it a bit if the pervert was taking pictures of naked female corpses and posting them on the internet.

He pulled into the parking lot of the funeral home and left the little Honda in the shade of a magnolia tree growing on an adjoining lot. His breakfast churned in his stomach and he dreaded just walking into the funeral home.

Inside he walked down a dimly lit corridor to a door marked "Office" and opened it.

J.R. Potts sat at his desk, a beautiful piece of furniture with a marble top and exquisitely carved sides and legs. Potts himself needed a beautiful desk to mask his ugly features. He was small, maybe five six, and wore his hair combed over from behind his ears to cover a bald head. He sported a small black moustache, one that looked like it had been penciled on with an eyebrow pencil.

"Burl Britton," Potts said, smiling his yellow toothed smile.

"Hello J.R." Britton said. "I'm not dead yet, so don't try selling me a funeral plan. I'm here to ask a few questions."

"About what?"

"The Banquells. When will the police release their bodies to you and when will the funeral be?"

"They haven't released them yet," he said. "Old man Banquell has ordered me to have the bodies cremated when I get them. He says he doesn't want to spend any more money than he has to on a funeral. I would have thought he'd want the best for his boy, Arthur, but by his phone call, he wants the two of them cremated."

"Has Lisa Banquell contacted you about funeral arrangements?"

"Yeah," he said, surprising Britton. "She called here yesterday. She wanted to know the same thing you just asked me. Poor girl. She was sobbing on the phone so bad I could hardly understand her."

"Crying?"

"Yeah. Real boo-hoo stuff. I feel so sorry for her. I'm going to see if she'll let me take pictures of her with her parents before I cremate them. If she will, I'll get the papers to publish them and they'll make good publicity for the business."

Britton wondered if it were Lisa or an imposter.

"Sounds like something you would do, Potts," Britton said.

"What's that suppose to mean?"

"Nothing," Britton said. "Well, thanks for the information, J.R."

"Good to see you again, Burl," Potts said. "I'll be glad to sell you a nice plan. We can put you next to Mindy, out at Forest Hills. I think I can get that plot for you for about $10 grand."

"No thanks, J.R." Britton said. "Mindy's parents wanted her there with her family. If I'd had my way there wouldn't have been a funeral and I would have spread her ashes on the golf course. That's what she wanted. Her parents don't believe in cremation, though."

"Well, have a nice day, Burl," Potts said.

"Yeah," Britton mumbled and walked out.

On a hunch Britton drove to the accounting offices of Arthur Banquell. He didn't know if it would be business as usual there since the head cheese, Art Banquell, had bit the dust, but he thought someone might be willing to talk about how Lisa would be supported by the estate.

He found another old friend there, another high school chum who had gone to Georgia Tech and played football before graduating with a degree in business.

"Marvin Grandy," Burl Britton said, as he walked into one of the cubicles in Banquell Accountants and Associates office.

"Hello Britton," Grandy said. "What brings you over my way? I'm pretty busy nowadays, trying to keep this place going. Art was the director and leader and never let things slide. I've got to try to fill his shoes, if that is possible."

"Just a few questions," Britton said.

"Ask."

"Did Arthur have a trust fund set up for Lisa? I guess what I'm asking is will Lisa be inheriting Arthur's money, or is she set to go to college and have a good life based on what Granddad is willing to put out?"

"Art had a will. In it he left Lisa a million dollars. She was to get it at age 21, if anything happened to him and his wife, Lisa would get $2500 a month until age 21 then she would get the full million."

"That doesn't sound like much a month for a girl to live on while going to college. Was her college expenses covered by that trust?"

"Oh, all of that was paid. She gets the $2500 in spending cash. All of her other expenses, dorm fees, books, tuition, grub, all paid."

"Well that's not bad," Britton said. "The old man would have something to say about that, wouldn't he? He loves that girl more than he loves his peanut butter."

"Funny thing about that," Grandy said. "The old man's business account has been here for years and I don't ever remember seeing any money set aside for the young lady. Lots of trusts and estate money was going to go to Art on the death of Jobe Banquell, but as far as I know, Lisa got nothing from the Grandfather's estate."

"Nothing?"

"Zip. Nada. Nada damned thing," Grandy said and laughed at his pun.

"So what you are telling me is that if Arthur changed his will, the young lady is penniless?"

"Well, I don't know what Grandpa will do, but the way I understand it, if, and that's a big "if" Arthur had his lawyer draw up a new will cutting the young lady out, then she gets nothing from his estate. Whatever the old man does in the interim is purely conjecture, but I'd guess he would take care of Lisa."

"Thanks, Marvin. How's the Missus?"

"Oh she's fat and sassy as ever. You'd never guess she was homecoming queen at Georgia Tech to look at her now. But I still love her to pieces. She'll always be my home coming queen."

"Yeah. Well, thanks again, Marv. Come see me sometime."

Britton left, knowing full well that Marvin Grandy would not come to see him. Neither would Rita Grandy, the fat and sassy home coming queen. Since the death of his wife, Mindy, no-one from the old crowd had set foot in Britton's house. It was as if Mindy had been the only one who ever had a friend in that town. When she died no-one called him and asked him to come for dinner, play golf or tennis, go to a picnic. Nothing. He could have died too, he thought.

"To hell with them," he told himself, and walked back to his car.

Ten minutes later he was back at Denny's, standing in front of the table where his partner of late, Noble Savage, was engrossed in telling Detective Beverly Miller, what his thoughts were regarding the Banquell killing.

"Jumping to conclusions, aren't you, Savage?"

CHAPTER 25

I was jumping alright, and I didn't much give a damn who knew it. All's fair, I figured. I didn't see any sign hanging on her saying, `Paws off!, Property of Burl Britton.`

"Hey, my man! What's the latest, Burl?"

"Well, I've been doing some digging...pardner."

It sounded like he was peeved. My guess was he thought I was up to something grossly unethical. He was partially correct. I was beginning to doubt whether I would be successful or not. See? I told you my middle name stood for, doubting Thomas.

"Oh, hi, Burl, Mr. Savage and I were just discussing the Banquell murders."

"Yeah, Burl, aint nothing wrong with that, is there?" My wolf retreated back into the forest.

"No, no, I suppose not." Britton replied with a subtle edge to his tone.

Ms. Miller felt uncomfortable at the strained moment. I felt like I had just been caught under the sheets in some sleazy Georgian flea-bag of a motel. She cut the tension by pulling out her make-up mirror, looking into it, only to say.

"Oh, my gosh, I look like the bride of Frankenstein! Gentlemen, would you excuse me, while I go and freshen up?"

"Certainly," we both said at the same time. It was an awkward moment. X had just met up with Y with intersecting complications.

We both watched her glide away into the ladies restroom.

"What the hell are you up to, Savage?" Burl pressed me for the truth.

"What ever do you mean?" I said like some pre-pubescent kid caught with a grimy girlie mag.

"I see the way you looked at her from the moment you met her!" He accused me rightfully. I didn't dare to flinch. I knew he could read me like the Saturday afternoon comics.

"Hey, forgive me for being a man." I shot back.

"Give it up, she's way out of your league, man!" he said like an outraged husband.

"What the hell do you mean by that? I'm no damn sub-human!" Said the Indian from Saskatchewan. Don't even try to pronounce it. It'll break your heart.

"Oh, shit! I didn't mean it that way. Honestly, can you see her living on pork and beans for the rest of her life in some hick town up near the North Pole?"

"Well, I suppose you might have something there." I had to concur. After all, I am a realist. But all I wanted was a slice. Not the whole pie.

"Alright, here she comes, just try to keep on track, and for heaven's sake, man, keep it in your pants. At least until we finish this case. O.K?"

"Alright, truce?"

"Yeah."

For the most part, I just sat there and listened as he dazzled her with his detective skills and obvious knack for finding the truth.

However, I was still convinced that she had found me interesting. I intrigued her. She said it in so many ways without saying a syllable. Her eyes gave her away. She kept flicking her glance back and forth between me and Burl. Once, I thought I caught a subtle wink thrown my way. It happened in a split-second while he was looking into his notebook to give her a fine detail regarding the M.O. of the shooters.

"Why so silent, Noble? she asked.

"Yeah, why?" Britton was gloating.

I was off in my own little world.

"When confronted with insurmountable odds, see yourself as the conqueror!"

"Yes, Sensei!"

"What the hell did you say?" It was Burl again.

"He said he sees himself as a conqueror! For heaven's sake, Burl, don't you have ears?" she said in my defense.

He blushed a slight shade of pink and looked sideways at me like he was contemplating premeditated homicide.

"Well, Savage, are you still in the game?"

"Oh, sorry, Burl, my mind was back on the flats again."

"Welcome back to Georgia! Can we just get on with it, now?"

I had never figured on Bev Miller to complicate things. In a sense, I kind of wished that I didn't love the thrill of the chase so much. It excited me as nothing else did. The eventual conquest was only part of it. If the truth be told her presence distracted me. Still in all, it was a pleasant distraction. Girly Girl was still there in the back of my mind. Even with her, it was kind of a long shot. Maybe, I was too old for her. But, you know what they say," There may be snow on the roof, but there's still fire in the belly."

"What were you saying about cremation of the bodies?"

"Yeah, Jobe Banquell is intending to put his son in a jar, as a family memento."

For some strange reason, I thought of his many trophies, mounted on the walls of the family ancestral estate.

"I've always thought of cremation as an indignity to the remains."

"Why's that?" She just had to ask.

"Well, if you must know, I've always felt that the human body is a beautiful thing."

Again, she blushed.

"Yes. continue."

"Oh, for Gosh sakes!" It was Burl. exasperated as all get out.

"Well, it's true! In the old days, our people never buried our dearly departed. Their remains were put on funeral pyres high in the open air."

"What a beautiful sentiment!" She looked at me with stars in her eyes. Burl, on the other hand was quietly seething with impatience.

"All right, open air, shmopen air, can we please stay on the same page, here?"

"I'm right on it, B.B!" I said, trying to sound gung-ho.

Another giggle tossed me back to my classroom prankery of yesteryear.

"Alright, I didn't find out Lisa was disinherited by her papa before Arthur Banquell went to meet his maker."

"And, so, we have no motive."

"Yeah." I joined in. "Something about it just doesn't feel right to me. It's too neat of a scenario for my way of thinking."

"What? You don't think the Black Prince would have the moxy to pull the trigger?" Burl was breathing the fire of dragons.

"Hold on, Burl, I'm getting the same message, although it's a little jumbled." Ms. Miller interjected.

"What's wrong with you two? Are you suggesting that there may be another unknown factor?" It was Burl, the Inquisitor.

"Anything is possible, after dusk, in Atlanta." I said, as though I had lived there for years. I tipped my fedora back, enjoying the rich baritone of my voice wafting in the cafe. I felt I had the exclusive right since it was the only thing rich about me these days.

"O.K. I guess it's only reasonable to keep all our options open. Although, quite truthfully, I still don't trust The Black Prince."

"What's the matter, Britton. afraid of the dark?" I could tell I skewed him with the soul search.

"Oh, yeah, would you trust the son-of-a - bitch who did this to you?" He pulled up his shirt to reveal an old war wound. His war, on the streets of Atlanta.

"Oh." was all I could say.

"The m.f....., tried to gut me like a fish!" He was trembling, and as livid as humanly possible without losing his cookies.

I was embarrassed for the man. He didn't have to be so dramatic. Was he trying to impress her subliminally, or what? I had the scars too.

But, please, let's not get into that. Just the facts, ma'am, just the facts.

"Alright, Britton, now that we've had our little show and tell, can we get it on? I mean, can we get on with it?"

Another muffled giggle told me that she was still with me. I don't know that he suspected anything. Time would tell.

Britton told us that Banquell's daughter was still in his will for a cool million bucks.

"Whew! What the hey is the interest on that kind of money?" I asked, preparing for my moment of awe.

"I expect that a young lady of her refined taste could live quite comfortably off of the interest alone, Savage." Burl hurled the fact at me, as a man might hurl a dog a bone. I thought I was a sly old fox, but it appeared that Jobe Banquell was the granddaddy of them all.

"And, so the plot thickens." I spit out my slim contribution.

"Spare me the theatrics, Savage. You're just echoing my findings, in case, you haven't noticed." Britton was getting sharper with each stab of innuendo.

"Aww, give him a break, Burl. This isn't exactly a case of cow rustling, you know." the angel rescued my manly pride.

"Alright, alright, but as soon as we're done with this case, you're on your own, Savage!" Burl was pee-ohed, that was for certain.

"Suits me fine, as long as I get enough cash to make it back to the flatlands, I'll be O.K." I asserted like a fella who was playing with a full deck.

Burl left to go to the little boy's room, and she attempted to apologize for his rude behavior.

"Oh, don't mind him, Noble, he's had a difficult time of it since he lost his wife. I guess he's trying to do the best he can under the circumstance."

Ms. Miller was a sweet thing. Deep down in my craw, I knew Burl would end up with her. I just wanted to have a little fun, that's all.

"O.K., I'll give him the benefit of the doubt. As long as he doesn't call me out. I don't give a damn! I`ll lay him low without giving it a second thought."

" Oh, you don't want to do that. He's not only a good P.I., but he's also proficient in martial arts." she warned me with a tone worthy of special note.

"Well, that's just my game!" the brightness came back into my eyes.

"Oh, here he is!" I said in as friendly a tone as I could muster. Burl walked back into our lives.

"Listen, Savage, I just went in to splash some cold water in my face, and I figured that woke me up to a little bit of maturity. I guess I should apologize from my rude behavior. Can we shake on it?" He held out his big, beefy hand. I shook it ,and I felt like I had been clutched by Paul Bunyan himself.

"Alright, I guess we forgot that we have a common enemy. It wouldn't do to be fighting amongst ourselves." I noticed the sweet smile on the lips of Ms. Miller.

"O.K. now what's next on the agenda?"

I caught the waitress by the hem of her apron and sweet-talked her into pouring us another round of java.

CHAPTER 26

Burl was cooled off enough when he left the restaurant that he felt that Noble Savage would be OK with Beverly Miller. Burl Britton was not a ladies man. He lacked the gift of gab that a lot of guys naturally seem to possess, that is the sweet talk that pours out of the mouths of some guys when it comes to women. Burl had always been a little shy, but his good looks and an effortless sense of confidence in his abilities had all worked well in his favor. He knew that Beverly Miller had taken a liking to him, and if Savage wanted to make a play, then may the best man win.

With that in mind, he got in his little Honda and drove away. He wanted to talk to Arthur Banquell's attorney and find out if Arthur had changed his will. He felt that Savage would be able to think on his feet long enough to interview the football coach at the high school and find out if Moose Moseley had missed some practice during the week, particularly the day that Jimmy Enderly was killed.

It was strange that Savage thought Moseley and Lisa had teamed up to put young Jimmy down. They had opportunity enough, but Burl was still a little unsure of motive. He did not want to think that Lisa and Moose had killed Lisa's parents, even though he could tell that Savage seemed to be walking down that road. Oh well, he thought, it won't hurt to investigate that possibility, particularly if I find that Banquell has changed his will. Money is a great motivator of practically anything, Burl Britton knew.

When Britton got to the office of Sanford, Slauson, and Thurmond, he parked the little car and sauntered through the doorway, grinning at the receptionist.

"Would you buzz Todd Sanford and ask him if he can spare a minute or two for me?"

"And who might you be?" the receptionist asked.

"Oh, Burl Britton," he said, blushing. "Todd knows me."

She buzzed Sanford's office. "A Mr. Britton would like a minute of your time, Mr. Sanford."

"Send him in, Gloria," Sanford's deep voice came back.

"You may go in, Mr. Britton," she said, rising from her desk and opening a door directly behind the receptionist area.

"Thank you, Gloria," Britton said, "I owe you one."

"Not at all, Sir." she said.

Britton walked into the plush office of Todd Sanford.

"What can I do for you, today?"

"Just a question or two, Todd," Britton said. "Did Art Banquell come to you wanting to change his will shortly before he was killed?"

"No."

"Did he say anything to you about changing his will?"

"Still no."

"Nothing at all? Not even at your usual Saturday night poker game, or at the golf course?"

"I'm telling you, Burl," Sandford shook his head from side to side for emphasis. "No. Nothing. He never mentioned it to me. His will has been on file here for six years. Everything goes to his daughter, Lisa. No changes, no codicils, no additions. No hits, no runs, no errors." Sanford smiled at his pun.

"What about the old man? Has he made any changes to his will?"

"Jobe Banquell? Well, I'm not sure I can tell you anything about Jobe, Burl. Client, attorney confidentiality, you know."

"Off the record," Britton said.

"If Jobe knew I told you any of his business I probably could never practice law in Georgia again, maybe not in the United States. Hell, he might even pull enough strings to get me banned world-wide. He's got connections all the way up to the United Nations."

"Yeah, yeah." Britton said. "I know he has friends on the state department, and his billionaire buddies all over, but hell, man, all I want to know is if he changed his will, that's not state secrets. Surely you trust me not to divulge anything like that where it could get back to Jobe."

"OK," he said, and Britton could tell that Sanford's resolve was weakening.

"OK what?"

"Well Jobe did talk to me about changing his will."

"He did?"

"Damn it, Burl, I just told you he did. Are you listening or what?"

"Oh, sorry, Todd. That just took me by surprise. What kind of change? Did he cut Lisa Banquell out?"

"No. He threatened to cut his son, Arthur Banquell out."

"What?"

"I swear if this gets back to Jobe Banquell, I'll personally put a bullet in your head, Burl Britton."

"Keep your shorts on, Todd. I'm just surprised by all of this. It may or may not play in the case that I'm working on. And if it does, it won't be any thing that I will let out of the bag. You know me better than that. I'd have been dead years ago if I told anything about my informants. I've got stuff on state senators that I wouldn't dare spill because my informants would cut my throat without thinking twice if that came to light."

"Which state senator?" Todd asked, all ears.

"You don't want to know, Todd," was all Burl said.

"Well, what I'm telling you is just as confidential," Todd said.

"Did he give a reason?"

"Jobe Banquell doesn't need a reason to do anything. He's always been a free soul. Even as a kid he didn't take any crap off of anyone. Rumor has it he's had more than one man disappear."

"Yeah, I've heard those rumors, too," Burl said. "I'm not sure I believe any of them."

"I don't want to take that chance," Todd said.

"So is that all you're going to tell me? You don't know a reason why he threatened to cut Art out of his will?"

"He suspects that Art has been cooking the books slowly, and that he, Jobe, may have lost millions to his son's ledger work."

"Art was cheating his own daddy?"

"I don't know about that," Todd said. "I'm not the bookkeeper, Art was. All I know is that Jobe stormed in here one day blowing off steam. He said if he found out that Art had cheated him, he'd fix it so Art would wind up on skid row, eating out of garbage cans."

"He must have had some reason to talk like that. I wonder how he got word that Art might have been dipping into the family pie?"

"I don't know, Burl. I've told you too much already. Now get the hell out of my office. If I find out you've leaked this, I swear I'll stick a tennis racket up your ass and re-string it with barbed wire."

"Thanks, Todd,"

"Get out, Burl."

CHAPTER 27

It was time for me to head back to school. High school. More specifically, Whispering Meadows High. From what I could piece together, that was the place where all the high flyers went. High flyers like Lisa Banquell and ,of course, her Moosey Baby. I intended on calling on the football coach to get the lowdown , on the "low- down," so to speak. I was never what you might call a jock back at my old alma mater. Hell, I never even made it as a water boy. That's O.K., I figured. As far as I was concerned, they were all a bunch of faggots, including the coach.

"Hey, where are you off to?" It was Burl.

"Jeez, I didn't think you cared. I'm genuinely touched." Was my sarcasm showing through my usual panache? I hoped so.

"Noble, give me your cell number, so we can....(ahem) keep in touch." It was the voice of the lady of my dreams.

"Soitenly," I said, clicking my tongue twice. "It's 981-7254, yes, that's 981-7254. Anytime, night or day. 24-7."

" Awright, awready! So where to?" Burl sounded like my old high school math teacher. The man never had any patience with me either.

"I'm going back to school. Whispering Meadows High, ready or not, here I come!" I said, serious as all get out.

"Well, I guess I better phone the poor sons-a - whores; and warn them you`re on the way!" he roared with booming laughter. I could be infectious that way.

" Yeah, well, you can tell them one more thing for me, nobody tries to hump me, without my consent, on or off the field." I heard her exhale sharply with unmistakable passion.

" O.K., keep us posted. You got my number, right? " the big lug shrugged his shoulders, embarrassed at his voice of concern.

"Yeah, I got it. But, I'd much rather have hers." This time she openly smiled as if she didn't care who saw her.

"Please do be careful. Sometimes, southerners can be exceptionally cruel in their dealings with outsiders. " she offered.

"Don't worry, it'll be a piece a` cake." I winked at her in such a way that old Burl wouldn't catch on.

The drive to Whispering Meadows was pleasant enough. I pocketed her phone number, which she had surreptitiously, smeared on a Denny's napkin. In fact, today, I felt like whistling. `Hmm,` I thought,` What'll it be, maybe a few bars of Melancholy Baby? ` Then, I decided against it. The sky above me was clear and there was not a cloud in the sky. But, I felt an inexplicable chill come over me. It was the inner man, I was quite certain of it.

"Listen for the voice in the wind. It will tell you of the danger ahead where your eyes cannot behold."

Why was the old man always so damn inscrutable in his dark sayings? Again, his calmly serene voice, dropped into my consciousness.

"There will come a time when you shall walk in a strange land. Listen with your heart. It will not fail you, when the Tiger poises to strike."

The voice of the old man came to me at the oddest of times. I heard him speak to me almost always when I was about to walk onto dangerous ground. I felt a tinge of sadness because, once again, I was about to put someone to shame, like a hundred times before.

I noticed that the place was rich. The grounds were manicured as there was not a blade of grass askew. Young people stopped to stare as if I was an alien from another world. A young, blonde girl of about 16, or so, laughed nervously when she saw me advancing up the sidewalk to the main entrance. I grew steadily aware of my weathered look and my shabby apparel. `Screw them," Ì thought, warding off the occasional pang of inferiority that I hadn't felt since my primary school years. I rubbed my chin and suddenly realized I hadn't shaven for a couple of days. I had gotten so preoccupied with playing the bloodhound that I was starting to resemble one.

She looked up from her bi-focal horn-rimmed glasses. Clearly, she had never seen one of us, except at the John Wayne film festival at the Bijou Theatre many, many years ago. Her jaw dropped as if she expected me to pull out my tomahawk, at any moment. I lifted up my right hand, and she drew back clutching the books she had been perusing. I grunted and addressed her as gently as possible.

"How!" I smiled.

That must have startled her. She dropped the books.

"I'm looking for Coach Kleats, ma'am." I tried as much as I could to put her at ease. "By the way, the Indian wars, are but a distant memory."

"Yes, yes...of course, I quite realize...." she was still not convinced that I had no intention of parting her hairline.

"What's the problem here?"

It was the distinctly sharp voice of authority. Principal Weatherbee stood there in all of his portly vainglory, tapping his yardstick on the perfectly polished limestone floor. He had on a pair of thick lens Teddy Roosevelt glasses. His conservative tent-size gray suit was complimented by a bright red bowtie, like the kind one might come across in an molding issue of Sears Roebuck. His toupee clearly did not match his bushy uni-brow. He waddled, rather than walked. Obviously, he was not a firm believer in the virtues of a daily exercise regimen. The tell-tale crumbs on his walrus moustache spoke volumes of his favorite pastime.

"And, who is this fine-looking gentleman?" I flattered the tub.

"Well...ahem...you may go, Miss Grundy," he dismissed her as one might give leave to a maid.

"Actually, I'm looking for a Coach Kleats, it's a police matter. If you please," I said striking up my professional decorum.

" I take it you have official identification ?" Weatherbee insisted.

I took out my pride and joy. It was a bonafide P.I. license, laminated with the official seal and signature of the head of C.I.S.I.S. Weatherbee looked at it and turned it over with an unerring scrutiny. A wry smirk of silent amusement flickered across his quivering jowls. Finally, he accepted it as genuine.

"Canadian, eh ?" the tub observed, looking down on the maple leaf emblem on the corner of my license.

"Yep, a genuine Canuck, through and through." I said with a matter of fact tone.

"Well, Mr. Savage, come with me." I followed him down the hallowed halls of WMHS. Up ahead of us, I could hear the sound of a basketball smacking hollowly on the gym floor. All along the way, people took sharply unwelcoming glances toward me. Hushed whispers were followed by a cacophony of cackling. I surmised that I was, indeed, in alien territory.

"Thanks, Mr. Weatherbee. Say, you haven't read the Archie comics, have you ? I'm a great fan!" I tried to dispel the obvious stink of racism lingering.

"Oh, goodness gracious, I get that all the time!" he laughed like a walrus enjoying life in the sun. He waved to Coach Kleats and made an informal introduction. With that, he waddled down the hallway and out of my life.

" Coach Kleats, I'm Detective Noble Savage, and I'd like to ask you a few questions about your boy, Moose Mosley, if I may."

" Yeah, and I'm the Lone Ranger of Atlanta, what is it you'd like to know?"

" Is your star player here abouts?" I probed.

"Nah...actually, he hasn't been around for about a week now." The cat came out of the bag.

"Where do you suppose he might be?"

"I don't know, maybe he's folding white sheets at the governor's mansion. How am I supposed to know? All I know is he'd better get his black ass back here if he doesn't want to lose his football scholarship."

I was beginning to dislike this cantankerous old fart more and more by the minute. Come to think of it, the only old fart I ever liked, was Grandpa. He was the only other human being I ever truly respected. Everyone else was suspect. Coach Kleats was a pig. He sweated like one and he had a turned up nose and you could see his boogers rattling around his nasal cavity. I'd wager that he didn't give a tinker's damn for Moose anymore than I did for Hush Puppies that gave off a horrific stink when wet. Bartholomew Kleats (no kidding) was a shit-kicking waiting to happen. He was a middle-aged balding, has-been athlete who thought he knew everything there is to know about affairs of the gridiron. You can usually tell those guys by their big talk and hot air.

"I just need a few facts that's all. Then, I'll leave you to tell your boys how they can take the State championship."

" Yeah, well, it aint all about chasing a pigskin around the field. Some of these cheerleaders are pretty sweet meat, that's if you haven't noticed, Blood."

" Hey, I may be Canadian, but I aint no wooden Indian!"

Bart let out a shrill, horse whinny which I surmised was glee of some sort. I was glad I could make his day.

"Listen, I'd like to stay and listen to some more of your stand-up routine, but..."

"What about Lisa Banquell ? Have you seen her at all?" The question hamstrung him, and he looked at me as though I had caught him spanking his monkey.

" Hey, Red, you're getting downright personal now. Who the hell hasn't seen Lisa Banquell! She came sashaying around here just before my boy split this groovy scene. Man, she's got some hooters on her! Hooo-ey!" The pig said smacking his thin pinkish lips.

"I'm trying to locate her in regards to a homicide in which she might be implicated. And, if your main man is with her, he may well be an accomplice."

"The only kind of murder Moose is capable of is on the football field. And, you can stick that in your peace pipe and smoke it.....Red."

"Anyone ever teach you any manners ?"

"Nope. Unless, you wanna try....Chief."

The daring of it intensified the air between me and the Pig. His team waited to see what I would do next.

"Alright, Kleats, no time like the present."

He rushed me with a full head of steam. I saw him coming a mile away. The clop clopping of his feet intensified and got louder as he approached. I danced a quick-silver two step out of his way. As his head breezed by my right arm, I grabbed it in a lock and squeezed as we fell headlong onto the grass. Just then, my cellular rang!

"Yeah, who is it?"

"It's Bev. Where are you, Noble?"

"I'm a little indisposed at the moment. Can I call you back in 5?"

"Okey-dokey," she said with sweet lips.

"Alright, Kleats, call your dogs off, or they'll be mounting your head on The Sports Hall of Shame, damnit!" I barked sharply.

"Alright, alright..boys,... let...him...g..g.g....go, I guess." He was choking on his Adam's apple. His face was beet red when I finally released him. Some smart-alec tried to rush me but I grabbed a Louisville Slugger from one of the baskets laying on the gym floor.

"O.K., any of you southern rebels want a lump to end all lumps, come and get er." I warned in deadly earnest. Having been sufficiently warned, they backed off.

"You haven't seen the last of me, Red," said the Pig, as I walked past him and out into the sun-shiny day.

I saw the wrench and a little puddle of oil by my tire on the driver's side, but I thought it was just coincidental. Looking in my rear-view, I ran a comb through my greased hair, straightened my tie and fired up Old Bess. Then, I called Bev just to let her know I was O.K. and that I was on my way.

I was cruising down this fair stretch of a hill, actually fairly long and steep and then, it happened! I was gaining momentum, going down the steep grade. I thought to step on my brakes to slow down, but there was nothing. Up ahead, I could see the train rushing by directly in my pathway!

CHAPTER 28

Burl was not happy. He didn't have any claim to Beverly Miller, although he was very much intrigued by her charms, and she was the first woman he had felt that way about since the death of his wife, Mindy.

And now he was faced with the possibility that she was intrigued by his partner, Noble Savage, the redskin from Canada. Burl was almost sorry that he had agreed to share his case with the Canadian investigator, but it was too late to cry over spilt milk. He just needed to think of a way to regain his lead in the dating game.

He stopped by a local florist and bought a dozen long stemmed roses and told the clerk to deliver them to Beverly at her home, and if there was no one at the house, to keep calling the number until Beverly answered, then deliver them. He picked out a pretty little card and wrote a note on it to send with the flowers. "More Veal Parmesan?" it said. After thinking about it, he had his doubts if that message was the right one, since she had told him she was trying to lose weight. She might construe it to mean that he thought she was getting fat.

"She's getting to be real popular now that she's lost a few pounds," the clerk said.

"What's that supposed to mean?" Burl Britton asked.

"Well she got flowers sent to her all last month by one of the richest guys in town."

"Is that right? Who might that be?"

"You mean who was it?" the clerk smiled. "Sorry, I'm not permitted to give names. You're a Private Detective, aren't you? You find out."

That puzzled Burl quite a bit. Too late now, he thought. The flowers, along with the card, were on their way to Beverly's home.

Something else was on his mind that he deemed more important, at least for the time being.

Who killed the Banquells?

He knew that Savage thought that Lisa had something to do with it. He wasn't sure. It seemed too pat for him. He knew, too, that Lisa had spent a lot of time with her father, and that there had never been any problems between them. He wondered if her association with the black football player had become a riff between them. Savage thought that it might have. Britton wasn't so sure. He decided to check on Art Banquell's past dealings with the black community. A good place to start, he thought, would be with the Banquell's former maid, Shauntell Jones. It was Shauntell who had discovered the bodies and called police.

He found her at home. She lived with her mother and her five children. Her mother watched the children while Shauntell worked. Britton opened the chain link gate and hesitated, waiting to see if the Jones family owned a dog. He glanced around the yard and noted that it was neatly mowed, a few toys were strewn around, but not a sign of dog droppings or dog toys, bowls, or any indication that there was a dog on the premises. He walked to the steps and up them to the porch. He noticed that a few of the porch planks had been replaced recently, and the entire porch had a new coat of paint.

He rapped on the glass panel of a storm door and waited.

The door opened slowly and a little boy looked out.

"Mama, some man's at the door," he said, still staring at Britton.

Britton heard footsteps across the room and the door opened wider.

"Hello," Shauntell Jones said. Britton had met her the day he went to the Banquell's and talked to Mrs. Banquell. It was the same day he had found the email message on Lisa's computer.

"Hi, Miss Jones," Britton said. "I wonder if I could ask you a few questions about the Banquells?"

"Come in," she said, and turned and walked back into the room.

Britton opened the storm door and followed her into the room.

"What you want to know?"

"Were you treated good while you were employed there?"

"Oh yes," she said. "Them folks always were nice to me. I work for them nearly ten years. That Lisa girl was just in first grade when I start there. That poor girl, now her mommy and daddy are dead, what gonna happen to her?"

"I'm sure she will be taken care of nicely by her grandfather," Burl said.

"Yeah, I s'pose. But I can't help feel sorry for her."

"So they were always nice to you? Did you ever get the feeling that Mr. Banquell might have been a racist?"

"A racist? Why I don't think so. He never said a word to me about me being black. Why on earth would you think he was a racist?"

"Did you know that Lisa was running around with Moose Moseley?"

"I knowed that," she said. "I seen them two together many time."

"How did Mr. Banquell feel about that?"

"Well, he knew about it," she said. "I couldn't say rightly one way or 'tother how he feel about it."

"Did you ever hear him talk to his wife about it?"

"I heared 'em talking a lot about it," she said. "They didn't seem to mind one way 'tother."

"They took it calmly that Lisa was going with a black boy?"

"A lot more calmly than his momma and daddy took it," she said shaking her head from side to side. "Mmm Mmm them folks were upset about it fo' shore."

"Moose's folks didn't want him to go with Lisa?"

"Now I just heard that through the grape vine," she said. "Mr. Moseley is the janitor over at Whispering Meadows High School. He's been there for a long time. I heard that he was worried that he might get fired if the school found out his boy was going with a white girl. Lotta folks round here don't like that idea."

"I understand," Britton said. "How'd you learn about that?"

"At church," she said. "Momma was sittin' behind them in church and heard Mr. Moseley say to Miss Moseley, 'dat football coach is dead set 'gainst black boys going with white girls. I'll prob'ly wind up getting fired.' Then Miss Moseley tell him, 'jes axe the Lord to keep watch over us, Daddy.'"

"So you think that the Mosley's were more upset about the match than the Banquells were?"

"Now I don't really know," she said. "Just I don't hear the Banquells saying anything 'bout it."

"What about the community as a whole, Shauntell. Did you ever hear Mr. Banquell say anything about the black community?"

"Nope." she shook her head from side to side. "Matter of fact, he give our preacher money to fix the windows that was leakin'. I was talkin' to my momma bout the windows on the phone one day and he heared me. He wrote a check for $500 made out to our church and gave it to me. He tell me to give it to Mr. Washington, our reverend."

"I see," Britton said. That didn't sound like a racist to him. He was starting to wonder more and more about Savage's theory that Art Banquell had threatened to cut off Lisa for going out with Moose Moseley.

"Was there somethin' else? I gotta go find me another job," Shauntell said.

"No, I guess that's what I wanted to know," Britton said. "Thank you for your time. He dug his wallet out of his front pocket and opened it.

"Take this money," he said, holding out some bills. "It isn't much but it might help you till you find another job."

She took it. "Thank you, sir."

Britton walked down the steps and across the sidewalk to the gate. As he opened the gate he glanced back towards the house. The little boy was standing at the door watching him.

"Thank you, sir," the boy said. He opened the storm door and a dog ran out, across the porch and down the stairs. It looked like a Doberman. A few low, throaty growls was all Britton needed to hear. He stepped through the gate and closed it behind him.

CHAPTER 29

Back in his office, Britton sat thinking about all that had developed in this case. He had listened to Savage's theory about Banquell perhaps threatening to disinherit Lisa, and at the time it seemed like it was a conceivable motive for a young girl to kill her parents. Now he wasn't sure. Shauntell had made it pretty clear to him that Banquell was not a racist, at least not in her eyes. Whether he was secretly a member of the Ku Klux Klan might be a matter of conjecture.

He was deep in thought when his phone rang.

"Burl Britton Investigations," he said to the mouthpiece.

"Mistah Britton, this is Shauntell. I just talk to you. I've got somethin' I need to tell you that I didn't tell the police." She pronounced police like pole lease.

"OK" Britton said.

"Well, when I found those poor fokes dead, I call the police first thing. Then I start lookin' round. On Mistah Banquell's night stand I find a little envelope with some white substance in it. I picked it up."

"Go on," Britton said.

"I went in to check on Lisa. Her bed hadn't been slept in. I'd heard Miss Banquell say that Lisa was spending the night with a girl friend, and I was glad that she wasn't there to see her Momma and Daddy dead. Anyway, I was standin' in Lisa's bedroom lookin' around when I hear the police come in the front door. I still had that piece of envelope in my hand, and I had a pretty good idea what it was. I didn't need no police spectin' me of takin' dope, so I thowed that envelope under Lisa's bed."

"You put the envelope under Lisa's bed?"

"Yassuh. I was goin' to get it back after the police left, but I forgot all bout it. When they told me I could go back the envelope was gone."

"Let me get this straight," Britton said, sighing. "I was there the day before the Banquell's were killed, at the request of Mrs. Banquell. She hired me to find Lisa. I looked in Lisa's room and found an envelope with some white powder in it that turned out to be cocaine. But that was before the Banquell's were killed. You're saying you put the envelope in her room AFTER you found the bodies?"

"Dat's what I'm tellin' you." Shauntell said.

"How did I find it there before you put it there?" he asked, although he knew the answer. It wasn't the same envelope.

"Don't know nothing bout that," she said. "I just thought it was important so I call you."

"OK, Shuantell," Britton said. "If you think of anything else, please call me again. And if you hear anything on the streets, let me know, OK?"

"Yassuh!" she said.

"Thank you, Shauntell," Britton said and hung up the phone.

Were the Banquell's taking cocaine? Was Lisa hooked on the snow? Britton's mind was spinning. It seemed like he was digging a hole that he couldn't crawl out of, and he didn't like the feeling. Something was wrong with the entire scenario, and he intended to straighten it out. Savage's speculation that Lisa was about to be disinherited, the possibility of Lisa being a coke head, how Jimmy Enderly was involved, the entire ball of wax was going to get unwound sooner or later, and Britton wasn't going to give up until he figured it all out.

CHAPTER 30

The wind got caught up in my throat as I made what felt like my final descent. With my right foot pumping wildly on the useless brake pedal, I realized in seconds that my brakes were gone! `Midas!...you lying sons of bitches..you aren't the best in the West!` I yelled in my frenzied state of panic. With the bottom of the hill rushing toward me, I heard the voice once again.

"It is said in the ancient writings, that when faced with certain death, save life, over saving face."

"Yes sensei."

The only thing I was interested in saving was my bacon. So, I resigned to letting go of Old Bess. She had been good to me. I heard the rumbling tons of steel thundering over the tracks and saw the lights flashing. The clanging of the warning bell rang sharply as I braced myself to kiss pavement. With one parting glance of this beautiful old car, I let go of the wheel, and whispered goodbye to the old gal. I hit the pavement, scraping off the pant leg of my Value Village six dollar and ninety-five cent , plus all applicable taxes, pair of slacks. I felt the burn of my red skin scraping off the pavement. Rolling out of the way of oncoming traffic, I whirled into a grassy hump of soft dirt. Somebody up there liked me. Somewhere down the canyons of my fading consciousness, I heard Old Bess crashing headlong into the rushing locomotive. I finally came to rest under a blanket of blackness. Today was not a good day to die, at least not for Noble T.!

When I came to, there was a nurse dabbing a cool, wet cloth on my forehead. In my delirium, I thought it was the twelfth of never.

" Girly- girl, is that you? Can you kiss the pain and make it go away? "I said and once again floated off into the land of Nod.

Her face was blurred at first, but I recognized her voice, even through the mist. It was Bev, and behind her was my nemesis and business partner.

" Is that you, angel cakes? "I cooed, feigning a mild state of shock.

"Yes, it's me, you stupid bastard! I knew you shouldn't have gone to see Kleats alone! Oh, Noble, you'll be the death of me yet!"

Something kind of rank also was in the air and I snuffed wildly against it. When Burl walked out of the washroom, I realized what it was.

"Allergies?" she said.

"No, it's nothing like that," I said, touched by her, and her concern.

"Well, what did Kleats have to say?" It was Burl, oblivious of my near demise.

"Well, I believe what you see before you is exhibit A, of the urgent message that he wanted to convey to my person." I tried to throw a monkey wrench into his cerebellum.

"For Gosh sakes, man, don't you ever speak in plain English?"

"Yeah, O.K., I saw the man, spoke to him, and I got zip. By the by, do I get reimbursed for my vehicle?"

"We'll talk about it later. What about Kleats?

"His face was turning redder by the moment.

"The fact is, he hasn't laid eyes on his monkey-in-training for about two weeks."

"That doesn't help our cause much, does it now?" He chomped at the bit.

" Accepting the fact that he had one of his preppy boys try to off me, indicates that he might have dark and sinister purposes on his game plan. Would you concur, Ms. Miller?

"Well, that is a distinct possibility...."

"What about the possibility of dinner and a movie?"

I loudly clicked my tongue twice. Ah, yes, I could see us alone, together, with a bottle of chilled root beer and a fresh can of pork and beans. Hmmm, it just made me salivate profusely, like one of Pavlov's mutts.

"Say, hold on, now, can you make a concerted effort to keep on task, here?" It was Burl, looming over my sinister plans.

"I'm sorry, Bev, I didn't mean anything by that.

My mind whirred and clicked with the silent machinery of reason trying to gain the favor that I thought I had won with her.

I was beginning to wonder about this roller-coaster we were riding. Was I even marshalling my efforts in the right direction? Or had Jimmy been used as a distraction? I smelled something rotten, and it wasn't trench foot. All I could do now was to limp out of the hospital and go hunting. Hunting Moose, that is.

CHAPTER 31

Not knowing for sure what Mona's last name was, Burl Britton asked at the high school. He parked his Honda at the curb next to where the bus picked up students, and waited. The first group of students that approached ignored his questions, staring at him like he was a pedophile or serial killer trying to pick up young girls.

A boy and a girl approached, walking slowly, hand in hand.

"Excuse me," Burl said. "I'm looking for a girl named Mona who was good friends with Lisa Banquell. Do you know her?"

The couple stopped. The boy looked anxiously at the girl, then back at Britton.

"You must mean Mona Manson. She's the only girl I know whose parents are in the same social status with the Banquells."

"Mona Manson? Reverend Manson's daughter?" Burl asked.

"That's her," the girl said. "Lisa hung out with her at lunch and stuff."

"The Reverend Manson would be a good place to ask about Mona," the boy said. "He's her father. What about Lisa? Do you know where she is? She hasn't been to school in four or five days. It's sad about her parents being killed."

"Yes, it is," Burl said. "I'm an investigator trying to find Lisa. I'll check with the Reverend Manson. Thanks for your help."

"Hope you find her," the girl said, glancing at the boy, then away. "She's pretty popular here. The cheer leading squad misses her."

"Are you a cheerleader?" Britton asked.

"I am now," the girl said. "I was an alternate until Lisa turned up missing, so I was asked to join. I still hope you find Lisa, though. Even if it means I'm off the squad."

"Thank you," Britton said, taken aback by the honesty and selflessness of the young lady.

The couple walked on and Britton started the Honda and drove away. He was familiar with Reverend Manson. The reverend was the head of the Episcopal Church in Whispering Meadows. Britton drove towards the church.

Five minutes later he parked at the curb next to the church's office and got out. As he walked towards the office he was met by Reverend Manson, walking towards the street.

"Reverend Manson?" Burl said.

"Yes."

"Are you Mona's father?" Burl asked, although he knew the answer.

"Yes, what's the problem?" The reverend was immediately concerned.

"There isn't a problem," Burl said, "I would like to have your permission to talk to Mona about Lisa Banquell, the daughter of Arthur and Dora who were murdered last week."

"Are you a policeman?"

"No, Sir. I'm a private investigator. I've been retained by Jobe Banquell to find Lisa, and to see if I can determine who killed her parents. May I talk to Mona?"

"Yes, anything to help find the killers of Art and Dora. They were marvelous people. Pillars of the community."

"Yes, Sir." Britton said.

"Let me get my car, you can follow me to my home. I'm sure Mona will be there," the reverend said.

Britton got back in his Honda and waited for the reverend to drive ahead of him, then pulled out behind the dark Lincoln and followed. At the edge of town they both turned right and drove towards the country club. A few blocks away from the gated entrance to the club, Reverend Manson signaled and then turned the Lincoln into a driveway and stopped. Burl Britton parked at the curb.

The Manson's home was a two story Victorian style home, built a few years before the country club estates. It had a small front yard, immaculately landscaped and trimmed. The house had faux stone front and large bay windows.

"Come in, Sir. I'm sorry, I don't know your name."

"Britton." Burl said. "I'm Burl Britton."

"Are you a Christian, Mr. Britton?"

"Yes, Sir," Britton said. "I attend the Whispering Meadows Christian Church."

"Oh yes," said the reverend. "I'm friends with your Minister, Todd Granger."

Britton didn't answer. He followed the reverend into the house, waited until he was asked to sit down, and took a seat on a plush couch. The reverend called out for Mona in a loud voice. Britton heard a girl answer.

"Please come down, Mona," Reverend Manson said. "There's a gentleman here who would like to ask you some questions."

"Be right down, daddy," the girl said.

Britton waited. A few minutes later he looked up as he heard footsteps coming down a winding stairway. He rose and waited for an introduction.

"Mona, this is Mr. Britton. He's an investigator. Please answer Mr. Britton's questions."

"Thank you, Sir," Britton told the reverend.

"Hi Mona," Britton said to Mona. "I won't take much of your time. Can you tell me where you might think Lisa Banquell would go if she didn't want anyone to find her?"

"I couldn't say, Mr. Britton," Mona said. "She's never told me anything that might even remotely relate to that."

"You were suppose to spend the night last Saturday, together, weren't you?"

"Yes. We did spend the night together. Lisa came over about four on Friday and we went to the mall. Then we came home and went to my room and talked and listened to music while we did our homework. Lisa spent the night. She left Saturday morning to go home, about 9 o'clock. That's the last I saw of her."

"She did spend the night?"

"Yes, Sir."

"Dora Banquell told me that she called and talked to your Mom and was told that Lisa did not spend the night here."

"Oh Mom probably didn't even know," Mona said. "She wasn't here when Lisa came over, and then she was gone again when we came home from the mall. I don't think she even knew that Lisa was here."

"But she was here."

"Yes, Sir, I told you, she spent the night."

"You're not just trying to protect Lisa's reputation are you? This is a serious matter. Lisa has been missing since Saturday, and her parents have been murdered. I hope you wouldn't try to mislead me."

"Mr. Britton, my daughter does not lie!" The Reverend said, coming back into the living room from the kitchen area.

"I'm not saying that she's lying," Britton said, apologetically. "Your wife told Mrs. Banquell that Lisa did not spend the night. Wouldn't she have known?"

"I'm telling the truth, Daddy," Mona said.

"I don't know where this is leading, Mr. Britton," the reverend said. "If you have any more questions, please ask them. I don't believe my daughter would mislead you. As far as my wife's telling a different story, Mona is right. My wife sometimes does not pay much attention to Mona's friends. She's busy with other ladies from our patronage and her mind tends to wander a bit when she gets real busy."

"Do you know anyone named Michelle Montague?" Britton asked.

"No, Sir," Mona said. "Should I?"

"Well, Mrs. Banquell told me that Lisa's best friend was a girl named Michelle Montague. It seems that you would know her, if you were Lisa's friend."

"Lisa had a lot of friends," Mona said. "I'm not a jealous person, Mr. Britton. If Lisa had another friend named Michelle Montague, I may or may not know her. Lisa had friends as far away as Atlanta. She didn't talk about all of them to me. I do not know Michelle Montague."

"OK" Britton said. "Thank you. If you hear from her, will you call me?"

"If I hear from Lisa, I'll call you right after I call Detective Miller."

"You know Detective Miller?"

"She was here today. She asked some of the same questions you just asked."

"She did?"

"Yes, Sir."

"Did she ask about Michelle Montague?"

"No, that name wasn't brought up."

"OK, Mona. Thank you. I'll keep in touch. Thank you, too, Reverend." Britton said.

"Nice to meet you, Mr. Britton," Reverend Manson said.

"Nice to meet you, Reverend, you, too, Mona." Britton said.

Mona nodded, and retreated back up the stairs.

"Thanks again," Britton said, and left.

Back in his old Honda, Britton drove to the library. It never seemed to change. The same librarian he had known for years, now nearly seventy, secure in her job, refusing to retire. She had hushed Britton and his friends when he was a senior in high school. He nodded to her as he walked silently towards the reference books.

He chose a big thick book, white pages for Richmond County. The city of Augusta encompassed a large percent of the area of Richmond County. The tiny suburb of Whispering Meadows was only an ink spot on the page.

He ran his index finger down the listings under "M" and found the name Montague listed several times. His first instinct was to start calling the numbers next to the names and asking for Michelle. But, as usual, his common sense took over and he looked for the precinct numbers in front of the telephone numbers. He found that of the entire list, only three names were in the same precinct as Whispering Meadows. He would start with those.

None of the three knew of Michelle Montague. He separated the remaining names into precincts and of the eleven remaining, six were in the same precinct. He used a mental "binary" search system, checking the names off with his ballpoint pen as he dialed the middle name on the first set of precincts, then the one above it, then the one below it. On his fourth try the phone was answered by a sultry female.

"Yes, I'm Michelle Montague," the voice said.

"My name is Burl Britton," Burl said. "I'm a private investigator, trying to locate a missing teen. Her name is Lisa Banquell. Do you know her?"

"Of course. She was one of my dance and cheer leading students," the voice said.

"I see," Britton said. "Did you give her a book with a note that read 'this is the book I told you about?'"

"Yes, I did," Michelle Montague said. "I recommended the book to all of my students, but

Lisa showed exceptional talent and I had an extra copy so I mailed it to her."

"She was a student of yours. Do you remember ever seeing her with a black football player named Moose Moseley?"

"No, Mr. Britton," she said. "I would certainly have remembered that. I don't think Lisa was the type to go out with black boys. She was the daughter of some very influential people, and her grandfather is the founder of one of this state's highly respected institutions that denounces mixed race relationships."

Britton thought about that for a minute. He knew, from what Shauntell had told him that Arthur Banquell was probably not opposed to mixed race relationships, but apparently Jobe Banquell was.

"You're speaking of Jobe Banquell?"

"Yes, of course. I don't know anything about Lisa's mother's family, but I know that Jobe Banquell is definitely opposed to mixed race relationships."

"Did the book you gave Lisa have anything to do with that subject?"

"Well, it was simply a viewpoint. It neither opposed or condoned inter-racial relationships. It just pointed out the pitfalls."

"The name of this institution isn't the Ku Klux Klan, is it?" Britton said, ironically.

"Of course not! Neither I, nor Mr. Banquell, are in favor of that organization."

"In that case, would you mind giving me the name of the organization?"

"It's really quite a benign group, Mr. Britton. It's the Georgia Family Research Society of Augusta."

"Georgia Family Research Society, huh?"

"That's right. Mr. Banquell's opinions are not necessarily those of this organization.'

"And what part do you play in the organization, Miss Montague?"

"I'm the director," she said. "My position is a non-paying one. I have my schools as my primary source of income."

"Schools? As in more than one school?" Britton asked.

"Yes, I am the founder. I own fifteen schools across the state. We enroll young ladies from the age of 8 and train them to be the best cheerleaders. Almost all of our girls are on cheerleading squads in high schools across the state by the time they are sophomores."

"Well, you've answered the questions I had in mind," Britton said. "May I call you again if I think of anything else?"

"Certainly. I've nothing to hide. Please call me if you find Lisa. I'm still coaching her, although she is already on the cheerleading team at Whispering Meadows. Our next format in my school is preparing the students for beauty contests. Lisa may be the next Miss Georgia when she graduates."

"You are aware that her parents were murdered last week?"

"Yes, how sad. But life goes on, doesn't it. Lisa may still want to remain in my coaching classes. She expressed a keen desire to one day be Miss America."

"Yes. Miss America." Britton said. "Well, goodbye, Miss Montague."

"It's Missus Montague," she said.

"Goodbye, and thank you, Mrs. Montague." He said.

CHAPTER 32

I pulled out the moose hide bag of medicinal roots and put them to work on my wounds. Unfortunately, there wasn't anything made that would soothe the sense of my beleaguered pride. Whoever it was that tried to cancel me out of the book of not so rich and infamous had something coming down their turnpike. There is nothing worse than a pissed off Indian from Saskatchewan who's just lost his ride. My first suspect would have to be Coach Kleats or one his faggot cohorts. And, yet that supposition didn't seem to make any sense either because I had just met the man. You'd think that murdering someone might take a little time and planning. It didn't take Conan Doyle to figure that much out. Who the heck would want me dead so much? A beautiful guy like me shouldn't have too many enemies.

I hadn't noticed any suspicious looking vehicles trailing behind me as of late. All I knew was I was in deep into this mystery. I don't much appreciate too many question marks hanging over my head for too long. It made me a little nervy. And when I get that way, I start to become dangerous. There's nothing worse than a cornered Indian. They get unpredictable.

"Hey, sleepyhead!" It was her. She smelled so good and she was as soft as a marshmallow.

"Hey, Detective Miller, you're lookin` mighty fly."

"You have any new revelations as to who might have wanted you out of the picture."

"Maybe...Burl? "I paused for dramatic effect.

Again, I heard the warm splash of girlish laughter.

"Oh, puhleeze, isn't that getting a little old?"

"Well, I kinda ruled out Kleats since he didn't know me from one of his holes in the ground."

"And what about Moose Mosley?"

"I have great difficulty suspicioning someone to whom I haven't been formally introduced . Do you mind?"

The truth was that I was beginning to wonder why Bev was trying to steer my thinking. I was almost to the point that she was beginning to make me feel that I was somehow incapable of deducing for myself. I had an almost disturbing 6th sense for that sort of manipulation. I could play that game too. Cat and mouse was not one of my favourite pastimes. I just didn't feel as though I had enough of the usual nine lives left to be dicking around in all the wrong places. I was healing fast and the son of a prick-head who tried to cancel my treaty card was in for a helluva surprise. I just hoped that my little accident wasn't just a diversion. At the most critical moment that I was trying to undress her.... thinly.. veiled... motives, my cell rang.

"Hey, it's Mr. Peanut Man! How the hell have you been, my friend?"

On the other end I heard the tired , rasping voice of Jobe Banquell.

"Noble, you've got to come quickly! It's Lisa."

"What is it? What's wrong, Jobe?" I was shocked to hear myself calling him by his first name.

"I'm afraid that....."

"C'mon, out with it man! I've never been good at charades!"

"It sounds like she's been kidnapped or something."

"What d`ya mean?" Where the hell was sensei when I needed a word of wisdom?

"She called me this morning. She was hysterical. It sounded like she was being held against her will!"

"Well, haven't you heard? Someone screwed with my brakes and nearly sent me off to the happy hunting grounds."

"I don't give a tinker's damn about that. Get your brown ass out of bed! This is not a time to be laying around! I'll have Clement pick you up in half an hour. You can do all your recouping at Blackstone. I'll have my own personal physician look after you."

"Oh, what da` hell, I'm getting tired of hospital food anyhow."

Bev sat there dead silent. She was a vision of loveliness, no matter what mood struck her. She turned her head at a slight angle when I told her I had to.....self-discharge.

"Adios, Bev." I said as I threw on my rumpled suit. Within the appointed time, Clement showed up at the front door of the hospital admittance room . I shuffled out of the hospital glad to be able to get away from the ever-present smell of death and antiseptic. I got into the sleek black Rolls and we sped of to the stately Banquell Mansion nestled in the hills overlooking Dark River.

CHAPTER 33

Cell phones are not one of Britton's favorite things but then a Private Investigator has to have one. He had learned a long time ago that stopping at telephone booths was both time consuming and a pain in the ass. Not only that but telephone booths were getting to be a thing of the past. Maybe that's why the crime rate was going up, Superman had no place to change.

When his cell phone rang, Britton angrily dug it out of his jacket pocket and answered.

"Britton Investigations."

"This is Savage."

"How you feeling, pardner?" Britton asked. "How are they treating you in the hospital?"

"I'm not in the hospital," Savage said.

"They set you free?"

"Funny," Noble Savage said. "I set myself free. I walked out. Right now I'm being escorted to talk to Jobe Banquell, the peanut man. He got a call from Lisa and it sounded like she's been kidnapped or something. I'm hot on it."

"You let yourself out of the hospital, Good God, man, you may be hurt worse than you realize."

"I'll take my chances. Right now I want to find out what Lisa told the peanut man, see if she gave him any clues as to where she can be found."

"Of course," Britton said. "Do you want me to meet you there?"

"No need," Savage said. "I can handle this. I've been out to the mansion before. Jobe

Banquell is a southern host and I could get used to sleeping on feather beds."

"Well, let me know what you find out. If there's anything I can do, I'll be on it. I'm just curious as to why he called you instead of me. I'm the one who has contracted with him to find Lisa."

"Hell, I don't know, Britton," Savage said. "Maybe he took a liking to me. Maybe he feels I can cut to the chase faster. How the hell should I know?"

"It doesn't matter," Britton said. Savage could hear a tiny hint of professional jealousy creep into Britton's voice.

"I'll call you as soon as I find out what's going on," Savage said.

"OK.   Meantime, I'll keep digging. We've got two parts to this contract. First is to find Lisa. Second is to find her parents killers."

"Yeah.   Wonder what the police have found on that matter? I just left Bev Miller at the hospital and she didn't seem to have anything new. If she did she didn't confide in me."

"I'll go see her." Britton said. He thought that would be a good excuse to meet with Bev Miller again.

One of the things that was bugging Britton was the alarm system at the Banquell home. How did the killers get past the alarms? Of course if Lisa and Jimmy were the killers, Lisa would know how to shut off the alarm.

Britton drove to the crime scene and talked to a uniformed officer who sat on the Banquell's porch in a canvas camping chair.

"How's about letting me go in, Joe?"

"Can't do it Britton," Joe said. Although he had known Joe since high school, Britton figured that Joe would not let him in the house.

"Well maybe you can do me a favor then," Britton said. "What company has the security system for this place?"

"There's a sticker on the garage door, Britton," Joe said. "I didn't read it, but I remember seeing it there the other day when I was assigned to guard this crime scene. I heard that we were supposed to take the guard down by the end of the week. Today's Wednesday, maybe by Friday you can get in."

"I'll check the sticker, Joe." Britton said. "I really don't need to go in, just wanted to check out the system."

"OK."

Britton walked around the huge porch and towards the garage. He saw the little shield type sticker on the bottom left window of the garage door long before the reached it. His eyes were still pretty good for an old man, he thought. As he got closer, he recognized the sticker. It was one of a company in Atlanta, Dependable Guardian Service. He took a notebook from his pocket and copied the phone number.

Back in his car he called the number on his cell phone and was soon connected to the agent that handled the Banquell account.

"Can you tell me if you had any hits on this account last Monday night, a week ago?"

"You mean the night the Banquell's were killed?" The voice asked.

"Yeah," Britton said. "That's what I'm asking. Did you get a hit that night, and if so, did you notify the police in Whispering Meadows?"

"Who wants to know?" the voice said. "We don't want any legal complications in this. Inquiries should be made through the local police in that area."

"I'm Detective Britton," Burl Britton said. He didn't tell the person on the line that he was a private investigator, just that he was a detective. No lie there.

"Just a moment, Detective," the voice said. Amazing how much co-operation a person gets when the police are involved, Britton thought, even though he hadn't really lied, he felt a little guilty about it.

"We did not receive an alarm notice on the night in question, Detective," the voice said. "Is there anything else we can help you with?"

"Can you tell me who the first response would be?"

"That would be Whispering Meadows PD," the voice said. "Our dispatcher has a direct line to their dispatch."

"OK," Britton said. "Thanks for your help."

He snapped the cover closed on his cell phone. If the person on the other end of the line was alert, they would make a note of his number, then verify that he was with the police. He hoped that the person he had talked to was not that alert. He didn't need to answer questions to the police.

Something wasn't fitting in, Britton thought. Why didn't the alarm on the Banquell home alert the dispatcher at Dependable Guardian Service? Had someone cut the wires or simply hit the code buttons and turned the alarm off? That was another question he filed away in the back of his mind that he intended to ask Beverly Miller. He thought that Beverly was a competent detective, otherwise she wouldn't be the sergeant. But Britton always felt that he was two steps ahead of most police investigators, and maybe that was something that Beverly Miller just had not had time to investigate.

CHAPTER 34

I missed Old Bess. The old gal had been a good old dame, at least as cars go. She probably rolled off the assembly line close to the time I was being hatched. However, this sleek ride made me almost forget her. In a sense, she had, at last come home to the place where she was...(ahem)..born. She would now be resigned to the auto graveyard, somewhere in this cold city. At any rate, I wasn't looking forward to riding back to the Prairies on the Greyhound. But a man has to do what an Indian has to do.

It didn't take long before we pulled up to the Banquell Estate once again. I could feel the desperation long before I saw him. It was somehow to me as tangible as a sharp slap to my face. Yeah, like the first fall of snow. The stressed face of the man who seemed to own this part of the South greeted me at the front door. It wasn't easy for him to explain that he was at wits end. This powerful mover and shaker seemed so lost and somehow pathetic, despite his obvious monetary solvency. By now, I knew that money couldn't buy an ounce of bonafide happiness. It could rent a whole lot, but it always seemed to fall short of heaven.

However, I still had to concede to the fact that I was trying to retrieve something far more precious than a stolen head of beef. This was precious and certainly lovely Lisa that we were trying to find. I guess the tough in me tried to shut out the possibility that she might be lost forever. However, I had to also admit that forever was a long time coming. Was her timely, and striated phone call a ruse to get the old man to shell out? Were her and Moose supposedly planning to suck the old man dry of his amassed fortune?

I suspected that her addiction to cocaine was insidious enough to make her turn on her own. Goddamn the pusher man for creating hell for so many lost souls on this earth. If ever there was a human cockroach, it would be the pusher man. And, I hear in some South American countries, a cockroach gets caught selling drugs, he dies. No questions asked. There, the drug pushing pimp may as well put his head between his legs and kiss his ass goodbye cause he won't be seeing tomorrow.

I had had a lot to chew on about this case. I was also fighting this relentless inner tension that I was somehow out of my element. One might call it self-doubt or just the feeling that the deck was just plain stacked against me. I was fully aware that I was somewhat of an anomaly in this white-man's world. It seemed that everywhere I went, I got "`the look."

When I say the look, I meant the kind of stare that tries to place you in the pages of history books and wants to bury you there. I kept expecting people to ask me what tribe I was from. The fact is, I wished they would step up to the 21st century. I rebelled at the thought of people trying to make me feel small and somehow less of human being. That was perhaps the main reason why I got a certain exquisite pleasure from ribbing white women. I knew most of them thought of me as something of a red devil.

Ah, so what! I thought. Someday, I hoped; that it would dawn on them that they had missed the chance of a lifetime to taste something of the exotic. If not...the erotic. With Bev Miller, this would take some work because she was an intelligent beauty. Those were the kind I found somewhat pleasantly disturbing. I was enticed by the faint possibility that I might lose out with her. I also knew that it was going to break old Burl`s heart if he ever found me and Bev locked in some kind of compromising embrace.

"Hey, Clem, ever have a white woman?" I said to the driver, on the way to the estate.

"That would be privileged information, Mister Savage." he said with a chuckle, sounding a bit like Uncle Remus.

I dropped the subject knowing full well that he had probably dipped into other men's private preserves for a time or two. I guess I was trying to stay the inevitable questioning of Jobe Banquell for as long as I could. It wasn't going to be easy, but, hey, I'm the tough guy, after all.

"What's up, my man?" I said to my old friend, trying to put him at ease. It was all I knew to do, given the circumstances.

"You don't have to feed me that line, Noble. Thanks, anyway. I appreciate your concern. Really I do."

"I guess, by rights, you should be consulting with Britton, since you hired him first."

"Britton's a good man, but I don't consider him a friend. He's a business associate. You, on the other hand...well, let's just say that if I were ever in a street fight, I wouldn't feel confident of the outcome, unless you were standing there beside me."

"Well, I must admit, sir, that is one helluva compliment. Thanks."

"I know that we just barely know each other, but do you believe in kindred spirits? It's just that I felt like I've known you forever. It's the damnedest thing. You know what I'm saying?"

"Yeah, I guess I do, even though you out-rank me by a few bajillion dollars."

He rolled his silver mane back and almost split a gut.

"You crazy bastard, you always seem to know how to crack me up!" He roared with laughter choking back the sorrow that comes with riches.

Speaking of sorrow, I just had to break the back of comic relief by asking him about Lisa and the mysterious phone call.

"So, you were saying that she phoned?"

"Yeah," he said, and I couldn't tell if those tears in his eyes were from my joke, or from thinking about Lisa.

"Can you tell me anything else about the call?"

"No, not really. Only that she was blindfolded and that she felt that there was three of them."`

"How would she know there was three of them, and why do you suppose they would allow her to disclose that information over the phone?"

"I guess I was too caught up in the moment to question anything. I mean, she sounded convincing enough. For Folly's sake, man! Do you have to question everything?"

"Well, Jobe, let's just say, it comes with the territory."

"Yeah, O.K, I know what you mean, I guess."

"Did you hear anything in the background?"

"Why, yes, come to think of it, there was what sounded like a fog-horn in the background."

"Don't you find it a bit odd that they would even absent-mindedly give away their location?"

"Hell, I never even thought about it. For all I know the sound might have come from a T.V. in the room where she was phoning from."

"How do you know it isn't a set-up?"

"That's the hell of it, I can't tell if it is."

"What d`ya mean?"

"Well, it seems to me I recall that Lisa won first place in a few of her high school plays."

"She's a drama queen, right?"

"Yeah, quite a bit like her mom actually."

"What else might have caused you to suspect anything?"

"Well...it's just that I thought I heard someone giggling close to her...as though, whoever it was. was listening intently to our conversation."

"If it smells like it and tastes like it then it probably is."

"You mean?....no, not my Lisa, she loves me. Noble, for shot's sakes don't break my heart by trying to tell me....."

"Jobe, I hate to break it to you, but she's hooked, man! She's in love with the snow."

"But, she loves me. I raised her since ....."

"Jobe! Wake up, my friend. She knows you cut her off of her allowance. In her eyes, you betrayed her! I'm sorry! That's just the way she stands!"

"You bastard! How dare you tell me the truth I can't bear to hear?"

With that, the richest man I ever knew became transformed into a wracking, sobbing beggar in a moment of time. I wanted to reach out and take a hold of him and extend a little bit of what remained of my humanity. But the tough stayed his ground. It was like I was dead inside. That part of me had worked only once in years, the day I watched them put Jimmy's body in the ground. All I could do was look away and let him have his moment as a tortured and grieving soul. Perhaps, in his mind and heart, Lisa was already dead. If not, she was certainly on her death bed.

"C'mon, old boy, let's go get us a drink." I said.

Outside, the night time was descending in beautiful shades of deep blue. We sat on the veranda, sipping on Kentucky's finest bourbon and waited for its` certain comfort to come creeping into our bones. Somewhere down in the surrounding fields of green, a lone coyote howled at the rising moon as it crested on the hazy Georgian horizon. I sat with the old fella and tried to comfort him with my tall tales from my world. I felt the ache to go home, back to the flatlands as never before. But before I made that trip, I knew I had to finish my unfinished business here, once and for all.

CHAPTER 35

Savage told Britton the whole story. He started with the ride back to the mansion, the meeting, the sob story, the phone call and ended with his belief that Lisa was hooked on the white stuff.

"We don't have any evidence of that, Savage." Britton said, shaking his head side to side.

"I've seen a hundred cases like it, Burl, old boy."

"That's not evidence," Britton said. "I'm surprised you would jump to that conclusion without really checking anything out. If Lisa was indeed a coke head, as you seem to have surmised, where is the evidence? Who was her source? Cocaine is still a controlled substance, you know. It's not all that hard to find, but a steady source that played that kind of role in Lisa's life would certainly leave a trail somewhere. Moose Moseley was an outstanding athlete. He couldn't have performed week after week in the manner that he did if he had been a coke addict, and by the same token, Lisa was an all-star cheerleader. Her teacher, Michelle Montague, said that Lisa was one of her best students. Could she have been a coke addict and accomplished that?"

"Well maybe you've got a point, Burl," Noble Savage said. "But you are the one that told me you found a package of the stuff in her room, and the maid found one prior to that. Didn't you say the maid dropped that pack after you found one? Couldn't have been the same pack if that's the case. Someone in the Banquell household was probably snorting the snow. If not Lisa, then who?"

"I'm not sure anyone was, Savage." Burl said. "And neither are you. You might want to lay off of that accusation until you have some facts that you can back it up with. Now you've got old man Banquell convinced that there is a cocaine source here in Whispering Meadows that was supplying his little sweetheart granddaughter. He'll be trying to hire me to find that source."

"He won't have to hire you," Savage said. "If the facts bear me out, and I think they will, Lisa was the family coke head. And if that is true, I'll find the source and when I do they'll silently disappear."

"You might be running up against forces a whole lot more powerful than you are capable of handling," Britton said.

"What's that supposed to mean?"

"I mean that the Atlanta area, like all big cities, has gangs that have well established ties, both to police and politicians. They operate pretty much under a blanket of protection. I've learned that much dealing with some of my snitches. I've also learned that it doesn't pay to pry to deeply. I'm a year or so away from retirement, and I'm not going to stir the waters much. It would get me killed; and if you pry too deep it will certainly give you a one way ticket back to the frozen north, or else to the happy hunting grounds."

"Oh that really scares me, Britton," Savage said. "Do you think for a minute that I haven't had my share of gangsters? I might not be a career PI like you, and most of my cases have been rustlers and shop lifters, I still know a bit about life in the fast lane. You've no doubt heard from Jobe Banquell about my abilities prior to hanging my shingle in Canwood."

"Yes," Britton sighed. "I know you were a combat veteran. I know you helped break up a drug smuggling operation in Quebec after you got out of the Canadian Army. I know you better than you think I do, Savage. I'm one who does his homework. You've still jumped to some conclusions, though. You don't know this Atlanta area like I do. The scar I showed you in Denny's is a reminder of how vicious these hoods are. I'm through trying to make the world a better place to live in, I just want to retire and play some tennis in Florida and golf in Augusta. I've said my piece. If you want to take on the world of drugs and gangs, be my guest. Just be careful."

Britton looked away when he said the last three words and Savage thought he heard a sincere note of concern in the old PI's voice. His respect for Britton went up a few points.

"OK" Savage said. "Let's assume that Lisa is not a coke head. Let's say she didn't enlist the services of Jimmy Enderly and Moose Moseley to do away with her parents because she thought she might be cut out of her millions. If Lisa didn't do it, who did?"

"Right now, your guess is as good as mine, Savage." Britton shuffled in his chair, straightened up and stood up.

"One thing is for sure," he said. "I'm not going to blame anyone for anything until I get a few more answers. My method of investigation may differ from yours. I go digging in the garden of reality. If I find a root, I trace it until it leads me somewhere. I don't just clip off the rose and put it in a book. I would suggest that you consider doing a little digging on your own, help me solve this case so we can collect our fee and you can buy a car and head back to Saskatchewan with your feathers still intact."

"I think you're a little jealous of me," Savage said. "You had a clear playing field with the lovely Beverly Miller until I showed up. Now you want to solve this case so you can shuffle me off to Buffalo and have that field all to yourself again."

"Bull crap!"

"Maybe, but listen to this, Burl. I'm here for the duration. Whatever it takes. Both to solve the case and to try my hand at winning over the fair maiden."

"Fine," Britton said. "Just do me a favor, will you? Solve the damned case first!"

Burl Britton left his office, leaving the door open. He trusted Savage to lock the door when he left, and wasn't worried about it. All of his past cases were locked in a file cabinet, and anything that was left out was regarding the Banquell case. Savage was welcome to look through that material. He was going home, have a beer, and watch a ball game on TV.

The little Honda car pulled into Britton's driveway and stopped just as the sun dropped below the horizon.

As he got out of the car he heard the gunshot and the windshield of the car exploded. Britton dropped out of the car and onto the driveway, scraping his left knee on the concrete. It burned like fire, but he was alive. A dark shadow ran behind his garage and he heard the sound of feet scrambling over the rear fence of his property.

He jumped up and ran towards the sound, hesitating long enough to glance around the far back corner of the garage to make sure no one was going to put a bullet in his skull. He heard the shuffling of footprints on the other side of his fence, in his neighbor's yard. He ran to the fence and jumped high, putting his right foot on the grape stake boards and catching the top of the fence. He swung his legs up and over and dropped to the other side.

He heard a car start up and race away. Britton ran as fast as his legs would carry him to the street behind his home and saw the red lights of the car reflected off of the street light as it turned the corner. Whoever had shot at him was going to get away. Britton knew that he couldn't get back to his car in time to give chase, and even if he could he realized the Honda was no match for anything other than perhaps a 1947 Studebaker.

He walked to the front door of the house behind his and knocked. No one answered. He knocked several times and waited but no one came to the door and no lights came on in the house. He glanced at his watch and in the dim light of the porch light saw that it was nearly 7:30.

He walked slowly to the corner, made a left and walked back to his street. He had just cautioned Savage about the dangers of prying into cocaine distributors and underground hoods. Now someone had damned near ended his plans of golf and tennis and early retirement. This made it up front and personal, and damned if he was going to give up retirement even if it meant taking on the entire Atlanta underground.

CHAPTER 36

I was feeling a bit restless and I took to the streets. And as I wandered about, I discovered that my feet developed a mind of their own. Wouldn`t you know it, I found myself hanging around her place. Her place was somewhat sumptuous. I tried to put 2 and 2 together and , damn it, I kept coming up with 3. On her salary? It was a bit of a stretch.

I was hoping against hope that she didn`t have some kind of sugar-daddy hidden away in a senior`s complex somewhere. Oh, well, maybe I`d been watching too many soaps lately. The allure of her bodily presence, albeit, from a considerable distance was intoxicating and almost left me less suspicious somehow. And as I pondered the deep significance of my one-sided love affair, I continued my pathetic, feverish vigil.

She cast a lovely silhouette through her sheer-veiled curtains. Her hourglass figure moved back and forth across the width of the window. The window was open a teensy of a crack, and I thought I heard something fall against the inside wall. It sounded like a vase or something smashing to pieces. I kind of shuffled up to the door of her place and knocked. After all, I was still recouping from my near-death experience. I moved with the measured grace of a three-legged scruff.

``Yeah, who`s there?``

``It is I, Sir Galahad from Saskatchewan! What goeth on, my lady?``

She opened her door just enough for me to see her beautiful peepers. On her ring finger, I noticed a big, glittering chunk of ice.

``Oh, I`m sorry, I didn`t expect you to come calling so soon. I thought you had a lead on Mosely. I just dropped a vase on the floor.`` She tried to hide the jitters in her voice.

``Can I come in?``

``Well...I was about to shower..``

``Aw...c'mon. 'My voice was as velvet as Torme. I'll huff and I`ll puff.``

``Savage, give it up. Come back tomorrow.``

``Bev, you know you can call me anytime, don`t you?``

``Yes..yes, I know. Can we talk tomorrow? Please?``

``O.K. Bev. Aw, reservoir.`` My French had always stunk to high heaven.

There was no question about it. I had competition. I was really beginning to wonder about her. The truth is, I don`t take rejection well. I had the sixth sense going like crazy when I left her little palace.

The voice of wisdom finds me at the oddest of times. I was dealing with some unfinished paperwork in the john when I heard him.

``If there is ever a seed of doubt, do not hesitate to engage your greatest enemy.``

``Yes, sensei. And that would be?``

``Yourself.``

The old Master was right. It seemed that he was always right. I had to look deep within myself to see what I had been missing all along. I had fallen in to the tender trap. It hurt to admit it. But, hey..don`t tell anyone I said it. If you do,

I`ll find you and I`ll tie you down to an ant hill. And, then, I`ll pour syrup all over your.... Oh, sorry, I just get kind of carried away in the drama of the moment. No doll, no matter how luscious, makes a fool out of Noble T., and gets away with it! Well, here I am, in No-Man`s Land, with a bummed out knee, and working for less than peanuts. Right about now, I sure could use a soft shoulder to cry on and an ice cold brew.

Well, with the world on my shoulder and my last fifty bucks, I amble over to the neighborhood bar. It`s about half a block away. Something about The Smiling Buddha made me smile inside. Or maybe, it`s just the few stiff shots of rye I`m not supposed to be drinking while on duty that's putting that silly grin on my mug. An old trash man is sitting three seats upwind of me and sporting one helluva shiner. The bag lady, sitting next to him is talking trash to him and is practically making him eat the 13 yellow roses he just handed to her. Another resounding smack and he has a matching coon eye! With that non-lady-like gesture of hurtful intent, she is quickly escorted forthwith off of the premises.

``Hey, Red, can ye give an old bastard a couple a bucks for a draft?` `It was Coon Eyes.

``Sure, pull up a stump.`` By now, my olfactory senses were numb. ``So, Bo Jangles, what in hell was that all about?``

``Oh, I just fished these flowers out of a dumpster just down the block and tried to give them to my missus.``

``Well, what`s so evil about that, pardner?``

``Aw....she was just bitchin cause she found another card in with the flowers and figured out I didn`t buy em` for her. Finders, keepers, is what I say. Ain`t that right, Red?``

``Damned sure, Mr. Bo jangles. Bah. You just can`t please women. Although, I never had a complaint.``

``Ha....heh..he..heh...he..heh..hehaaa!! ``That`s a good one, Red!``

``Is that the card right there?``

``What the....I reckon it is. Here, can ya read it?``

Well, I near shit my brown drawers when my eyes beheld the rapturous note attached. It was embossed with exquisite golden fancy script. It read, 'To my dearest Beverly, Signed, yours....A.J.B'. Holy Toledo! Could it be? Arthur Jobe Banquell?

The next morning I woke up at The Junk Man`s humble abode. I had succumbed to the Sandman in the backseat of an abandoned 84` Oldsmobile. My head felt swollen and I felt like Ira Hayes. My host must have made up with his hag, because they were both sleeping soundly over in the next car when I left. The fog slowly left my cranium. After breakfast, a coupla fast-acting Tylenol and a few cups of steaming java, I felt like a brand new Indian.

Next on my agenda was tracking the place of purchase in regards to the big, honkin` chunk of ice on the hand of my lady fair. I hounded the diamond down to Chez Pierre's one of the more exclusive jewelry stores in Atlanta. I told the manager that I was on official police business, but that I wanted everything said to be kept off the record because I was working on a particularly sensitive case.

The dealer was a weasel. In fact, he looked very much like a blood-sucking weasel. And, I suppose when one deals in such humungous amounts of filthy lucre, one tends to take on a certain ``look`` about them.

``So, tell me, Henry..``

``No, Monseiur, that`s Henri.``

``Yeah, yeah, so tell me, Henry, about that particular purchase.``

``Ah, yes, the Cartier transaction. Let me assure you, Monsieur, only the privileged few....``He looked down on my previously enjoyed attire from Value Village with a raised eyebrow. "That ring was fashioned after a mystical ring called "The Ring of Gerges."

``And, who was the gentleman that signed the bill?``

``It was an Afro-American gentleman, by the name of Clement Duvalier.``

Holy Toledo! It was the chauffeur! But where in the Congo Hell would he get that kind of moolah? It didn`t figure. Unless the old boy had put him up to it.

It was then that the voice of the Ancient chimed in.

``It is written in the scrolls of the Silent One, that what glitters to one may ultimately seem tarnished brass to another.``

``I cannot understand what that means, Sensei.``

``That is excellent, for in understanding the deep things, there is much sorrow.``

The mud was starting to get a little clearer now. I hoped against hope that I was wrong, but the truth kept nagging at me. I knew then that there was something bad about to transpire for all concerned. As to who would be left standing was in itself the damndest mystery of all.

CHAPTER 37

Burl had never been to Jobe Banquell's mansion. He rolled the little Honda car through the swinging wrought iron gates and drove the mile back to the house. When he got to the door it opened, as if by magic. Clement stood there, as big as a barn, and smiled at Britton.

"Good morning, Sir," he said.

"Is Jobe ready to see me?" Britton asked.

"Yes, Sir, right this way." Clement walked away and Britton followed. The inside of the mansion was more intimidating than the grounds. It was so big that Britton thought the Braves must take spring training there when it rains.

After what seemed like a hike along the Appalachian trail, they finally arrived at a study that held more books than the Library of Congress. It amazed Britton that anyone would even consider building a house as big as a stadium. You can only set in one room at a time. You don't need 30 bedrooms because you can only sleep in one at a time. You don't need 15 bathrooms, you can only pee in one at a time. Britton's mind was wandering. He needed to snap out of it, concentrate on why he was there.

He had called and talked to Jobe about the phone call received from Lisa. During the conversation, Jobe told him that he had recorded the phone call, and Britton wanted to hear exactly what had transpired.

"Good morning, Mr. Britton," the rich man said.

"Good morning, Mr. Banquell."

"I've got a machine set up right here to listen to this tape, if you're ready?"

"Go ahead," Britton said, sitting at a long walnut table. Jobe Banquell sat at the end of the table and punched some buttons on a machine that Britton estimated must have cost eight or nine grand.

Lisa's voice poured out of the speakers.

"I'm being held somewhere," then a long pause.

"Three people are here," more pause. Britton could here clicking sounds coming from the speakers as each phrase ended.

He sat and listened to the tape. It wasn't long, the entire call lasted only a total of twenty or thirty seconds. The old man's voice could be heard at the beginning, saying hello. Then the phrase "I'm being held somewhere" by Lisa, then some shrieking sounds and the old man asking "Where are you, Lisa, sweetheart? Who's holding you? Tell me, I'll come and get you."

The voices of Jobe Banquell and Lisa were not in sync with each other. Britton noticed right away that the voices overlapped as if one could not wait for the other to finish their questions before the other person started relating something different. Lisa's voice sounded strange, disjointed.

"Have you turned this over to the police," Britton asked.

"No. I wanted you and Savage to hear all of this first, see if you can find her. I don't want any publicity if I can help it."

"Can you make a copy of that for me? I'd like to have a friend of mine listen to it."

"I've got four copies ready," Banquell said. He motioned to Clement and the big man handed Britton a tape.

They talked a few minutes, Britton purposefully did not tell Banquell about being shot at the night before. The shooting might not even be remotely related to the Banquell case, he thought, but no need muddying up any waters by telling about it.

"I'll keep you posted on what I find," Britton said, "Thanks for your time, and I'll get this tape back to you soon."

"Burn it when you're through with it," Banquell said. "I don't need it, as I have the one I recorded direct the night I got the call."

"OK." Burl said. "I can find my way out. Thank you."

"Thank you for coming," Banquell said. "Find her, Britton. Whatever it takes, find my granddaughter."

"I'll do my best sir," Britton said. "For now, don't let the police in on this. I don't want them muddying the waters. Wait and see if the kidnappers contact you again. Record everything. OK?"

"I'll do it," Banquell said.

Britton left and drove back into town and got on the interstate. A half hour later he was at the office of a friend of his who ran a recording studio in Atlanta. The studio had done some important demo work for some top recording artists and Britton knew that if anyone could help him, his friend could.

Stacy Fields was not a college graduate. He didn't have a degree in sound reproduction, recording arts, or electronics. What Stacy had was the ability to hear frequencies and pitches that most humans can't even describe. He had worked his way through the college of hard knocks, waiting tables to buy his next piece of recording equipment, living in one room flop joints to get enough money to buy CD reproducers. He was considered one of the best in the field, and Britton admired him for his tenacity.

Now Stacy Fields owned an office building, a very comfortable home in the suburbs, and a Corvette. He was still single, enjoyed his relationships with rock groups that he had helped advance, and in his middle age, still acted like a teenager hooked on rock and roll.

"What brings you to the big city, Burl?" Stacy asked when Britton walked into his studio.

"I've got a tape I want you to listen to, if you can do me that favor," Britton said.

"You finally decided to record some of those songs you wrote?"

"Not that kind of tape," Britton said. "And I quit playing and singing years ago. I found out that it was not my bag."

"Let's have it, then." Stacy said.

Britton gave him the tape. "This is the property of a friend of mine who thinks his granddaughter has been kidnapped. We don't want the cops to know about anything yet. Can you keep this confidential?"

"Quiet as a zero."

"Thanks, I owe you one."

Stacy inserted the tape in a machine that was comparable to the one that Britton had seen at the home of Jobe Banquell. He adjusted a few knobs, fiddled with a few more, and the tape began playing.

Britton started to say something and Stacy held up one hand with the index finger pointing up. Britton clammed up.

They sat listening to the short tape.

"It's a fake," Stacy said.

"What?"

"Fake, F as in Funny, A as in Altered, K as in 'I kid you not', and E as in Extracted."

"Can you elaborate?"

"I don't know what you want me to say," Stacy said. "The voice is the same throughout, but the clicks and pauses are sounds made when a recording instrument is either turned on or the volume is changed rapidly. The barely audible ticks are segments where the tape has been spliced."

"Spliced?"

"Yeah, you know, clipped and pieced together. This recording is definitely a fake."

"So my friend's granddaughter didn't record that?"

"I'm not saying that this voice is fake, the harmonics of the voice are the same throughout. What I'm saying is that this tape was made from bits and pieces of the girl's voice as recorded on other tapes. Is she an actress?"

Britton thought a minute. Something that Michelle Montague had said was hammering at his gray matter. She had told him that Lisa was a good candidate for Miss Georgia and had definite acting ability.

"Thanks for your help, Stace," Britton said. "You're the best!"

"You're welcome, Burl. By the way, here's some tickets for Wonder's concert next week. They gave me a bunch of them, and I've given out some to friends."

Britton knew that 'Wonder' was a rock group that Stacy had helped hit the big time.

He took the tickets. Maybe he could convince Beverly Miller to attend the concert with him.

"Thanks, Stacy," he said. "If I can ever do you a favor, call me."

He left the recording studio and on his way back to his car he was thinking of how and where the dubbed tapes might have been made. Lisa Banquell had definitely made some tapes at some point, but this tape, and the call to her grandfather, were as phony as tissue titties.

CHAPTER 38

He drove slowly back to Michelle Montague's residence. If anyone could tell him about any tapes that Lisa might have made to practice for a play, it would be Michelle, her coach and mentor.

"I'm sorry to bother you, Mrs. Montague," he said, not really sounding apologetic. "I've got a taped recording I would like for you to hear. It concerns Lisa Banquell's disappearance."

"Come in," she said, holding the door open and stepping aside. Britton went in and was mildly shocked by the disarray that he saw in the Montague home. There were books everywhere, a lot of paper stacked up in loose-leaf binders.

He handed Michelle Montague the tape that had been given him by Jobe Banquell.

"I've come to you because I believe you are the one best suited to help me understand this," Britton said.

She took the tape and walked across the room to a machine similar to the one Britton would have used at home to play a cassette tape. His was an older boom box that played CDs as well as cassettes. Hers was similar, only bigger. She put the tape in the slot, hit a button and the door to the cassette reel closed.

The voice of Jobe Banquell saying hello. The voice of Lisa saying that she'd been kidnapped and that there were three people. Some startled exclamations by Jobe. Lisa's voice continuing. The entire tape wasn't more than 30 seconds long.

It stopped.

"What do you want me to tell you?" Michelle said.

"I've got it on pretty good grounds the tape is a false recording." He said. "Do you have any idea as to where or how someone might have got their hands on tapes Lisa used to practice her lines for a play?"

"I have a collection of tapes that match that description," she said. "I've coached Lisa on several plays that she's been in, all through middle school and up until now."

"May I see that collection?" he asked.

"Its right here," she said, bending over and sliding a panel beneath a window. It was a long storage space built to look like part of the entertainment center. Britton stepped closer.

He looked at plastic bound containers, each had the month and year on the spine. The first thing that caught his eye was that one of the containers was missing. It was the month prior to Lisa's disappearance.

"It seems as though one is missing," he said, pointing to the spot where the missing volume should have been.

"Yes, you're right!" Michelle said. "I have no idea how that volume got out of the set."

"You live here with your husband?" he asked.

"No. I'm Mrs. Montague because it is better for my students to think that I am. There's a Mister Montague in my life but we've been apart for several months. He was jealous of my work."

Sounds like someone else he knew, Britton thought. Beverly Miller's husband.

"So no-one would have access to these tapes except yourself?"

"That is correct. But then I'm not here all of the time. I suppose someone could have came in when I was out and taken that volume. I lock my doors but anyone with burglary tools might have been able to get in. I keep nothing extremely valuable here and have never felt the need for deadbolts."

"Have you ever suspected that someone might have been in here while you were out?"

"Well there was once." She said. "About a month ago I remember coming home and there was a strange scent in the air. At first I thought that it might have been the lingering perfume of one of my students, but it seemed like a perfume that would have belonged to an older woman, someone my age. I never thought much about it until now."

"Not a scent that Lisa would have worn?" Britton asked.

"Definitely not. She always wore the same scent, something that was light and smelled like white ginger."

"Can you tell me what tapes were in there? Anything about them? What plays might have been practiced? Anything?"

"I might be able to tell you," she said. "I keep a journal. Let me see if there's anything I've written on those dates."

She opened a drawer and got a book. It was a simple diary type of book one that you can buy at a stationary store, with blank pages.

Specifically a journal entry book or a diary. She opened it and glanced through it.

"That's really coincidental," she said. "Last year Lisa had a part in a play based on the TV series, "Kidnapped". It would have been part of the tapes that are missing."

"Kidnapped, huh?" I said.

"Yes. It was not a big hit. Only ran one season, 12 or 13 episodes if I remember correctly. I remember the episode. I helped her memorize her lines by reading the other parts of the script."

"Do you remember any of the lines?"

"No, not right off hand, I'd have to look them up."

"Would you mind doing that for me? It's pretty important."

She walked away from me to a book case that was built on one side of a massive fireplace. It had always struck Britton as odd that modern homes in Augusta, Georgia, where the U.S. Open Golf Championship is played, would have a huge fireplace. Most winters were mild enough that a fire isn't necessary.

"Let me see," he heard her murmuring. "Oh, here it is." She picked a book off of the shelf.

"Do you mind if I take this with me?" Britton asked.

"Not as long as I get it back. I like to keep certain books and that is one of them."

"I'll make sure to get it back to you." He said.

"Is there anything else, Mr. Britton?"

Britton thought for a moment then on impulse he asked, "Do you happen to know a

Detective Sergeant Miller on the Whispering Meadows police department?"

"No, I don't know her," she said, shaking her head. "I don't know anyone from the Meadows except Lisa and her mother...and now that poor woman is ...."

"Yes," Britton said, hurriedly. "Well, thank you, Mrs. Montague. I appreciate your help, and I'll make sure you get this back."

She walked him to the door and he left, thinking that Mrs. Montague was a very attractive woman.

As he walked to the rented car he was thinking that he hadn't mentioned that Detective Sergeant Miller on the Whispering Meadows police department was a woman.

He wondered if that was a Freudian slip on the part of Mrs. Montague.

CHAPTER 39

Something about this case was rubbing me the wrong way. I felt like there was something that I should have sensed, seeing as how I always relied on my sixth sense and intuition. But whatever it was I couldn't lay a hand on it.

I still felt like I had enough of a sense of how things really work in life to justify believing that Lisa Banquell was walking on the wild side. Bags of cocaine found in her room, sudden disappearance. Telephone calls to her rich grand pappy.

The one thing that was bugging me about that call is that Lisa did not ask for money. She didn't even mention the word. The call had ended rather abruptly, but if she were being held somewhere against her will, wouldn't her kidnappers ask for dough? Lisa had done all of the talking and there wasn't a mention of money, so why didn't the kidnappers talk? What was the purpose of the call if not to wrangle money from the old man?

There would be a second call to Jobe, of that I was certain.

My cell phone tinkled and vibrated in my pants pocket. Danged thing.

"Yours truly!" I yelled into the phone.

"Noble?" It was Britton.

"What's up, my man?"

"Well I've done some preliminary work on the phone call that you told me about. Here's what I've found."

He blabbed on for a few minutes about having a friend in the recording business, something about a trip to see someone named Montague, and in the end, made the not so startling announcement that the phone call was a phone E.

That didn't surprise me. It didn't surprise me either that Britton had gone to a lot of trouble to discover that fact. His method of investigating things differs so much from mine. You might say I go on instinct. My end didn't stink any more than anyone else's but that was my sixth sense, not the sense of smell.

I sat in a rented car, provided by Britton Investigations, and thought about the situation at hand. Lisa was either being held captive somewhere, maybe for future ransom, or she was dead and the killer or killers of her parents just wanted the old man to think she was still alive.

Or the third scenario is that Lisa is alive and well, holed up somewhere with Moose Mosely, waiting for the right time to show up and claim the estate of her late parents.

My instinct told me that it was time to add things up. I dug in my medicine bag and pulled out a yellow lined legal size tablet. In it I had started a letter to "girly-girl" back in Saskatchewan, but it clung to the pages like yesterday's pizza, and I ripped it out, crumpled it up and tossed it in the back seat.

I dug out an old ball point pen and started to scribble in my barely legible handwriting.

1. Kid disappears in Georgia.
2. Kid disappears in Chicago.
3. Kid number 1's parents killed in home.

4. Kid number 2 turns up poisoned in Chicago

5 Indications are that the fair maiden, Beverly Miller was having an affair with the father of Kid number 1. (Flowers and diamond ring.)

6. Indications are that somehow Kid number 1 found out about the affair and decided to leave home. (speculating).

7. How does Kid #2 get mixed up in the whole scenario?

I sat there a few minutes chewing on the ball point pen, finally tucked it away in my Salvation Army reject jacket and dug out one of my cheroots. It tasted better, so I chewed on it as I thought.

Was it coincidental that Jimmy disappeared from Chicago and showed up in Atlanta at about the time the Banquells were shot? Was the e-mail that Britton found on Lisa's computer important?

A little tingle of excitement scattered nerve receptors in my brain. Either that or the nicotine from the cheroot I was chewing had just hit home. I felt a little tinge of dizziness.

I suddenly had the feeling that Britton had overlooked something in the computer bit. He had examined Lisa's computer but he hadn't really done anything about the computer from which Jimmy had sent the mysterious e-mail. Where was that computer? Jimmy's parents said he didn't own one, that he might have used one belonging to a friend or at a library somewhere. To find it would mean I had to make a trip back to Chi-town. Windy City, home of the Bears and Cubs. They do things there that they don't do on Broadway, according to Ol' Blue Eyes.

I dug out my cell phone and called my associate, Burl Britton.

"Hello, Noble," he answered.

"Will your business cover my airfare to Chicago and back?" I asked.

"As long as it is business, I can charge it to the old man."

"Then I'll be gone a couple of days," I told him.

"What's up?"

"Just a hunch at this point," I said. "I'll keep in touch."

"OK, Noble. Have a nice trip." He sounded almost jubilant. He'd have clear sailing with the lovely Beverly while I was gone. Oh well, can't be helped, I thought.

CHAPTER 40

Burl Britton was thinking of Beverly Miller. He hadn't stopped thinking of why the lovely Michelle Montague would lie about not knowing Beverly. He ran the conversation back through his mind carefully to make sure that he had not mentioned Detective Miller's gender.

Britton had a very good memory. In school he had been one of those kids who could read the textbook ahead of the course and never open it again. He could memorize poems and parts for plays readily. He was not an "A" student because he didn't really care about the grades. It never made a difference to him what the teachers or others thought about his scholastic abilities as long as his parents were OK with his report card.

Now he was absolutely positive that he had not mentioned gender in reference to Detective Miller, yet Michelle Montague had said "No, I don't know her" when asked if she knew Detective Miller.

Britton decided to put the question in reverse to Beverly Miller to see what kind of reaction he got. He punched in Whispering Meadows PD number on his cell phone and was put through to Beverly.

"Whispering Meadows Homicide, this is Miller."

"Hello Beverly," he said. "I am tracing down some leads on Lisa Banquell's disappearance and one of the people I've spoken to is a dramatics coach named Montague. Does that name ring a bell with you?"

"Should it?" she asked.

"Well, I don't know if it should or not, that's why I'm asking," Britton said.

"Let me think." There was a prolonged silence and Britton was thinking that it shouldn't take someone that long to answer that question. You either knew someone or you didn't. It was as if Beverly was trying to decide whether she should answer the question or not.

"I'm not sure," was the eventual answer. "What are you doing Friday evening? I'm thinking about the Italian restaurant we went to the other night. And the place we went afterwards."

He voice was silky, inviting.

Britton noticed how smooth she had evaded his question, however, and filed that information away in his mental filing cabinet.

"Sure. I'd like to have dinner with you. Shall I pick you up, say around 5:30?"

"Why don't I meet you there?" she said. "I've got a meeting late in the day, do you mind?"

"Not at all." He said.

"OK. It's a date then? Say around 6 at the restaurant?"

"Sure, Bev."

"See you then, Burl."

He flipped his cell phone shut and started his car and headed for home. Suddenly an idea popped into his head. He keyed the Whispering Meadows PD number again but this time asked to speak to Sgt. Joe Miller. The dispatcher put him through.

"Miller."

"Good evening, Mr. Miller," Britton said. "This is Burl Britton. We talked not long ago."

"Yeah, I remember."

"I'm following up on a lead and came across a name that you might recognize. Would you happen to know a dramatics coach named Montague?"

"Sure, I know her." he said. "Beverly and I had our daughter in one of her classes a few years back. What's up with her?"

"Oh, just a hunch for now. It's related to the Banquell case. I'll let you know how it pans out."

"That would be appreciated, Sir." Joe Miller said. "If I could bust that one I'd be sure to beat my ex-wife out for a candidate for Major."

"Still throwing your hat in that puddle?" Britton asked.

"As I told you, Sir, I've always had a desire to go into public service, maybe even run for Congress, at least state representative. I think that's the main reason Beverly divorced me, my ambition and hers were too similar. Mine for public service and duty, hers for the money and power."

"Well, thanks for the info, Joe. I'll definitely call you if I get anything definite."

"Thanks."

Britton snapped his phone shut and thought about what he had just been told. Beverly Miller did know Michelle Montague and the reverse was true. Michelle Montague had lied about not knowing Beverly. Britton wondered why.

CHAPTER 41

I don't often look backwards. I remember a guy named Willy Mays, I think it was, who said, "Don't look behind you, the ones behind may be gaining on you." Hell, I don't know, it might have been Jesse Owens, or even Jim Thorpe that said that, although if it had been a redskin, I'd probably remember.

There was, however, something that kept evading my senses, like a bit of a dream that pops into your conscious mind at times, nagging you, you remember just a part of it but not the whole dream.

I was sipping a cup of coffee at the Airport wondering what Britton was doing, and pondering the case in general when suddenly it became clear what was nagging me. Did Lisa Banquell kill Jimmy? If so, why? I sat there thinking about it for quite some time. I'm sure the waitress thought I was just another bum, lingering over a last cup of coffee.

I pulled out my wallet and dug out the business card of the police sergeant who had given me the information about Jimmy being bailed. I punched in the number on my cell phone and when it rang, I asked for "Casey O'Donnell", the name on the card.

He didn't remember me and it took some sweet talking to get him to pull Jimmy's bail info up on his computer.

"Who signed the bail release?" I asked.

"Lisa Banquell," he said. "Paid cash. It wasn't that much, car theft isn't a high risk bail for teens. Now once they get to be adults, the bail goes up. Teens are usually first time offenders, and bail is set pretty low."

I listened to him explain all of that, then asked what I really wanted to know. "Do you remember her? Can you describe her?"

"Yeah, I remember her pretty well, she was a little flirty and a good looking woman."

"Woman? Not a teen ager?"

"Hell no, man. This one was fully grown. I don't pay that kind of attention to teen aged girls."

"How old?"

"I'd say mid-thirties. Maybe a little older. she was well preserved and built like a, well..you know..nicely endowed."

"Hair color? Did she remind you of anyone you might have known? Actress or TV personality, anything like that?"

"Give me an address and I'll send you a picture of her. We have a security camera on the bail sergeant's desk and if that hasn't been erased, I'll print out a shot of her and mail it to you."

"I'm at the Atlanta airport waiting for a flight to Chi-Town now. I can pick it up when I get there."

"It may take a week or ten days to get it," he said.

"Hang on a second," I said, and pulled Burl Britton's P.I. card out of my wallet, and gave him the address.

"Mail it first class, attention Noble Savage, if you will."

"Sure, Mr. Savage. Nice talking to you."

"Yeah," I said and closed the connection.

I got off of the plane in Chicago and was waiting in the Avis line to rent a car when my cell phone rang.

"Savage," I said

"Noble, I just got another call from the kidnapper!" It was Jobe Banquell.

"Did you tape it?" I asked.

"Yes. This time they gave me the ransom demand."

"Ransom? How about the delivery instructions?"

"No. Said they'd call again."

"Did you have the call traced?"

"Yes, it came from one of the few public telephones left in Whispering Meadows. A small bar over on the dark side of town."

"Give me an address."

"Twelve oh one Washington Street."

"Call Britton and give him the details, I'm in Chicago. I'll check out the bar when I get back tomorrow and see if anyone remembers the caller."

"Chicago?" he said loudly. "What the hell are you doing there. I need you here, Savage."

"I'm checking on something I just remembered about the kid that sent e-mails to Lisa. I'll be back tomorrow. Keep a lid on it!"

"OK," he said. "Should I pay the ransom?"

"How much?"

"Two hundred and fifty thousand."

"Talk to Britton about that," I said. "Don't go to the police. Let's think this out first."

"OK, Noble." He didn't sound the least bit concerned about paying the money, but his voice started to crack.

"If they've hurt Lisa, I swear I'll spend a thousand times that much to track them down and when I find them, there won't be enough of them left to run through a meat grinder."

"I'm with you on that," I said. "I'll call you."

I signed the rental papers, took the key and headed out into the windy city.

My first instinct was to contact Jimmy Enderly's parents, make arrangements to spend the night with them, and find out more about where Jimmy might have used a computer. But memory of watching them at graveside while they buried their son came flooding back, and I didn't want to face either of them right yet. Not until I found the one responsible for Jimmy's hideous death.

The rented car came equipped with a GPS and I took my time until I was able to understand how to use it. New fangled technology always hits Saskatchewan last and I hadn't owned a cell phone long enough to figure out how to get "missed calls" yet, but I soon was able to key in the Enderly address and then from a "find" menu typed in the word library.

There were two libraries within 10 miles of Jimmy's home, but one was only a few blocks away from the pizza parlor where he had worked. I tried it first.

I showed the "information" librarian a picture I had of Jimmy, provided in the letter I had first received from the Enderlys.
"Ever see this kid?" I asked.

She looked at me like I was a pervert trying to find a young victim to seduce.

"I'm a private investigator," I said, showing her my credentials. She didn't seem impressed, but opened up a little.

"He used to come here a lot to use the computers but I haven't seen him in a long time."

"How can I tell which computer he used?" I asked.

"He always waited for the same one," she said. "He seemed sort of manic-compulsive about that. It was number 8, over by the window."

I glanced at the row of computers on a long table.

"Do you have a log in sheet where he might have signed in?"

"Yes," she said and looked in a drawer. she pulled out a book and flipped through it. I could see enough to know it was a standard "register" book found in stationery stores everywhere. She ran a dark red fingernail down the page and then glanced up at me.

"Every time he came he signed in," she said.

"Can you make copies of the pages where he is signed in? I'll pay you."

"Xerox copies are twenty five cents each," she said, looking me up and down. "That may amount to a few dollars."

I laid a twenty on the counter.

"If that isn't enough, tell me."

She took the book and walked towards a copier. I walked to number 8.

A young boy was using it. He had long hair and pimples. His hands were milky white like he'd never picked up a wrench or a screwdriver in his life.

"This computer is being confiscated for evidence in a murder trial," I told him. "I'm sorry but you'll have to wait until I screen it."

That accomplished what I had hoped. He jumped up and scurried away like a mouse being chased by a cat. He left so fast that he was still logged on to the internet.

I sat down and looked at what he was logged on to and decided that I might want to wash my hands after using the keyboard. The pictures on the screen were pretty vivid pornography. Somehow he had bypassed the libraries screening locks and accessed a free porn site.

I closed the screen and sat wondering where to start. It dawned on me that I didn't have the foggiest idea where to begin.

Back at the desk I told the information clerk that I would be taking the computer for some police work.

"I'm sorry, sir," she said, "you can't just take a computer from here. You aren't even connected with the police department here in Chicago. Private Investigators from out of the United States must be licensed to practice here, and to confiscate one of our computers you will need a court order."

I walked back to the computer, unplugged the power cord and the ethernet cable, left the monitor on the table but tucked the tower under my arm and walked past her desk on the way out. I picked up the Xeroxed sheets she had prepared for me.

"I'll bring you your court order, sweetheart. Meantime, I'm taking this computer."

I could hear her calling the police before I got to the door, and before I got to the corner in the rented car, I could hear sirens.

CHAPTER 42

The jingling of the phone in the office of Burl Britton Inquiries ended just as Burl unlocked the office door.

The tape machine started and he could hear the voice of Jobe Banquell, rambling something about ransom money.

He quickly picked up the phone.

"Burl Britton," he said.

"Britton, I'm glad I caught you. This is Jobe Banquell. I've received another call from the kidnappers, this time they've asked for ransom."

"Slow down a bit, Jobe," Britton said. "Let me sit down. I just got in."

"Well sit your ass down and listen," Jobe said.

Britton sat down.

"OK."

"They want 250 grand. I asked your partner Savage if I should pay it, he said to talk to you."

"Mmmmm." Britton said.

"What?"

"Just thinking, Jobe," Britton said.

"Dammit, Britton," Jobe yelled. "I'm telling you I need to know whether to pay the ransom or not. I don't give a crap about the money, just tell me yes or no."

An idea suddenly arose like a tennis lob shot coming over the net in Britton's mind.

"Pay it," he said, "but pay it in counterfeit money."

"Counterfeit?"

"Yes, counterfeit"

"Did you say counterfeit or confederate?"

"Counterfeit, Jobe, as in phony. You know, worthless paper money printed by people who want to get rich quick."

"I've got a million times that much money, Britton. Why should I risk Lisa's life by paying the ransom in counterfeit money?"

"I'll tell you why if you'll calm down and listen," Britton said.

Silence.

"You listening?"

"OK Britton, what reason do you have in your head for paying in counterfeit money?"

"First, and you aren't going to like this, most kidnappers will kill the victim as soon as the ransom is paid. If we want to find Lisa, we watch for counterfeit money to appear somewhere and trace it back to the person spending it. When we find that person, we'll have Lisa."

"Now the second question, Einstein," Jobe Banquell said, growling. "Where the hell do you think I can get 250 grand in counterfeit cash?"

"How long have you got to get it?"

"They didn't say. No instructions for delivery. Said they'd call back."

"You've got connections, Jobe. Use them. I don't know where you'd get it, but I do know that you could call in fifty agents from the CIA if you wanted them. I'm surprised you haven't done that. You figure it out."

"Damn, Britton," Jobe said. "You're smarter than I gave you credit for. You're right, I might be able to come up with the phony cash."

"Call me back when you've got it, and let me know the delivery details."

"OK, Britton," he said. "And thanks. You make me feel better about getting Lisa back in one piece."

"That's what you're paying me for, Jobe."

The line went dead and Britton sat staring at the tape. It hadn't shut off and all of his conversation was recorded on it. On impulse he took the tape out of the answering machine and stuck it in his desk and inserted a clean tape in the machine.

There was something Britton needed to do and he dreaded doing it. He needed to talk to the elderly couple behind his home to see if they had seen anything the night he was shot at.

He had only seen the couple a few times, they'd entertained in their backyard once and invited him and his wife over. He had reflected on the sad state of urban life when people do not even know that someone's wife had been dead for four years. He politely told them that he and his wife would not be able to attend.

What were their names? He thought it sounded like Fred and Ethel, the image of the Lucy show hung in his mind. Fred and Emma? He was pretty sure it was Fred and someone. What was the last name? Mertz?

Be serious, Britton, he told himself. It wasn't Mertz and didn't even sound like Mertz. Seems like it started with an R, though, he vaguely remembered thinking of Ricardo, tying the whole incident to the Lucy show.

He sat there for a few minutes and thought of that day, then his mind drifted to the night his windshield exploded when hit by gunfire.

He picked up the phone and called the body shop to see if his car was ready. They told him it would be one more day, they had painted some trim work around the edge of the windshield and that paint needed to dry and be rubbed out before they released it.

"By the way, Sir," the body shop guy said, "my guys found a rumpled slug embedded in the front seat of your car. How'd you avoid getting drilled in the chest?"

"A slug? As in bullet?" Britton asked.

"Yeah, you know, lead. As in why ain't you dead, lead."

"Thanks, Jake," Britton said. "I'm coming over. Hang on to that slug for me, will you. Maybe I can find out who owes me for a windshield."

"Sure, Burl." Jake said.

Burl hung up the phone and headed for the rental car. He had, for the time being, forgotten all about the people he didn't know who lived behind him. Then out of the clear blue sky it came to him...Ricketts. Fred Ricketts.

He went back inside the office and found a phone book. Ricketts, Fred...1808 West Hillside Rd. Whispering Meadows, GA...555-1212. He dialed it.

"Hello."

It was a woman's voice.

"Mrs. Ricketts?"

"Yes."

"Hello, my name is Burl Britton. I live behind you on the next street. We share a common fence in the back of our houses."

"Yes, Mr. Britton?"

"Well, I was just wondering if you and your husband heard or saw anything out of the ordinary Friday night."

"This past Friday?"

"Yes."

"We were not here, Mr. Britton," she said. "We were out of town. It was our anniversary."

"Well, thanks anyway," Britton said.

"Maybe our house sitter heard something," she said.

"Your house sitter?"

"Yes, my niece was here. She stayed the week we were gone, just keeping watch on things in our home while we were away."

"Is she there, and may I speak to her?"

"One moment, Mr. Britton, I'll call her."

The line went silent. He waited. He could hear Mrs. Ricketts calling for someone. He couldn't hear the name but it sounded like Caroline.

"Hello."

"Hello. I'm a neighbor of your aunt. I'm curious if you might have heard or seen anything this past Friday night around 6:30, just about sundown."

"I did hear something," she said. Britton was suddenly very acutely aware.

"What did it sound like?" he asked.

"Gunshots," the voice said. "I had just turned on the 6:30 news and I thought I heard gunshots, I at first thought it might have been on TV."

"Did you see anything unusual?"

"I went to the back door and I saw a woman running towards the street, up the side of this house."

"A woman?"

"Yes. I'm sure it was a woman, or a man with nice long hair."

"Did you see the car the woman got in?" Britton asked.

"No, by the time I got to the front of the house the car was headed down the street. All I saw was the tail lights."

"Could you tell what kind of automobile it was?"

"Not for sure," the voice said. "Might possibly have been a BMW, but I'm not sure. My boy-friend's Dad drives a Beamer and I remember thinking that the car tail lights looked like that."

"Anything else you saw that you remember?"

"No. I hope I've been able to help you. My Aunt Ellen says you are a good neighbor, and would like to meet your wife some day."

"Give my regards to your aunt. Tell her that my wife would like to meet her too."

"Anything else, Sir?"

"No. I think you've given me all you know. Thank you, and good day."

The party he had been speaking to hung up the phone without saying anything further. He pondered what he had learned. A BMW? He didn't think he remembered anyone who drove a BMW.

He got his computer logged on to the internet and looked up BMW car photos. A long list of pictures appeared, posted by a guy in California who collected BMW's. Must be nice, he thought.

Half way down the list his eyes caught the flicker of a red BMW. He scrolled back up to the page and clicked on it. He opened it in a photo viewer and zoomed in on the tail lights. He had seen a car recently with tail lights just like that. Where had he seen it?

Just as he started churning brain cells to remember where he'd seen those tail lights, his office door opened and there stood his partner, Noble Savage.

CHAPTER 43

"Top of the morning to ya," I said.

"How was your trip, Savage? Did you learn anything?"

"I've got a computer out there in my rental car that might give us some answers. It's the one Jimmy Enderly used to email Lisa."

"How'd you get that?" Burl asked me.

"You don't wanna know. If I told you, I'd have to kill you."

"Yeah, sure," he said. It was almost like he didn't believe me or something.

"I just took it out of the library where I found it. The librarian insisted on a search warrant, but I convinced her I didn't need one."

"How'd you do that?"

"I just put it under my arm and walked out with it."

I could tell by the look on his face that he didn't approve of my evidence collection tactics, but hell, I didn't really give a crap what he thought. I just wanted to get the case settled, collect my fee, and get back to girly-girl in Saskatchewan.

"Can you have your computer friend analyze the hard drive?" I asked.

"No problem." he said, "You ready to roll?"

"Now?" I asked. "I just got back in town and I thought I'd call on the fair maiden, Bev Miller, maybe see if she's open for dinner tonight."

"I believe in striking while the iron is hot," Burl said.

"Speak to me in English," I said, "me no speakum white man parables."

"Come on Noble," he said, rather heatedly, "Can the clown act for a change, and let's take that computer to Augusta. You drive, I've had a hard day."

An hour later, and four near misses caused by my lack of knowledge of the Augusta road system, we arrived at an office shop that Burl had guided me to, with a series of "turn left, turn right, take the next exit, turn left....." I was getting dizzy making so many turns.

I was introduced to Roger and he didn't look at me like most of the people I'd met on this caper. He actually smiled and stuck out his hand as he spoke his "glad to meet ya."

"Got another job for you, Rog." Burl said. "I wonder if you can access the email sent from this computer, and tell me anything about it. I'm particularly looking for email from a Jimmy Enderly to Lisa Banquell."

"I remember that name," he said. "Didn't I just do a job for you that found some email address or something?"

"That was then, this is now," Burl said roughly. "Got time to do it?"

"I'll make time," Roger said. Now that is the kind of guy you want on your side, one who'll make time for you when you need help.

I watched as Roger took the computer hard drive out of the tower case I had confiscated from the Chicago library, attached a few cables, wires and ribbons to it. He then clicked on a monitor, typed a few commands on a keypad and "viola" there were the messages from Jimmy to Lisa.

"Do you want to read them?" he asked, "I can make them bigger."

"No, I'll read them later," Burl said, I was thinking I'd like to read them now, but I didn't know what I was looking for anyway, so it didn't matter.

"Can you print them?" I asked.

"Sure," he said. He typed a word or two on the keypad, switched on a printer and it whirred a couple of times and started spitting out pages.

"What I would like to know is who received these emails?" Britton said.

"Looks like they were received by a network in Whispering Meadows." Roger said. He clicked in a few more commands and suddenly turned to face us.

"That's funny," he said.

"What?" Burl and I said, almost simultaneously.

"These went to the Whispering Meadows library."

"Not to Lisa Banquell's computer?"

"Nope. They were received by a computer registered to Whispering Meadows Public Library system."

"What about the one that I brought you, I took it directly from Lisa's computer." Burl was looking as puzzled as I felt.

"That I can't tell you," Roger said. "All I know is that every message originating on this computer was received by a computer in the WMPL system."

"What's the date on the first one?" I asked.

He gave me an answer.

"And the last one?"

He gave me another answer.

"How about the date on the one you found on Lisa's computer, Burl?" I asked.

Burl took out his notebook and flipped through the pages.

"Makes sense," he said.

"What?"

"This message was received more than a week after all of those. This may have been the only message actually sent to Lisa's computer."

"Right you are, friend," Roger said.

"How can that happen?" I asked.

"Someone with a good working knowledge of computers, let's say a competent hacker, could have re-routed all of these emails to the library system. For some reason, that one got through to Lisa's computer."

My limited knowledge of computers was showing and I didn't want to appear any dumber than I felt so I kept my mouth shut and listened.

"Every computer that is logged on to the internet has a unique address," Roger was saying. "Everything that computer sends or receives is stored on its hard drive."

"What if someone deletes their email?" I asked.

"Nothing is ever totally deleted without a disk wipe," he said. "When you delete something, you're just telling the computer to erase the file address where the item is stored, and the next time you try to access it, it is gone. By special codes, however, all of those file addresses can be accessed. It takes some time and a little knowledge, but all is possible."

"A little knowledge?" I said. "Sounds like you'd need a teepee full of knowledge, and three or four wickiups full of medicine men."

"What's a wickiup?" Roger asked.

"Same as a wigwam," I told him.

"Oh."

"What's a disk wipe?" I asked.

Burl Britton was standing there. I could sense that his mind was two steps ahead of me, thinking about what to do next, the systematic, step-by-step analysis of the investigation.

"That's a complete disk deletion, where everything, including the operating system, is deleted and has to be reinstalled."

"Let's get going, Noble," he said.

"Glad to make your acquaintance, Roger," I said, extending my hand.

He shook it. "Same here," he said, and handed me the printouts from the printer. I folded them and stuck them away for safe keeping in the inside pocket of my Salvation Army rescued suede jacket.

CHAPTER 44

Burl Britton and Noble Savage, partners in crime analysis, got back in Noble's rented Chevy and with instructions grunted by Britton, managed to find their way back to Whispering Meadows. Britton then directed Noble to an auto body shop where he got out and left Noble listening to country music on the radio.

Britton spoke briefly with a man dressed in white coveralls, then followed him inside. Noble watched as they disappeared into an office beyond the waiting room. He wasn't gone long, and when he returned to the car and slid in, Noel asked,

"Where to, Kemo Sabe?"

"It's late, Tonto," Britton said, grinning. "Just take me back to the office, I've got some thinking to do. I'll finish up this little bit of business tomorrow, and then we'll meet for lunch somewhere to review the case and see what we've got. OK?"

Noble couldn't help himself. He busted out laughing. "OK," he said. "I asked for it. But when we meet tomorrow, you drive. I'm tired of being a chauffeur. OK?"

"Deal," Britton said.

In his office, Britton sat at his desk and turned his computer back on. He found the website with the BMW pictures and scrolled down to where he had left off. By the time he viewed all of the pictures, he had firmly implanted in his mind an idea of what BMW tail lights looked like on all of their models.

He then searched for pictures of Audis, looked at their tail lights. Then Cadillacs, Chryslers, Chevrolets, Dodge, Ford, Infinity, Isuzu, Jaguar, Jeep Cherokee, Kia, Mazda, and Mercedes. He was getting tired and once caught himself drifting off to sleep, sitting upright in his office chair. He glanced at the clock on the right bottom side of his computer and to his surprise noticed that it was nearly 10. He turned the computer off and locked up.

As he started out the door he remembered that he was supposed to meet Beverly for dinner that evening. Oh crap, he thought. Now I've ripped it with Mrs. Miller and left the door wide open for Noble.

He found himself reminiscing about his first date with Beverly, how they had met at the restaurant, how he had walked her to her car, and she had invited him to follow her back to her place. He visualized the trip from the restaurant to the country club estates where she lived.

In his mind's eye he saw her car in front of him as she pulled into her driveway and stopped before opening her garage door. Her tail lights had been on all the way but when she braked they glowed.

The car was a BMW!

His blood suddenly chilled in his veins. Could he be mistaken? Was it a BMW or just a car that looked like one?

No, he was convinced. Bev Miller drove a BMW. That bit of information in itself didn't mean a thing, he told himself. There had to be at least fifty BMW sedans in Whispering Meadows, and probably another 200 or more in nearby Augusta. Why did he get a sudden chill when he thought of Beverly's car being a Beemer?

And what of it? It wasn't Beverly Miller who had taken a potshot at him, shattering the windshield of his old Honda. She was a police officer working a case that he happened to be involved in, what logical reason could she have for shooting at him?

Nah..it had to be someone else.

But his neighbor's niece had said it was a woman, or a man with long hair.

Or a man with a wig, he thought, who might purposefully have driven a BMW to disguise his real identity, in order to assassinate a Whispering Meadows private eye.

He had to find out for sure.

He locked the office, gathered up a few things he would need and made sure that he had the slug that had been found in the upholstery of his car. The one that had shattered his windshield on its intended path of shattering his old gray head.

He used his cell phone to call an old friend of his, a man who was part of the Whispering Meadows police department years ago, but who had left and became a part of America's police department, the F.B.I.

"Sorry to call you so late, Ernie," he said when a voice answered. "Can I bring you a slug to identify?"

"Britton?" the voice queried.

"Yep, in person," he said.

"Working late aren't you?" Ernie said.

"Well, I am on a teen kidnapping case that will make headlines when I solve it," Britton said. "Someone took a shot at me, probably trying to scare me off of the case, and I want to try to find the gun that fired it."

"Bring it over," Ernie said. "I've been keeping late hours since I retired. "Speaking of retirement, when are you going to quit playing Matlock and start playing more tennis?"

"I'd like to," Britton said truthfully, "Maybe after this one I'll be able to afford retirement. I'll be at your house in fifteen minutes. Can you access FBI files from your home computer?"

"Yes," Ernie said. "I've still got my password, until someone decides to pull the plug, I can still get in to the system."

"Good," Britton said. "See you in a little bit."

CHAPTER 45

There were some things that just didn't add up.

Jobe Banquell called me the day he paid the ransom. He told me that he had managed to get the $250 G in counterfeit bills, according to Britton's suggestion, and took it personally to the drop, a Club Car golf cart sitting on the 13th fairway, next to the green.

But Lisa was not released and Jobe had heard nothing from the kidnappers.

No counterfeit money had showed up in or near Whispering Meadows. It had been three days since the drop and still nothing.

I got another call from Jobe. He was whining and complaining that neither I nor Britton had made any headway in locating Lisa.

I feared the worse, that Lisa was dead.

Then I sat down with a bottle of my home-made firewater and got a little pie eyed. As I drank I went over things in my mind.

One of the things that bothered me was the ring. Why was Beverly Miller wearing a ring purchased by Jobe Banquell? One that had a price tag on it for enough money to buy half a warehouse full of the old man's peanut butter.

I decided to ask her.

She answered the door on my third ring and smiled. She looked very beautiful in the dim light of the street lamps radiating from the street that ran parallel to the 13th fairway of the golf course.

"My ain't you the purty one, Miss Beverly," I said in my southernmost Rhett Butler imitation.

"Why thank you, Noble. you look right pleasing yourself," she said.

"I'm not interrupting anything am I?" I asked. "No interference from the hometown PI?"

"Why, what on earth could you mean by that?" She asked.

"It's no secret Britton isn't happy about me calling on you, Miss Beverly," I said, still with a hint of Rhett Butler in my voice.

"Britton can lump it," Beverly said, and that set my mind at ease. "He's not one of my favorite people at the moment."

"Old Burl rile you up, did he?"

"He didn't so much rile me up as he did stand me up," Beverly said. "We were supposed to meet for dinner the other night and he didn't show."

"That's too bad," I said, although I was thinking "that's too cool."

I glanced at her ring hand and sure enough she was still wearing the multi-carat diamond ring.

I took that hand and bent low over it and kissed it.

"Anyway, I'm glad you are alone, my lovely lady," I said. Then I switched gears. "My, my, sweet potato. That's a pretty ring you've got on your finger. I hope that isn't a gift from my arch rival, Burl Britton?"

"Burl would have to rob a bank to afford that ring," she said laughing.

"Then may I ask who the gentleman is who robbed the bank?"

She laughed.

"No one robbed a bank, Noble. A friend of mine gave me this ring. You wouldn't know him. His name is Paul Montague. My ex-husband and I were friends with Paul and his ex wife at one time. I don't like to think ill of him, but I don't think his wife knows that he gave it to me."

"Does that mean that you and Mr. Montague are engaged to be married?" I asked.

"Heavens no," she said. "We're not much more than good friends. I think he would like to make it more, but I'm not ready for that. Funny, when he gave it to me he called it 'The ring of Gyges' any idea what that means?"

"Nope", I said. I was thinking in my mind that Jobe Banquell didn't buy the ring for Bev Miller, he bought it for someone else, and it came in the possession of Mr. Montague by hook. I was also thinking that I needed to have a chat with Paul Montague.

"Might I ask what business Mr. Montague might be involved in to afford a rock like that?"

"He's the biggest peach grower in the peach state," she said.

I thought for a minute then decided to go full speed ahead.

"I don't know any other way to ask this, Beverly," I said, "but were you ever romantically involved with Arthur Banquell?"

"Arthur?" She gave me a funny look. "I don't find that remotely funny, Noble. If that was intended as a joke, it failed."

"No offense, my lady," I said hastily.

"It's just that I had some doubts. My theory was that Arthur might have been having an affair and got caught with his pants down, killed by a jealous husband, or boyfriend, or maybe even a wife."

"Be serious," she said.

"Oh I'm serious enough," I said. "I even stumbled on a bunch of dried up flowers that had a card in them. If I remember the greeting was something like 'To my dearest Beverly, Signed, yours....A.J.B'.

"Oh that wasn't Arthur Banquell," she said hastily. Those were from an old high school classmate of mine, Alex Bishop. We had our 15th reunion last week and he played up to me at the dance. I got those flowers the next day, promptly threw them in the dumpster on my way to work. The creep is still married, left his wife at home, and thought he could seduce me with flowers. I didn't tell him that I'm a detective sergeant for the police department, and that I have ways to check on people."

"Oh, well, that's another lead that I have blown completely out of proportion," I said. "Sorry to mention it."

"Don't be," she said. "I'd call that being pretty attentive to circumstantial evidence. I wish I had more people on my staff like you."

"Well thank ye." I said, reverting back to my Rhett Butler imitation. "I'm right proud that you feel that way. I wish I had something better to do than chase down false leads, though."

"What did you have in mind?" she asked, half grinning.

"Maybe a candlelight dinner?" I said, grinning like a raccoon eating persimmons.

"Why, Mr. Savage, I do believe I am inclined to accept that invitation." She said, causing my red face to blush even redder, and my cold blooded heart to skip three or four beats.

We left in her car. But something still puzzled me. I had learned that Jobe Banquell purchased the glittering gem that adorned Beverly's finger, and she told me it was a gift from Paul Montague, a peach grower, and the ex-husband of Michelle Montague. This Whispering Meadows bunch was beginning to look like a little Peyton Place or Harper Valley PTA to me.

CHAPTER 46

Burl was thinking that he was getting too old to be dodging bullets and digging for clues.

He wanted desperately to wind up the Banquell case and retire. It had started to work on his subconscious. He woke up in the middle of the night with a different perspective, tried to think it through logically, then the next night he would wake up with an entirely new slant on the case. Nothing seemed to make sense.

"I'm getting too old for this job," he said to Noble Savage, as they had breakfast at Denny's.

"What's up, my man?" Savage asked. Even that phrase was starting to get a little old to Britton. He'd never quite understood the meaning of the question.

"The sky is up, my blood pressure is up, taxes are up, cost of living is up, government spending is up, and you're asking me "what's up"," he said. "I wish to hell this case was up."

"Yeah, me too," Savage said. "I would like to hang around a little longer, but all of my leads are disappearing."

"What leads?" Britton asked.

"Well, the ring that Beverly Miller wears, for one," Savage said. "The Ring of Gyges, she called it. She told me it was given to her by Paul Montague, I traced the diamond to a dealer who sold it to Jobe Banquell."

"When did you see Beverly Miller?"

"Last night," Savage said, smiling. "We had dinner at an Italian place. Talked for an hour or so afterwards."

"So you want to hang around Bev Miller a little longer, or you want to chase down leads a little longer?"

"Now don't get your tit in a wringer, Britton," Savage said. "We had a friendly dinner and I learned a few things. What's wrong with that?"

"What did you learn?"

"Well, for one, Beverly Miller received some flowers from an old high school chum and that killed one of my leads." Savage told Britton about the flowers the old man had found in a dumpster, the card that had been attached, and waking up with a hangover in an 84 Oldsmobile.

"And the other thing?"

"She's not interested in a permanent relationship." Noble Savage pushed his chair back and picked up his coffee cup , motioning with it to a passing waitress.

"So what do we have to go on to get this case finished?" Britton asked.

"I just told you, I'm out of leads," Noble Savage said, "What do you have?"

Britton hauled out his worn notebook and flipped through it. He told Savage about being shot at, about what the neighbor had told him regarding the BMW, about remembering that Beverly Miller drove a BMW. He mentioned the alarm system, and that the one person who would have access to the code was someone within the Whispering Meadows Police Department.

"Whoa, my man," Savage said. "You ain't thinking that the lovely Beverly had anything to do with the kidnapping or murder, are you?"

"I don't know what to think," Britton said. "I've just about ran out of clues myself."

"What about the kidnapper call? Any further leads on the tape?"

"No," Britton said, then suddenly he got a strange look on his face, as if he'd just thought of a new invention that would rid the world of drug dealers

"What?" Savage asked.

"I just thought of something. Did Beverly say anything to you about counterfeit money showing up anywhere around here?"

"Nope."

"That's funny. You'd think by now that the kidnappers would have spent a little of the ransom money."

"Maybe they're from out of state, or out of the country, as far as that goes," Savage said.

"Maybe, but I'm thinking that they are local."

"What makes you think so?"

"They knew about the golf course, the green on thirteen, the secluded spot that is hidden from view of the road. Hell they even knew what kind of golf carts the course uses."

"What's your point?"

"I'm at a loss as to why we haven't seen any of the money. No further calls to Jobe and no Lisa."

"Aha. The whole thing was a fake, not just the calls?"

"What are you thinking?" Britton asked.

"Maybe the kidnappers went through all of that rigmarole to throw off the police or to get them to look in a specific direction while things were moving in a different direction? Drug deal maybe? Holding off for something bigger, baiting the old man with a paltry ransom, then banging him with something huge?"

"What if there never was a kidnapping?" Britton asked.

"What?" Savage nearly yelled. "What are *YOU* thinking?"

"I'm thinking back to what you pointed out a long time ago. Maybe Lisa set the whole thing up and is sunbathing on a tropical island somewhere, waiting to hit grandpa up with a demand for several million?"

"Along with the black football player?"

"Could be. Have you found anything on him?"

"No, I thought you were working on that angle."

"Hell, Savage, I can't do it all!"

"No one's asking you to," Savage replied, in a calm manner. "I just didn't follow up on Moose because I assumed you were doing that."

"Well let's don't argue over it," Britton said. "Will you check with his parents and find out if they've heard from him?"

"Sure, Britton," Savage said. "What's your next move? Not that you have to confide in me, but just so I know what bases you've covered and don't spin my wheels looking for something that isn't there."

"Let's think a minute, Savage," Britton said. "Suppose Lisa did set this up. Suppose she's the one who killed her parents. Where would she go, and how would she get there? If she's still in the U.S. she probably isn't smart enough to hide her movements or spending. If she used credit cards, she'd be easy to find. If she left the US she would have to have a passport to get in another country, and even then her spending would be a beacon light to her location."

"So where does that leave us, Pardner?"

"Maybe she didn't set it up after all, or maybe the old man knows where she is."

"Grandpa Banquell?"

"With his money it would be easy to cover spending, he'd just use cash. And with his connections, he could get her out of the country without a trace."

"For what reason?" Savage asked. "He wouldn't have anything to gain by demanding ransom from himself. Maybe to keep her safe from the people who killed her mommy and daddy?"

"That's possible, but why would she turn up missing *before* the murders, if that is the case?"

"That's a good question," Savage admitted.

"Well, we're not getting anything done sitting here talking about it," Britton said. "You check out Moose Mosely, and I'll be checking out a few other things, mainly the alarm system."

CHAPTER 47

I took the main thoroughfare from Denny's and turned the rented Chevy on a street that ran north and south out of Whispering Meadows. I drove North.

Maybe it is just my imagination but it seems like every town I drive through in the U.S. of A. the colored folks lived on the north side of town. Whispering Meadows was no exception. I'd got Moose Mosely's address the first day I visited Whispering Meadows High.

The house was a well kept brick veneer home in a nice neighborhood. I parked in front and knocked on the door.

A portly black gentleman opened the door and looked me up and down.

"Can I help you?" he said.

"I'm looking for Moose Mosely," I said. "Is he in?"

"No, Sir," the man said. "I'm his father, Moses Mosely. What is it you want with my son?"

"I'm from the University of North Carolina," I lied. "I'd like to talk to him about a scholarship to play football there."

"Well, Sir," Mr. Mosely said, "You're a little late. My son has signed a letter of intent to play at Notre Dame. He's been there since the middle of the month, participating in their pre-season drills."

"That's where he is now?" I asked.

"Yassuh." he drawled. "He left the day after those white folks were found dead, you know, the Banquells?"

"I see," I said, although I didn't. "Did he tell his coach where he was going, and that he'd signed with Notre Dame?"

"Didn't have to," Mr. Mosely said. "The coach knew about the offer. He was eager to let Moose go. He has a son that he wanted to play in Moose's position, and was afraid of black backlash if he did, so he was eager to find a school who wanted Moose. Even wrote a great letter to the Athletic Director at Notre Dame."

So my trip to talk to the crotchety coach was for nothing. He'd already set it up so that Moose was gone when I went looking for him. That left a bad taste in my mouth, but there was nothing I could do about it now. Maybe the next time I saw him I might leave him with a bloody taste in his mouth.

"Well thank you very much for the information, Sir." I said, politely. "Good luck to your son at Notre Dame."

I turned and walked back down the sidewalk, got in the rented Chevy and sat for a long time complimenting myself on being such a top notch detective. Something I should have known two weeks ago was now revealed to me by the source I should have visited first.

"Oh well," I told myself. "Like Bill Gates said, 'life isn't fair, get used to it'."

So Moose wasn't part of the plan to either kidnap Lisa or murder her parents. Apparently he had nothing to do with any cocaine matters either. I berated myself for rushing to judgment. I'm always critical of people who look at me like

I am a second class citizen from Saskatchewan, but I had formed an opinion about a black football player that I didn't even know, based on a hidden prejudice that had crept into the picture. I vowed to change my bigoted self because of the bigotry I had seen around me.

Sensei had told me once, "Show respect to all, get respect from all."

Now I know what he meant.

I drove the rented Chevy back to Whispering Meadows High School and walked the halls to the bigoted coach's office. I pushed on the door and it swung open.

Coach was sitting at his desk. He looked up at me with a startled, surprised look on his face and his upper lip started to tremble a little.

"What the hell do you want now, Redskin?"

"I'll ignore that temporarily," I said. "What I want is you to tell me why you shipped Moose Mosely off to Notre Dame and didn't tell me about it when I was here last."

"Didn't think it was any of your beeswax," he said.

I leaned across the desk and got a handful of red hair and slammed his face down hard on the desk. When I lifted it, his nose dripped bright red blood on his desk blotter.

"I'm making it my beeswax," I said.

"You're crazeeee.........."

He pushed his chair back away from his desk and started to stand up. I put my left hand on the desk top and vaulted over it, landing with both feet in his chest. The chair, with him in it, slammed hard against the wall behind him.

"Tell me, you dumb piece of dog crap," I said. "Who gave the orders to get rid of Moose?"

His breath escaped his lungs with the sound an 18 wheeler makes when the driver lets up off of the air brakes.

"Go to hell," he said.

I got behind the chair and pushed it up hard against the desk, stepped to one side and grabbed his hair, slamming his nose down hard again on his desk.

"Not before you tell me what I want to know," I said.

"All right, already...." he sputtered. "I got a hand delivered note from Jobe Banquell, delivered by his head chauffer. It told me to find Moose a place in college football and get him out of Whispering Meadows."

"Banquell?" I asked, suddenly taken aback.

"I didn't stutter," he said.

I let go of his hair and shoved the chair back to the wall and stood in front of him.

"If I find out you're lying to me, I'll come back and pull every hair out of your head, one at a time," I said.

"I got no reason to lie," he said. "I don't owe allegiance to him or you."

"You don't have to fear me," I said. "But I'm thinking that if you've betrayed the peanut man, you might not last long as coach here in Whispering Meadows."

I turned and walked to the door, opened it and looked back.

"Good Luck with the rest of the season," I said. "And the rest of your life."

CHAPTER 48

What had seemed like an easy thing to do was starting to get harder. The main office at the alarm company didn't want to talk to Burl Britton. He tried bluffing his way in with a sly reference to the Whispering Meadows Police Department, but that didn't work. The clerk asked for his identification. He changed tactics hurriedly and was about to withdraw when an idea occurred to him.

"How long have you had the contract for the Banquell residence?" he asked.

The clerk who had asked for his identification glanced up at him and smiled.

"That information is confidential, Sir." She said.

"Oh is it?" He smiled back. "I just heard that the house was built four years ago, and wondered if you folks got the original contract. Surely that information can't hurt anyone."

He opened his wallet and extracted a twenty, holding it between thumb and forefinger. He made sure the clerk was watching then released the bill. It floated gently to the floor on the other side of the counter at which he stood. She looked over her should to see if anyone in the office was watching, and confident that none were, she shifted slightly and put her foot on the bill.

"Ever since Jobe Banquell presented the plans," she said, "we have been the sole security company for that address." Her voice was several decibels lower than it had been.

Realizing that he had extracted all of the information that he could for his money, Britton thanked the clerk and left the office.

Something she had said was buzzing in his mind. She had told him that the plans were submitted by Jobe Banquell, not Arthur.

He drove to the county court house and checked with a friend who worked in the building codes department. Sure enough, the plans filed for permits had been presented by Jobe Banquell. It wasn't a problem for Burl's friend to give him the code for the alarm system. It had been given to the building codes people so that they would release the permits and provide the homeowners insurance company with proof of an alarm system.

So almost anyone who had seen the plans would have known how to turn off the alarm. The surprising thing to Britton was that it was Jobe Banquell who had handled that detail, until he learned that the construction company that built the home was owned by Banquell Industries, one of Jobe's many companies.

Some tiny little details were starting to trickle down. The kidnappers had knowledge of the layout of the country club, there had been no counterfeit money passed, Jobe Banquell knew the code to the alarm system on Arthur Banquell's residence.

Maybe it was time to pay another visit to the peanut man. Britton drove back to his office and sat at his desk for several minutes thinking about everything he had learned to this point. As he sat there, the mailman opened the door and stepped in.

"Morning, Burl," he said. Britton smiled and returned the greeting.

The mailman laid a handful of mail on Britton's desk and turned to leave. "I see you've been busy, Britton. There's one there from a detention center in Chicago. It's addressed to Detective Noble Savage, but in care of you, here at your office."

"Thanks," Britton said, picking up the stack.

He shuffled through it and took out the one the mailman had commented about, got a letter opener from his desk drawer and slit the envelope.

Inside he found a brief note from the Chicago jail that had released Jimmy Enderly on bail. A picture slid out as he opened it. He read the note and then picked up the picture.

A curious look of amazement fell over Britton's face like the sun blinking through the venetian blinds on his office door.

The picture of the woman who had bailed out the Enderly kid was one of Michelle Montague.

Suddenly things started to click in Britton's mind.

CHAPTER 49

What I needed to try was a bluff. It involved getting some help from Britton, since I am way out of my bailiwick in Georgia.

We met at Denny's for lunch and I asked him if he knew anyone who could get a handful of counterfeit $100 bills.

"What have you got in mind?" he asked.

"I'd like to set up a bluff, Old Chap," I said. "Take a wad of counterfeit money to the Peanut Man and tell him his ransom money has started to show up here in Whispering Meadows."

"You think the ransom call was fake?"

"I think the whole thing is fake," I said. "For some reason, the likes of which I have yet to uncover, I think the old man wanted Lisa out of the household of her parents. I think he has her stashed someplace, with his contacts and money it could be anywhere, but he's faking the kidnapping to cover her absence."

"I think I know why," Britton said.

"You do?" That was a shock to me. It told me that Britton and I had been thinking along the same wave length, but he had uncovered something that had tied it to reality.

"Didn't you tell me that it was Jobe Banquell who financed getting the black football player an early start at Notre Dame?"

"Ah...I'm beginning to see where you're coming from," I said, my thought processes racing ahead of his voice like a rabbit running from a puma.

"Let me hear what you're thinking," Britton said

"Jobe is the real racist in the Banquell family," I said. "He tried to persuade Art to put Lisa in a private school, away from black football players, but Art refused. So Jobe first tried to buy off the Moseley's by sending Moose to Notre Dame. When Lisa threw a fit and threatened to follow Moose, the old man had her abducted and shipped somewhere for her final year of high school, and at the same time, hired a crew of professionals to re-frame her mind to fit his beliefs."

"You've hit the nail right on the head, Savage," Britton told me. "That's exactly the way I see it."

"But who murdered Lisa's parents?"

"I'm still working on that one," he said. "When I figure it out, we'll have this case wrapped up tighter than a papoose in a saddle bag."

I let the comment slide. It seemed to me like people make remarks all the time that aren't really meant to be "digs" or "slurs" but just comments. They hurt people's feelings unintentionally, often without even knowing that they are doing so. That was a new lesson I had just started to learn, but learning was important to me, so I didn't say anything.

"Well, can you get me a few $100 counterfeit bills somewhere?" I asked.

"When do you need them?"

"The sooner the better," I said. "I don't know if I can get the old man to slip up and say something incriminating, but I'm going to try."

"I'll contact a friend in the printing business," Britton said. "He might be able to print up some for us that will pass without close examination."

"Good deal, Lucille," I said. "In the meantime, I'm going to put some feelers out with some old friends of mine in Canada. They may be able to shed some light on whether Lisa is still in the United States, Canada or somewhere else."

"I didn't know you had contacts like that," he said.

"There's a lot about me you don't know," I said. "Maybe that's why we are starting to work good together."

"Could be, Noble." he said. "Keep in touch. Do you need back up when you confront Jobe?"

"Nah," I said. "If I can't handle an 85 year old peanut farmer, I'm in deep *caca*."

I left.

CHAPTER 50

Britton was able to get a friend to print a hundred counterfeit $100 bills after he signed an agreement to hold the friend harmless in any Federal or Civil lawsuit that might arise out of the use of the counterfeit money. Britton signed it without any thought as to whether he might face prosecution if the bills fell in the wrong hands.

He called Noble Savage and arranged to meet him briefly at his office to give him the bogus bills, then drove to the home of Michelle Montague.

She answered the door bell after the third insistent ring.

"What is it, Mr. Britton?" she asked, perturbed.

"Just a question or two, if you don't mind," Britton said.

"Come in."

He entered and got right to the point, extracting the picture that he had received from the Chicago Police Department.

"Recognize this picture?" he asked, holding it up for her to see.

"Yes, it is a picture of me," she said.

"Taken by an automatic camera the day you bailed Jimmy Enderly out of a Chicago holding tank."

She stepped back quickly, a look of absolute terror in her eyes.

"Second question. Did you kill him?"

Her composure was still slipping, but she managed to compose herself enough to answer.

"I don't know what you are talking about," she said.

"I'm talking about a kid that came to the rescue of a young girl that he thought needed rescuing. According to emails found on his computer, Lisa Banquell was being physically and sexually abused by her father, Arthur. Those same emails convinced the vulnerable teenager to steal a car, drive to Georgia and fall under the spell of a woman intent on murdering the Banquells."

"What are you saying?"

"I'm saying that you wanted the Banquells dead. You tried to convince them to stop the romance between Lisa and Moose, but they wouldn't listen."

"Your nuts!" She hissed. "Prove it."

"I don't have everything I need yet," he said, "But the proof is often in the pudding. I found a copy of a book you gave to Lisa. You and your husband have been associated with the top level KKK members here in Georgia. You saw a rising star in Lisa Banquell and was determined to cling to that star to advance your own interest."

"That's absurd," she said. "You can't prove any of that!"

"Not all of it. No need to, but I've got a lot of circumstantial evidence. I traced those emails to a computer in Whispering Meadows library. I've got a description from the librarian on who used that computer on the dates that the emails were sent. That description matches you to a capitol T." he said.

"I'm not here to arrest you. That's a job for the cops. I'm just here to tell you that if you ever shoot at me again, I'll kill you."

"Shoot at you? I suppose you can prove that?"

"A neighbor got your license plate number the night you shot at me," Britton rattled off a license plate number. He had read it and memorized it from her car parked in the driveway. He was bluffing, lying through his teeth. He knew that she would probably not fall for it.

"Bullshit!" she said.

"Nice language," he told her. "I also had the slugs you fired at me examined by a friend. He said they came from a .38 Police Special purchased by the Whispering Meadows police department. That gun was issued to Beverly Miller. I think her husband provided it to you to take care of me, am I right?"

"Get out," she said, calmly. "If you don't leave, I'll call the police."

"Your lover, Joe Miller?" Britton asked.

She turned and walked to a low coffee table where Britton saw a telephone. What he didn't see was the gun.

She reached for the gun and as she turned, Britton saw it.

"So now you can finish the job you started at my house, you can't miss from that range."

She raised the gun enough to point at his chest.

"You bastard," she said. "You meddling fool of a bastard. For years the Negroes have gained in politics and keep pushing their agenda.

People who should have been promoted, elected or selected have stood silently in the shadows, waiting for their chance, but people like you and Art Banquell who believe in equality for all, regardless of race, have kept pushing the more qualified, beautiful people back into the shadows."

"So, you were the chosen queen of The Thule Society? Or The Georgia Family Research Society, as you prefer to call it?" Britton asked. "Jobe Banquell is the King and you are the Queen?"

"I have my own opinions, you fool," she said. "I answer to no-one."

"I figured as much when I researched you and found that you had been Miss Georgia in your teen years, right out of high school, but you were not selected as Miss USA, a black girl from North Carolina got that title."

"She didn't deserve to be Miss USA, I was the leading candidate," Michelle Montague hissed. "The judges were all under scrutiny from the NAACP and gave in to their political pressure."

"So you were going to make sure that pressure was not applied to Lisa Banquell. You were going to ride her coattails back into the spotlight. Your schools would be Nationwide, your chances of being a big screen star would also soar."

"You don't know anything, Britton," she said, quietly. "You can't prove anything, and you are going to get shot while attempting to rape me." She reached for her blouse top and ripped it from top to bottom, Her breasts were exposed, one scratched by her own fingernails.

"Maybe you can tell the police that I stole that magnificent ring that Jobe bought you." Britton said.

"My ring?" she had a look of sudden shock on her face. "What about my ring?"

"You haven't missed it?"

"Why should I miss it? It's in my jewelry box, in my bedroom safe, locked up securely."

"Better look again, Michelle," Britton said. "The ring that Jobe Banquell bought at Chez Pierre's is now on the finger of Beverly Miller."

"What?"

"Yep. My partner asked her about the ring just a few nights ago. She told him your ex-husband gave it to her."

"He gave her my ring?" Incredulous disbelief sounded hollowly in her voice.

She held the gun steadily on his belly button and motioned with her other hand.

"In there, Britton," she ordered, pointing to the bedroom.

He walked in the direction she pointed, through a partially open door. His nerves were tensed like mandolin strings. He had a few minutes to live unless he acted fast.

As she started to follow him through the door, he sprang quickly to his left and swung his right hand in a quick arc, like returning a thigh high serve in tennis, hit the door solidly and it slammed against her gun hand. He followed that with a quick spin and slammed the door behind him, turning the lock at the same time. Now he was locked in her bedroom, He looked quickly at the floor but the gun was not there. A split second decision made him drop to his chest on the floor just as the gun roared and wood splintered as a slug ripped its way through the door, penetrating the air where his chest had been.

He crawled on hands and hips, swiveling to her bed, as another shot rang out and more wood splintered. Keeping as low as possible, he rolled across her bed and dropped to the floor on the far side, between the bed and a window. He grabbed a pillow from the bed and used it to shield his fist as he ran his hand through the glass, then brushed loose glass away and dove head first, shielding his face with his arms, through the broken window.

A shard of glass ripped into his thigh right above his right knee as he landed in the grass on the outside of her bedroom. He rolled to his feet and ran as fast as he could to his Honda.

He got his key out of his pocket as he ran and jammed it into the ignition and twisted. The little car started without hesitation and he peeled away as fast as the car would go, expecting at any minute to hear more shots.

What he heard, instead, was sirens. Someone else had heard the gun going off and called the police.

He didn't care what the police found when they got to Michelle's address. No doubt she would tell them the phony rape tale, expose a scratch mark on a bare breast, and they would be looking for a Honda with a deranged, rapist PI driving away.

CHAPTER 51

At about the same time that Burl Britton left to confront Michelle Montague with what he suspected, I was on my way to see the Peanut Man, armed with a briefcase full of blank paper masked by $100 counterfeit bills.

What I suspected was foremost on my mind as I stopped at the gates to Jobe Banquell's magnificent mansion. Here I was, a mail-order PI license in my wallet, about to confront the richest man in the state of Georgia about a fake kidnapping.

I'd be lucky to get back out his front door, let alone out of these gates.

I pushed the button and waited. A servant asked my name and who I wished to see, and I knew that a closed circuit TV was beaming my smiling face in to somewhere. I smiled my best subservient smile and humbly requested audience with the great man, Jobe Banquell.

The gate swung open as I was being told to drive to the main entrance where I would be greeted by Mr. Banquell's butler.

I hadn't noticed in my previous trips to the old boy's multi-roomed wickiup just how opulent his surroundings were. On my right was tennis courts, on my left a huge swimming pool. The driveway my rented Chevy was rolling on was paved with slabs of metal that were polished to look like gold. In the front of the house sat two cars, Jobe's Lincoln and his Rolls Royce.

Ever wonder what you would do with more money that Carter's got peanuts? Well whatever you dreamed up, Jobe Banquell had already thought of it, in spades.

I stopped the car and got out as the front door to the mansion opened. Clement, Jobe's number one manservant, approached.

"Good morning, Sir," he said. "Mr. Banquell will see you in his study."

"Thanks, my man," I said, saluting him. I was wondering what Clem would think if he knew what a real racist, bigoted man he was serving.

He led me in, down one hall and up three steps, on carpet so thick a giraffe might get lost in it. My stomach was starting to quiver a little. Not from fright, but because I had started to like this old man, and now I realized just what a creep he had been all along.

After what seemed like a trek across the Kalahari, we arrived at the study. Solid mahogany doors, taller than basketball goals, arched at the top, stood in front of us. Clem knocked and I heard the deep voice of Jobe call from within.

"Come on in," he roared.

We went in.

"Well, if it isn't my favorite investigator, Noble Savage. What can I do for you? Have you got some good news? Did you find Lisa?"

"I've got some good news and some bad news," I said. "Which would you like first?"

"Come, come, Noble," he said. "I don't have time for games, what is it?"

"Well, the good news is this," I said, raising the briefcase to the top of his massive desk. I set it down and opened it. "We've recovered nearly fifty grand of your ransom money."

I watched his face closely. His left eyebrow went up first, then his right, then his eyes got considerably bigger. His upper lip started to tremble slightly, and his left ear twitched.

"I see," he mumbled.

"Yep," I continued. "It wasn't hard to track down, a Mercedes dealer in Atlanta was where it showed up. Apparently the kidnappers tried to use it to buy a new Mercedes."

"But, but..."

"But?" I said. "As in derriere, or as in the Miriam Webster definition, used in speech at the beginning of a sentence that expresses surprise or shock?"

"What the hell are you gibbering about, Noble?" He asked, gaining some of his composure.

"You act like you are surprised that someone would try to spend your counterfeit money."

"Were they apprehended?" He asked. "What about Lisa?"

"The man was arrested for possession of counterfeit money but he bailed out within hours of his arrest," I lied. "I'm sorry to say that the kidnappers are still free. The name he used in arrest records was from a phony driver's license."

"I see." Jobe said, again.

"You know what puzzles me, Jobe?"

"No, please tell me, Noble. As if you weren't going to tell me anyway."

"Well it really puzzles me how the kidnappers got a bite on your confederate money that you paid for Lisa's ransom."

"What's so puzzling about that?"

"Well Jobe, Ol' chap, you didn't pay any damn ransom. Surveillance videos of the 13th green area at the golf course on the night you said you paid the ransom doesn't show anyone. Nada, Zip. Nothing."

"And on top of that, there's a warrant out for your arrest for passing counterfeit money, even though it was part of the ransom." I was lying again. Getting to be a bad habit with me.

"What? Why those sonsabitches can't do that to me, I didn't pass any counterfeit money."

"You didn't? You mean you didn't pay the ransom?"

"Oh I paid it all right," Jobe said. "But I disregarded Britton's suggestion that I pay it in counterfeit money, and paid it in real money."

"Why didn't your old mug show up on the surveillance videos?" I asked.

"I purposely gave you the wrong information regarding the ransom drop because I didn't trust you not to tell the authorities. My instructions were to keep the police out of it, and I was protecting my granddaughter's life by keeping that information to myself."

"You PAID the ransom? Someplace other than the 13th green?" I asked.

"I didn't pay it in person," he said. "Clement took the cash to the drop. He was disguised as me, I drove my limo and he got out of the back seat and made the drop."

"So that brings up an interesting question, Mr. Savage. Where did you get this counterfeit money? What makes you think I am stupid enough to fall for a trap like the one you just tried to spring?"

"I, I, I don't know what you're talking about, Jobe, " I said, hastily.

"Oh, I think you do," he said. "You apparently had it in mind that I faked my own granddaughter's kidnapping, faked the ransom calls, and that I have her stashed away somewhere. What reason would I have to do something like that?"

I thought about that for at least two seconds and made up my mind to try to shake him a little more before I put him down.

"I think you are lying through your ten thousand dollar capped teeth, you black dirt peanut farmer."

He stared at me with a surprised look.

"Why, Savage..after all I've done for you, put you up in my own home, fed you breakfast and treated you like a man instead of a damned Injun. Now you turn on me? Call me a liar?"

It didn't take two seconds to know he was trying to turn the tables back on me. Ball was in my court.

"I know you better than you think I do, Jobe," I said. "I know that you are a member of the Georgia Ku Klux Klan. I know that you have spent a lot of money promoting the idea that minority races should be exterminated, like rats. You see, you really don't know me as well as your dossier indicates. I had people in Canada and Britain rig my dossier long before you checked me out. You got what I wanted you to see. "

"You're nothing, Savage." He said.

"Meaning I'm just a redskin Injun? Yeah, I'm an Injun, alright. My father and grandfather before me were Injuns. Just like your father and his father were Klan members, and secret organization members, like the Skull and Bones society. Arian brotherhood organizations. Tell me, Jobe, does Clem know you as well as I do?"

"Clem's just another servant to me," he said. "He does as I say because I pay him well."

"Like you paid him to buy that ring for Michelle Montague? Like you paid him to cut the brake lines on my old car? You knew I was getting close to figuring you out. Right after I went to see the high school coach. Coachy didn't tell me that day that it was you who had Moose suddenly whisked away to a Notre Dame football program, all expenses paid, to get him away from your sweet Lisa. You'll have to give him credit for that, he didn't tell me till I beat it out of him."

"Here's the way I see, it," I said, and took a long breath. "You hate black folks. It damn near killed you when Arthur decided he didn't want to be a racist. His decision to let Lisa date a black boy was more than you could take."

"You had Michelle Montague get a boy from Chicago to thinking that Arthur was molesting his daughter, by pretending to be Lisa and sending him e-mails. She built up enough hate in that boy that he stole a car and drove to Whispering Meadows and met Michelle Montague, who, of course, told him she was Lisa. She took him to Arthur's home and he shot Arthur to death. She then told him to kill Dora

Banquell, but he balked at that. Dora wasn't the one he hated. Dora hadn't molested Lisa."

"So she shot Dora. To make the whole thing look like a drug deal gone wrong, she dropped a bag of cocaine there. She was going to get rid of Jimmy Enderly but decided that his presence in the Atlanta area might somehow be linked back to her, so she fixed it so he was picked up in his stolen car, taken back to Chicago, and she flew there. He still thought she was Lisa when she bailed him out and took him to a motel room where she fed him cyanide."

"You'll never prove any of that, Savage," Jobe Banquell said through clenched teeth.

"Think not?" I said. "Britton is at Michelle Montague's as we speak, telling her the same thing I'm telling you. She'll break, Jobe. I won't have to prove it."

"You misunderstood me, Savage," he said, "I didn't mean you can't prove anything, I meant, as I said, you will never prove anything."

A door opened behind me and Clements entered silently.

"Dispose of this piece of trash, Clements." Banquell said.

"Yes, Mr. Banquell," Clem said, as if he were a robot, programmed to obey at all cost.

I was unarmed. I've always relied on my ability to talk my way out of a fight rather than shoot my way out. I didn't have a gun and my martial arts techniques might be useless against the big fellow who stood facing me with a .45 aimed at my belly button.

"Watch him, Clements," Jobe said. "He's a sixth degree black belt in Kung Fu."

"Seventh," I corrected him.

Jobe pushed a button and spoke into hidden microphones. "Bart, you and Dawahn get in here. I don't want this man to leave the premises."

Like ghosts, two more men entered the room, one a huge Latino looking fellow, twice as big as Clements, the other smaller than Clem, a black man with a big gun, an Uzi.

"Cuff him," Clements said. The Latino giant spun me around like I was a ballet dancer and I felt the cuffs go on my left wrist first, then my right. My resistance would have proven futile, if not fatal. I had to talk my way out of this one, and I had an idea.

I remained silent as they pointed the way down the hall and ushered me out.

CHAPTER 52

Britton knew that it was just a matter of time before he would have to face the Whispering Meadows police department and try to defend the phony rape charges. He really had nothing he could give the WMPD to convince him that it was Michelle Montague who was the mastermind of the Banquell killings. It was all purely speculation on his part. He did know, however, that someone had taken a potshot at him. He headed for the home of the former FBI agent who was checking the slug fired at him.

He rang the bell and waited. Ernie answered the door and stood back looking at Britton's bloody trouser leg.

"What the hell happened to you?" He asked.

"I fought with a glass window and the window won," Britton said. "Can I come in? I promise not to bleed on your carpet."

"Let's treat that leg out here, then we'll talk," he said. "I'm in no mood to watch someone bleed out on my couch."

He closed the door behind him as he re-entered his home and Britton stood there feeling a little dizzy and waited.

The door opened again and Ernie went to work on Britton's leg, cutting the pants leg off above the knee, applying a tourniquet, and then antiseptic and a bandage. When he finished he led Britton in and told him to have a seat.

"What in the hell have you done now?" He asked.

Burl Britton took a deep breath and told Ernie the entire story, starting with the day he went to the Banquell residence. He finished with his description of the scene he had just left and his concern that WMPD might believe Michelle Montague's story.

"What is it you want from me?" Ernie asked.

"I can't prove anything on her about the Banquell killings yet, "Britton said, "But I thought you could help me prove she fired a shot at me. How can we tie that slug I gave you to the gun she just fired at me again?"

"We would need to get our hands on either the gun or one of the slugs she just fired," He said.

"That's a tall order," Britton said. "You told me the gun was one issued to the WMPD. Can you back that?"

"I think I can," he said. "The guns purchased by police departments for issue are all fired and the lands and grooves for each gun are recorded. When I ran a search on FBI computers against the lands and grooves on the slug you brought, it matched with a gun purchased a few years ago by the WMPD."

"Beverly Miller!" Britton said.

"Who?"

"The homicide sergeant at WMPD!" Britton said. "She would be able to dig up those records."

He reached for his cell phone but couldn't find it. He must have dropped it in his escape from the Montague residence.

"Can I use your phone?"

Ernie handed Britton a phone and stood patiently while Britton connected with the WMPD and asked to speak to Beverly Miller.

Britton put the phone on 'speaker' and waited.

"Whispering Meadows Police," Beverly Miller said, after what seemed like an eternity.

"This is Burl Britton, Beverly," he said. "I have got some information for you about the Banquell affair."

"You are a wanted man, Mr. Britton," she said. "There's a warrant out for your arrest. I suggest you turn yourself in immediately. Where are you now?"

"Not yet," he said. "I have some information. Before I tell you anything, hear this. Whatever Michelle Montague told your officers is a lie. I was there to confront her about the Banquell killings."

"Go on," she said.

He told her what had transpired. He didn't leave anything out except the connection between Michelle Montague and the KKK. He related the entire scenario as best as he could remember. Then he got to the reason for the call.

"Do you have access to the records where service revolvers are issued to WMPD officers?"

"Of course," she said. "Why?"

He looked at Ernie and Ernie went to his desk and returned with a piece of paper, pointing to a serial number. Britton read it into the phone.

"Slow down, Britton," she said. "Give that to me again."

He repeated it. Silence.

He stood holding the phone, thinking that something had happened to the connection. Several seconds went by. He held the phone away from his ear and looked at the screen for a "call ended" message but saw none.

"Whoa!" he finally heard her say.

"What?"

"That serial number matches the gun issued to my ex husband," she said.

"No!" Britton said.

"Yes," she said. "It was Joe's gun when he was a rookie cop. When he bought a Glock semi-automatic, he turned it in."

"Where is it now?" Britton asked.

"Locked up in the gun cabinet here at the office, I guess," she said.

"Can you check that, please?"

"Hold on."

The phone made a sound like it was being placed on hold and Britton waited. After what seemed like 10 minutes, but couldn't have been more than 1, she returned."

"Not there," she said.

"Who has a key to the cabinet?"

"There are several," she said. "Each shift commander has one, I have one, the chief has one. I'd say there's at least six or seven. Joe had one, since he is a shift commander."

"Let me ask you something, Bev." Britton started. "What are Joe's views on minorities?"

"Very conservative," she said. "As a matter of fact, that's why we divorced. I have always seen every race as equal under the law. Joe was adamant that they created more problems and caused more crime."

"Would you say he was conservative to the point of being paranoid?"

"More than that," she said. "One night he came home late and when I asked him where he had been, he said to a KKK meeting, and laughed. I thought he was joking until I got to checking around and found out he was telling the truth. He had a white sheet and hood hidden in his truck in the center console compartment."

"KKK, huh?" Britton murmured.

"Yep." She said. "Can you come in and talk about this, Britton?"

"Not yet," he said. "I'm a wanted man, you told me that. I've got some more work to do before I give myself up. Just do something for me, will you? Check on Michelle Montague's background. I think you'll be surprised to learn that she's got a connection to the KKK as well."

"Will do," she said. "I still think you should turn yourself in, though. It'll go better than being a fugitive from justice."

"I'll call again as soon as I have something firm," he said, and snapped the phone shut and returned it to Ernie.

"So who has the gun now?"

"Probably the one Michelle Montague used to shoot at me," Britton said. "Would you mind doing me a favor?"

"What's that," Ernie asked.

"Go to her place and show her your FBI badge. Ask her if she owns a firearm that used to belong to the WMPD. See if she'll loosen up. If possible, get the gun. Tell her you will need the gun to prosecute me on the rape charge. She doesn't know you so it might work."

"It's worth a try," he said, "but she'd have to be pretty dumb to hand over the gun. From what you've said, she's no pushover."

"So you'll do it?"

"Yeah, Britton, Ol Pal," Ernie said. "Leave it to me, I'll try it."

CHAPTER 53

I didn't have any idea what method the three men who were told to get rid of me might use to accomplish that task.

What I did know is that I was in a hell of a bind. My hands were cuffed behind me, I didn't have a gun, and my martial arts against these guys would probably wind up getting me hurt. The only prayer I had was my ability to talk to people.

"So what are you guys going to do with me?" I asked.

"What we do with anyone the boss says to dispose of," The smaller black man said.

"Don't you know that when he gets tired of using you, he'll hire someone to get rid of you?"

"That won't happen," the man said.

"Shut up, Dawahn," Clement said.

"Man, I aint hurtin' nothin' answering this Dude's questions."

"Why won't it happen, Dawahn?" I asked, eager to try to drive a wedge between him and Clem. Divide and conquer.

"We know too much," Dawahn said. That was one of the dumbest answers to any question I've ever asked.

"Don't you think that would make it more of a reason to have someone else dispose of you?" I asked him.

"Well, I don't know," he said, and shook his dreadlocks. "I'm bettin' on him keepin' me around a while. I can do things for him. I know people he needs."

"Clan members?" I asked him.

"What clan, man?" he said.

"As in Ku Klux Klan," I said.

"Shut the hell up, Dawahn," Clem said again.

"You might be better off to listen to him, and me," I told Clem. "You are in the same category."

"Que habla es?" The Latino muttered.

"Ahora que me estaba diciendo a esos chicos que cuando el jefe se prepara a alguien, deshacerse de usted como usted son para deshacerse de mí." I spoke directly towards the Latino in my best Spanish. It had been years since I'd studied and I hoped he'd understand enough to get the drift.

"Si, you may be right, man," he said.

"So I tell you what I'll do," I began. "If you guys will let me go, I'll make sure nothing he does will ever result in your demise."

"Speak English," Clem told me, and for the first time, I thought I might be on the right track.

"I've got almost enough on your boss to put him away for a long time," I said. "But if you guys dispose of me, someday you will be disposed of too. No one likes three witnesses to a murder."

"We ain't killed no-one," Dawahn said.

"Not yet, maybe," I said. "But what about me?"

"We ain't gonna kill you," he said. "We're just going to dunk you in the lake with a heavy weight tied around your neck."

"That wouldn't kill me?" I asked, dumbfounded.

"But it would be the lake that kills you, not us," Dawahn said. Talk about your logical thought processes. This guy was three turnips short of Lil Abner.

"I'm listening," Clem said.

"Did you know that Jobe Banquell is a high ranking official in the Georgia Ku Klux Klan?" I asked.

"You're shittin' me," Clem said.

"Couldn't do that if I wanted to," I said, hastily. "He got rid of the football player by having him shipped off to Notre Dame to keep him away from his granddaughter, Lisa."

Clem scratched his big head and looked at me.

"That's why he sent that Mosely kid to college? I thought it was because he *liked* him."

"He doesn't like anyone who is black, or red, for that matter," I said. "If he gets rid of me, you'll be a danger to his existence. He'll have to hire someone to get rid of you, and that won't be far away."

"He'll get rid of us if we *don't* get rid of you!" Clem said.

"Not if I can get rid of him first," I said.

"Here's the thing on being a racist," I said, talking fast. "The people you hate are your main target. He hates black people, Clem. You think he likes you? Tell me, how much money does Jobe pay you?"

"Fifty grand a year," Clem said. "I'm the manager of all of his home security people, I'm the boss over these two clowns."

"Any idea how much a security man with your capability is worth in Chicago?" I asked.

"Probably a little more," he said.

"I'd say a lot more, probably closer to a *hundred and fifty grand.*"

"Do you think so?" Clem asked, a look of doubt spreading across his dark face.

"Hell, man, do you know how much Michael Jordan's bodyguard makes?"

"No."

"*Five hundred thousand a year.*", I said, even though I didn't have the damndest idea of how much Jordan's bodyguard made, or even if he had a bodyguard.

"And that black TV weatherman, you know who I'm talking about? He pays his bodyguard *two hundred thousand a year.*

I could see that Clem was thinking. He scratched his big head again and took me by the arm. We had walked maybe two hundred yards from the mansion to a boat house on the lake. He motioned me towards a door.

"I'm going to lock you up in here for a while," he said. "The boss won't know that you're still alive, he'll think we drowned you. Then I'll wait and see if what you said is true."

"I'll starve to death out here before he gets someone to get rid of you three," I said.

"No you won't, I'll see to that," he said.

He pushed me into a room, spun me around and took the cuff off of one wrist and motioned me towards an old steel radiator. He picked up a rusty piece of chain, clipped the loose cuff around it, and padlocked it to a radiator pipe.

He took his foot and slid a 5 gallon bucket close enough that I could sit on it.

"That bucket will be your toilet. I'll have someone empty it before it gets full."

"I'll be back tonight with some food," he said. "If you scream or try to escape, I will kill you, then I'll dispose of your body in the lake."

He turned and motioned to the other two goons. "We'll leave him here for now. Don't do anything till I tell you to. Chico, you stay outside this door, if he tries to leave, shoot him."

"Si, cabron," Chico said. He turned off the lights in the room and closed the door behind him as he stepped outside. It was as dark as pitch in the room. After a while it got quiet.

CHAPTER 54

It was 6 in the evening when the former FBI agent returned. Britton was asleep on the couch but sprang up wide awake when the front door opened.

"Piece of cake," Ernie said, and showed Britton the pistol. It was a 38 Police Special.

"How long will it take to compare the grooves?" Britton asked.

"I've got all of that on file," he said. "I can fire a slug through this barrel and have the results in an hour."

"Thanks, I owe you," Britton said.

"You look like you'd been shot and missed and shit at and hit," his friend said.

"I feel like it too," Britton replied. "Can I shower and use your razor?"

"Sure. What's your plan if this is the gun used to fire at you?"

"I'll take the gun and what I know to the Whispering Meadows PD. Let them handle the rest."

"Good idea, Burl. You've covered a lot of territory, they should be grateful for your work."

"It's one of the toughest cases I've ever had since getting my PI license," Burl told him. "Good enough for someone to write a book about."

He found his way to the bathroom of his friend's home and lathered his face and scraped a day's growth of beard off with a multi-blade razor. He wondered how many blades a razor would have in ten years time. His old trusty razor at home had only one.

He sat on the stool and took his shoes and socks off, removed his pants and dropped them on the floor, his underwear on top of them. He'd have to borrow a pair of pants to replace the ones with the right leg missing above the knee. The bandage that his friend had applied was bloody but dried and he knew the bleeding had stopped.

He stood in the shower for several minutes, relaxing, then soaped down, rinsed and stepped out. He caught his reflection in the mirror and was surprised at how old he looked. It was if the last 20 years had suddenly disappeared and he had gone from 40 to 60 overnight. He felt good, but his mind was tired.

"This is it," he told himself. "My last case. I'm done. Stick a fork in me."

He walked back into the living room in his shorts, carrying the ruined slacks in one hand and damp towel in the other.

"Where to put these things? he asked.

"Toss the trousers in the trash under the sink," Ernie said.

"I'll need a pair of pants, can you loan me some Dockers or Levis or something?"

"Sure," Ernie said and disappeared into a bedroom. He returned with a pair of Dockers. Burl sat on a kitchen chair and put them on and stood up. They were a little tight, but he sucked in his stomach and buttoned the top and zipped them up.

"Thanks again, Ernie," he said.

"No problem, friend." Ernie said. "The gun is a match."

"It is?"

"Yep. Didn't take long to figure that one out. The lands and grooves are a perfect match. It's the gun that was sold originally to the WMPD, and the one that fired the slug you brought me."

"Great," Britton said. He clapped Ernie on the back and asked for the gun.

"You off to the WMPD now?"

"Yep!"

Britton was afraid he'd get pulled over by a squad car before he got to the WMPD building. He drove very carefully, obeying all the speed limits and watching other traffic with more attention than he normally did.

As he drove, his mind wondered back over the events of the past few days, back to the day he first arrived at the Banquell's and looked through Lisa's room for clues. He remembered the envelope he'd found near the book. Cocaine.

It still bothered him how an envelope of cocaine had shown up after the murders. The more he thought of it the more it bothered him. He had turned the one he found over to the police department the day after he found it. The second envelope showed up the morning after the murders. It hadn't been there when he searched the room and he remembered Shauntell's explanation and the tale she told him about finding it, picking it up, then tossing it because she heard the "pole-lease" coming. Something just didn't feel right about that. The more he thought about it, the odder it seemed.

She had been an employee of the family for several years and background checks surely were done prior to Art Banquell's hiring her.

Why would she be afraid the cops would book her for possession? It didn't make sense.

A light began to come on in Britton's mind. It started as a flicker, then got a little brighter. He tried relaxing and letting his mind think it out. He had experienced the feeling in the past and knew that he was on to something.

The light in his mind flickered again, came back brighter than before. Suddenly he realized that Shauntell was the only person who could have planted the envelope that he had found, but since it was not there when the WMPD showed up after she found the bodies, she had planted another one.

He flipped on his turn signal indicator and made a right hand turn at the next street and headed away from the police building. He needed to talk to Shauntell about why she would plant two envelopes of cocaine in Lisa's room.

He knocked on he door, looking around for any sign of the Doberman. She opened the door and stared out at him, a quizzical look on her face.

"Hi Shauntell," he said. "I've got a couple of more questions about the Banquell's if you don't mind? May I come in?"

"I'm kinda tied up right now," she said.

"It won't take long," Burl said.

She stepped back and Burl opened the screen door and went in. The furniture that had been there when he visited first was missing. The room was practically bare. Two folding lawn chairs, a small folding table with a briefcase on it, that was it.

Burl glanced at the briefcase and noticed it was very similar to the one he and Noble

Savage had crammed with blank papers and counterfeit $100 bills. Odd, he thought.

"Wha you want, Mr. Britton?" She asked.

"I was curious about that envelope you said you found, remember, the one you thought might be cocaine?"

"Yassuh."

"Well, it occurred to me that there was an envelope of cocaine in Lisa's room the day I examined it before the Banquells were murdered, and you found an envelope in their room and took it to Lisa's room and threw it under the bed, the day you discovered the bodies?"

"Yassuh, I done told you that."

"You said you knew it might be cocaine? That you was afraid the police would bust you for possession?"

"Yassuh. I didn't want no part of that."

"But why would you think they wouldn't believe you, Shauntell?"

"Huh?"

"Why did you think the police wouldn't believe that you found the envelope on the night stand in the Banquell's bedroom?"

"I just don' think they'd believe me," she said.

"Had you ever found evidence of cocaine use by the Banquell's prior to that day?"

"No suh!"

"I'd like for you to tell me the truth, Shauntell," Burl said. "Did you take that envelope with you the morning you found the bodies?"

"Why in the world would I do that?"

"My idea is that someone told you to."

"No."

"No what, no-one told you to, or you didn't take it with you that morning?"

"Wha' for?"

"To make it look like the Banquell's death was a drug deal gone wrong," Burl said.

"Y'all excuse me just a minute," she said and retreated through a door and closed it behind her.

Britton didn't know what was going to happen next, but he took the moment to open the lid on the briefcase. Inside was the counterfeit money, still neatly arranged on top of blank sheets of paper, just as he and Noble had stacked it.

Just then the door opening caught his eye, and a deep throated growl reached his ears.

The Doberman took a few running steps and leaped for Burl Britton's throat.

CHAPTER 55

I woke up to the sound of the big door opening. A beam of light shined in my eyes and I couldn't see who was coming through the door. I smelled something that smelled like cooked meat and I realized that I was hungry.

The overhead single bulb light went on and I saw the smaller of my three captives standing near the door with a tray in his hand. It was Dawahn.

"I bringed you sumpin to eat," he said.

"Great, Dawahn. Thank you."

"Yassuh!"

He sat the tray down near me and I got to my knees and tipped the five gallon bucket upside down with one foot, then raised my hind end enough to sit on the bucket. The chain kept me from reaching the tray with my right hand but I could with my left. I picked it up and set it across my knees.

"Did you bring me any silverware?" I asked.

"Oh..yassuh. I forgotted. Here it is," he pulled a knife and fork from his pants pocket and handed it to me.

I took it in my left hand.

"I hate to ask for a favor, Dawahn," I said, "but can you cut up this steak for me, I can't hold the fork and knife with one hand.."

"Oh, yeah." He said.

But to my amazement, instead of cutting the steak for me, he took out a key and opened the padlock that had my right hand hooked to the radiator.

I might be a little slow at times, but I'm not stupid. Dawahn didn't realize what he was doing, I'm sure, or he wouldn't have done it.

I swung the heavy chain with the padlock still on it. The lock caught Dawahn in the side of the head and a spurt of blood covered the potatoes on the tray. Catsup on my potatoes? No thank you.

He staggered but regained his balance and pulled a 38 snub-nosed revolver from his waistband. Before he could level it at me, I slashed out with the chain again and it landed across his gun hand, at the tender spot right below his wrist. He screamed and the gun went flying.

I wrapped the chain around his neck and head butted him on his nose. He went out like a light.

I fished in the right front pocket of his gabardine slacks and found the key to the handcuffs, unsnapped the one on my wrist and quickly cuffed Dawahn to the radiator where I had been, moments before.

As hungry as I was, I wasn't going to eat that steak with Dawahn's blood on it. I like rare meat but that was just downright sickening.

Instead, I glanced outside. Chico was gone. They must have had a changing of the guard, and I was glad of it. I closed the door and looked around the room. I found Dewahn's gun and stuck it in my pocket.

I turned the overhead light off and opened the door and stepped outside into the cool night air. There was no moon, and it was pretty dark near the building. I couldn't decide whether I wanted to get the hell out of there completely or go back for my rented car. It was a long way from the boathouse to the front drive where I'd left the car.

I started for the car. After fifty feet, I was suddenly bathed in a brilliant light and the sound of a high powered rifle was preceded by the whine of a slug that missed splitting my melon by inches. I dove for darkness.

The light flicked over my prone body, continued for twenty yards towards the drive, in the direction I had been headed, then started slowly back towards me. If it found me again, the next shot might not miss.

I got up and ran like a deer away from the driveway. Ahead of me now was the lake. The beam of the high powered light was gaining on me as I ran, and I shifted to high gear and ran like an antelope.

By the time the light was a foot behind me, I heard another shot. The slug made a chunk sound as it hit the grass behind me. Then another shot. Closer.

I turned it up a notch and ran like cougar.

When I reached the boat dock I flew down the planked gangway like a cheetah.

Kaboom, followed by the sound of splintering wood. Kaboom, more splintering wood. Then the cool dark waters of the lake enveloped me. I came up for a quick breath of air and saw that the spotlight encircled me. Kaboom, splunk..the sound of a slug hitting the water. I dove.

Under water I swam towards the bottom at least 6 feet, then tried swimming parallel, as powerfully as my legs and arms would let me. I could hear the splunk of slugs hitting the water above. I changed directions and swam at a 90 degree angle to my right. After 50 or 60 feet I ran out of air and had to surface. The spotlight was making sweeping motions to my left, and twenty yards away. I took a quick deep breath and dove again.

This time I headed for what I thought would be the center of the lake. I had no idea how far the water reached in the direction I was headed, but the more distance I put between myself and whoever was shooting at me, the better I liked it.

When my lungs screamed out for air again, I let myself ease to the surface, and a foot below, I rolled over on my back and floated very quietly. face up. The searchlight was now 50 or 60 yards to my left and 40 or 50 yards behind my location. I thought I'd be safe to relax a bit and catch my breath. That's when I heard the sound of a powerful outboard motor roar to life, what sounded like a pistol shot, and the spotlight went out.

CHAPTER 56

Britton had worked for a short time before college as a meter reader. He had been taught what to do if a dog attacked while reading someone's meter.

He grabbed a large stack of counterfeit $100 bills and held them at arm's length towards the charging Doberman.

The Doberman clamped down on the paper and immediately shook its big head.

Shauntell screamed.

"Dat dog's eatin' my money!"

Britton slammed the briefcase down on the dog's massive head and headed for the door.

He made it just as the surprised Doberman shook its huge head and spit the phony money out on the floor and refocused its attention on him.

"Get him, Shark!" Shauntell screamed.

Britton had the door open and stepped through, slamming the door behind him.

He ran as fast as he could to the gate and opened it just as the front door opened and Shark streaked off of the porch and down the sidewalk. Britton opened the gate just in time and slammed it after he went through. The dog leaped towards the top of the gate and sank its teeth in the briefcase that Britton still had in his hands. Britton yanked and the case came free, a canine incisor stuck in it.

Shauntell was still on the porch watching the dog leaping at the gate. The gate rattled each time the dog's massive muscled body slammed into it. Britton opened his car door, flung the briefcase across to the passenger seat, and got in as fast as his aching leg would let him. He twisted the key in the ignition, yanked the gear shift lever down to low and stomped on the accelerator. The little Honda engine roared like a banshee, wheels barely turning, the car finally crept away like a mouse trying to sneak away from a cat.

Britton thought that if he didn't quit his PI business, he'd take the money from this case and buy a bigger, faster car.

Ten minutes later he was in Beverly Miller's office with the door closed, telling the WMPD detective the whole story.

"You need to get some officers out to Jobe Banquell's mansion ASAP," he said, "Savage went out there with this briefcase, intent on rattling Jobe's cage enough to get a reaction. The Peanut Man will probably be gone, but we may get there in time to save Noble Savage's life."

"Damn, I hope your conclusions are right, Britton," Beverly Miller said. "Jobe Banquell will wind up owning me, you and the whole damned town of Whispering Meadows if you are wrong."

"Get someone to pick up Michelle Montague too," Britton said. "She'll crack when you tell her the gun evidence."

Beverly picked up her phone and said something that Britton didn't catch, then spoke clearly and distinctly, telling the dispatcher to send units to pick up Michelle Montague, Joe Miller, her ex-husband, and Shauntell.

"I'm off the Jobe Banquell's place," she said. "You want to be in on it?"

"Wouldn't miss it for love or money," Burl Britton said.

CHAPTER 57

I heard the motor start up and strained my eyes to see the boat house dock. Sure enough, a tall figure stood in the back of a boat, hand on the tiller. He was too far away to see if he was armed, but I figured he had a definite advantage over me. I was in the water, tired, clothes getting heavy, out of breath, hungry, and the only weapon I had was the .38 that I had taken from Dawahn.

First things first, I told myself. Get rid of some of this wet clothing that keeps dragging me down.

I wiggled out of the Salvation Army reject jacket and dug the Colt .38 out of the pocket. Just as I started to let go of it and let it sink, I thought of something. If I could get that jacket tangled up in the prop of the boat, either its occupant would be dead in the water, or I would. I preferred the former.

I held on to the jacket. The powerful outboard was roaring and the boat was throwing up a rooster tail as it left the dock. I watched, and waited. One good thing was that the spotlight had gone out. The boat occupant held a high candlepower torch in one hand, the other hand on the rudder, throttle control of the boat. I was on my back, relaxing as much as I could, moving my arms gently to stay afloat.

When the boat was 1000 yards away, and headed right at me, the roar of the motor diminished to a healthy growl. He was slowing to look for me. I knew I had a chance. I waited. Then it was 150 yards away. In order for my plan to work, I had to slow the boat to a much lower speed. When the growl of the motor diminished to a gentle purr, I raised the jacket as high over my head as possible and splashed it down on the surface of the water.

Immediately the boat speed slowed. It was now 50 yards away. Then 25. It's forward motion was enough that if I stayed in the same spot it would run right over the top of me. I submerged, pulled my arms down then to my sides, still holding the jacket. I was two feet below the surface when I saw the dark shadow of the boat pass where I had been.

I eased myself back to the surface, arched my back and watched as the boat skimmed by. It started a slow circle and the motor hummed a little louder. The tall figure in the boat turned the beam of the torch at the spot I had been when I slapped the surface with the jacket.

Now the boat was headed back towards me. I waited until it was 20 yards away then quietly let myself sink below the surface, took the jacket by the ends of the sleeves, and when the boat passed over my position, I kicked my feet and raised my arms high over my head. I knew I probably had just one chance. This had to work.

The prop hit the jacket and jerked it out of my hands, twisted it around and around and as I surfaced I could hear a grinding sound like metal on metal. The boat eased to a very slight forward motion away from me, the tall man turning towards my position. I raised the pistol.

I had the barrel pointed right at his chest. My finger started the squeeze. Then I heard a familiar voice.

"SAVAGE!"

It was Burl Britton.

CHAPTER 58

It was over.

I had stayed alive and more or less revenged the death of Jimmy Enderly, and The Peanut Man was in jail, the cheerleader teacher, Michelle Montague, was in jail, Shauntell and her boyfriend, Clement were in jail. Dawahn and Chico were in jail. Hell, the whole damn town of Whispering Meadows could have been in jail, including Joe Miller, the ex-husband of Beverly Miller. Beverly, by the way, at the moment, was leaning comfortably against my side as I drove away from the town in my "new" ride.

I'd taken my cut of the money Burl Britton paid me and purchased a honey of a car, one damned near exactly like the one I'd almost been shredded in. A 56 Pontiac. Same color as Old Bess had been. Velour seat covers and all.

I won't go into detail, but I had won the fair maiden, Beverly Miller. She told me that she had liked my style from the beginning of our introduction, that she had grown tired of life in the big city and wanted to retire to a quiet village somewhere far away, have a few dogs for pets, and give up the country club life.

It hadn't taken much to convince me to ask her to go back to Saskatchewan with me. Britton didn't even flinch when she told him she was going with me.

The task force she had put together that night saved my life, even though it was Burl Britton who took the initiative to come out on the lake and look for me. She had men from the Atlanta PD, some FBI guys, her own crew from

Whispering Meadows, and maybe even some from Homeland Security as far as this old Tonto knows. I didn't care.

She told me that when they got to Jobe Banquell's place, armed with a warrant, they heard the sound of a high powered rifle coming from the rear balcony. Someone had the brains to shoot out the search light, and Britton, bless his peanut picking heart, had taken the boat and started searching the dark water for my body. Fortunately that body still had me in it. My spirit, at least.

Shauntell had 'fessed up that her and Clem had been about to fly the coop. They had the briefcase full of phony money that Britton grabbed. It had been payoff for her part in trying to make the murder of Art and Dora Banquell appear to be a drug scene. Truth of the matter was that Clem and Michelle Montague were the ones who gunned down the Banquells.

Jimmy Enderly had refused to follow the lead that "Lisa", who was really Montague, tried desperately to play out. So Jimmy, may the Great Spirits rest his soul, was innocent; only guilty of following his heart and falling for a girl he'd never met.

The real guilty party was Jobe Banquell. He confessed that he wanted to get rid of his son because Art had systematically skimmed money from the peanut business and funneled it to organizations responsible for furthering the NAACP. He had discovered that millions of his hard earned money from the peanut butter business had been given to the United Negro College Fund, and that was enough to send him over the deep end. All of his hard work, all of his hatred and animosity against people of color got the best of him.

I have my own opinions on the race issue.

I see men as men. Some are good men, some are bad. Any man who fathers a child and walks away from it, never provides for its education, its health, its station in life, is not a man. That, in my way of thinking, is the problem in the black community, and in some white communities as well.

I'm against taking money from those who work hard for it and giving it to those who have found a way to siphon it from the system. In a lot of ways I agreed with old Jobe Banquell, but not to the point of murder. Jobe just hated black folks. I hate people who are parasites, I don't give a damn what color they are.

On the other hand, I didn't agree with the mindset of Art Banquell either. It seems like the more you give to minorities the more they demand. Maybe Art had a guilty conscience for the years he had helped his father acquire massive amounts of money, and paid the farmers peanuts, literally.

Oh well, enough of the way I view that situation.

I am tooling through Chicago. I'll stop long enough to pay my respects to the Enderly family, visit Jimmy's grave, and then it is on to the sleepy little town in Saskatchewan that I call home.

I drive as though there is no tomorrow. When I get tired, my lovely lady, Beverly, takes the wheel. You might say we are accomplishing a joint effort.

What about the lovely Lisa?

The FBI and Interpol had found her in an all girl's school in Switzerland. She had not been aware of the death of her parents. Jobe Banquell had faked her kidnapping, flew her out of the country and to a psychiatric hospital where she was brainwashed for days.

Early attempts by her cheerleading teacher, Michelle Montague, had not convinced Lisa to stay away from people who were not white. Lisa had her own life. She enjoyed the notoriety of being Moose Mosely's girlfriend, and had no intention of letting him go. After Jobe had Moose whisked away to Notre Dame, Lisa had left on her own free will and went to Indiana to be with Moose. Jobe had her picked up and to cover his own ass, let everyone think she had been kidnapped, including her parents.

The ransom demand was his downfall. It didn't take the FBI long to uncover that plot after Britton's brilliant detective work found that the ransom telephone calls were phonies. Got to hand it to old Burl, he's a helluva detective.

CHAPTER 59

Burl was in a limousine. He thought of Beverly Miller on occasion, particularly when he took Beverly Boulevard out to the Hollywood studio that was filming "Joint Effort in Death". But with a beautiful blonde on his left, and a cell phone in his hand talking to his agent, he wasn't burning many brain cells in regrets.

After the dust settled on Whispering Meadows' biggest news story in its history, Burl had been granted his fee for solving the case. It didn't take his attorney long to file action and win against the estate of the late Art and Dora Banquell, and for some strange reason, old Jobe Banquell had not contested Burl's suit to collect from him.

Burl started writing "Joint Effort in Death" a week later. It went smooth from the start, and he wrote with a fervor, egged on by some people who had never came around before, but now were suddenly eager to be his friend again.

He found that his best friend and assistant in writing his true crime adventure was his old FBI friend, Ernie. Ernie seemed to have a knack for words that often eluded Burt. Six weeks after he started "Joint Effort in Death" it was a finished manuscript. A local English teacher had edited it for him and he submitted it to an Atlanta publishing company.

They paid him a hundred thousand in advance royalties. A week later "Dreamer" pictures had picked it up and gave him a sweet deal. One million dollars plus ten percent of the net proceeds on a movie.

His "secretary", the beautiful blonde on his left, made him his favorite morning drink, a Tequila Sunrise, and as he sipped it, he fondled a watch fob that had been sent to him by Noble Savage.

It was a woven platinum chain with a single object dangling on it. Encased in gold was the tooth of a Doberman.

THE END

OF A JOINT EFFORT

By: Don Yarber, author of the Kip Yardley series.
By: Allen Clarke, first time PI author.

About the author: Don Yarber is a native of Harrisburg, Il, now residing in Morganfield, KY. This is his 7th book. He is the author of Bodies and Beaches, Corpses and Canyons, Death and Deep Waters (featuring LA Private Eye, Kip Yardley) and The Sign Killer, a mystery with more twists than the law allows. Don's first attempt at a Western Novel, Train to the Sun, is a venture into the Old West dished up with the flair of Zane Grey and served with a mystery and surprising finale.

First time PI novelist, Allen Clarke, hails from Saskatchewan, Canada. Don and Allen are friends from Scribeslice, an online writing group.